# Aal the way to
# LUNDON

## Dennis Forster

First published in Great Britain as a softback original in 2021

Copyright © Sarah Gedney and Jonathan Forster

The moral right of this author has been asserted.

Typeset in Sabon LT Std

Editing, design, typesetting and publishing by UK Book Publishing

www.ukbookpublishing.com

ISBN: 978-1-914195-18-1

*'To Biffy and Fat Man (they know who they are)'*

# Aal the way to Lundon

The four married couples, all pensioners, called themselves the 'Ensemble'. Their names were:

Debbie and Geoffrey
Beryl and Roger
Flora and Jock
Shirley and Ravi

It was Geoffrey and Debbie's idea that the 'Ensemble' should start a 'reading group'.

Discussing their embryonic idea while sharing the chore of washing-up after a boozy, at-home dinner – Debbie, washing and Geoffrey, drying – Geoffrey said to his wife, 'I know how they think. If we are to get our idea of a reading group up and running, we will need to ambush them. You know how they can take against something if they are given time to think.'

'And, Roger won't like the idea on principle,' said Debbie.

'Because it's not his idea?'

'Yes, and, you know how mean he is; he's bound to want to know how much buying a book a month will cost.'

'Not if we get him pissed first, he won't. Why don't we invite all of them round for a meal? I think it's our turn. When they are all a bit woozy from drinking our cellar dry, that's when we'll mention, en passant, as it were, what about the 'Ensemble' starting a reading group? Whatever you decide to cook for them, Debbie, remember, use lots of salt. Roger always complains you don't use enough salt.'

'There are more palates to satisfy than his.'

'He thinks he's the centre of the universe.'

'Not in my house he isn't. I will use as much or as little salt as I think the dish I am cooking, requires.'

'I wish we weren't old.'

'But, Geoffrey, we are and there's nothing we can do about it. And, be careful you don't drop that milk jug; it belonged to my mother.'

Geoffrey sighed and, looking at the cages of bird food he could see hanging from the silver birch in his back garden, pondered where all the food he put out, went. He never saw any birds.

*******

Geoffrey and Debbie's Victorian terrace house had a west-facing back garden. A vine grew in a greenhouse. A gardener came in once a week to do the heavy work, Geoffrey's back no longer up to bending.

The evening they 'ambushed' their friends with their 'idea' was warm and sunny.

After the meal Geoffrey said, 'Let's take our drinks outside.'

'Is it warm enough?' said Flora.

'Of course it is,' said Beryl.

'I hope, Geoffrey,' said Roger, 'you're not forgetting I'm on tablets to thin my blood. I've had a heart attack. I feel the cold.'

'Roger, dear boy, fear not, it said on the radio this morning we are having a heatwave.'

'Fake news. It doesn't seem that hot to me.'

'Cuddle in to Beryl, Roger,' said Shirley, 'isn't that what we wives are for? Hot water bottles to keep thin blooded men warm.'

'I don't think what the weatherman said on the news this morning was "fake news",' said Jock, 'I'm sweltering. I'm all for taking our drinks outside.'

'Fake news,' repeated Roger.

'Roger, if you want to sit and sulk inside all by yourself, that's up to you. I'm going to sit outside,' said Beryl.

'Let the people speak,' said Geoffrey, 'let's take a vote.'

'And if we vote to stay inside,' said Roger, 'you'll want a second vote like you do about us leaving the EU.'

'Now, now, Roger, no politics. We have things to discuss,' said Debbie.

'Have we?'

'Geoffrey and I want to … I'll tell you in the garden.'

They sat on comfy, high backed wicker chairs placed round a table with a furled sunshade in its middle.

'That was a very nice meal, Debbie,' said Roger, dragging his chair into the sun, 'just one thing wrong with it … like a lot of cooks you don't use enough salt.'

'Up or down?' said Geoffrey, hands on the sunshade.

'Down,' said Roger, 'I need the sun to keep me warm.'

'I've had a melanoma removed,' said Flora. 'I shouldn't sit in the sun … doctor's orders.'

'Experts … what do they know?'

'They know we shouldn't be leaving the EU,' said Shirley, 'and I'm Welsh.'

'What's that got to do with leaving the EU?'

'I'm asserting, Roger, that it is perfectly possible to be a member of a group of countries and still retain one's identity.'

'I'm a Scot,' said Jock, 'I voted to stay in the EU.'

'You still a druid, Shirley?' said Roger.

'That was a long time ago. When we were young we all did silly things. You still in favour of fox hunting?'

'Why not?'

'You know where you should be? In one of those trolleys you see in supermarkets full of out of date items at reduced prices.'

'The sunshade,' said Geoffrey, 'up or down?'

'Geoffrey,' said Debbie, 'put the sunshade up, and … please, no more politics. Roger, move your chair more into the sun … there, sun for those who want sun and shade for those who want shade. Geoffrey, serve the champagne.'

Geoffrey disappeared into the house.

'Why the champagne?' said Ravi, a magnificent specimen of a Brahmin Hindu. He'd lived and worked with the British for over fifty years … they never ceased to amuse him. 'What are we celebrating? That the Toon is still in the Premier League?'

'We're safe this season,' said Jock.

'Not like poor Sunderland,' said Flora, 'they'll soon be playing Wallsend Wasps.'

'I can never understand,' said, Jock, adopting a meditative pose by fluttering his fingers on his chest, 'why there is a "sun" in, Sunderland; it's not more sunny than anywhere else in the North-East; funny things, names.'

'I once knew someone who had a Pekinese called Hercules,' said Shirley; then, her mind wandering to more important matters, 'I'm glad I stopped smoking; if I hadn't, I don't think I'd be here now.'

'Calling a Pekinese Hercules, is a misnomer,' said Jock. 'Funny things, misnomers.'

'Like Brexit,' said Roger. 'Brexit should be called, "Liberation".'

'More like, "Lemmings' Leap",' muttered Jock, looking at Roger and shaking his head.

'Please,' said Debbie, 'no politics. If you must be disputatious, talk about football.'

'We are all Newcastle supporters,' said Ravi. 'Howay the lads!'

'Shearer! Shearer!' chanted Jock.

'Season tickets for the Toon, please god, keep the price of them doon,' said Roger.

'I'm not a snob,' said Debbie, 'but keep your voices down; please, remember we are in Jesmond, not Byker. The garden is large but, on a warm summer's night such as this, voices do carry. I know you will find this difficult to believe but, my neighbour – that way – has leanings towards Liverpool; or, so I've heard.'

'It's football,' said Flora, 'it brings out the best and worst in people. When I'm at a match and shouting, "Howay the lads!" I forget I am old. It releases all my inhibitions. I'm like a car going downhill when its brakes fail; quite out of control. I say naughty things. In a fit of passion I once used the F-word. Football brings out the worst in me. It makes me say bad things.'

'The priest always knows when Flora's been to a football match,' said Jock.

'I'm glad I'm not religious,' said Beryl, 'can't imagine telling someone all the naughties I've done. If Roger was a Catholic he'd never be out of the confession box.'

'Stop picking on me, Beryl. You are always doing it. I don't like it. I think Geoffrey is going to propose a toast that we all start a campaign for a second referendum … if he does, I'll not be raising my glass.'

'But you'll drink what's in the glass?'

'Of course. I was brought up during the war … waste not, want not.'

'Brexit,' said Ravi, 'is splitting the UK the way you Brits partitioned India in forty-seven.'

'That's when we had an Empire,' said Roger, 'those were the days … Britain ruled the world. Now we have an aircraft carrier but no aeroplanes … sad.'

'We have a tank,' said Jock.

'It's getting painted … sad, very sad. To think we have come to this. Taking orders from the French.'

'Please, no politics … here comes the champagne.'

'So,' said Ravi, 'what are we celebrating?'

'That we are all still here,' said Shirley, 'that our prosthetic knees are all in working order?'

'Don't forget my hips,' said Beryl.

'I know what we are celebrating,' said Ravi, 'obvious ... Geoffrey is going to get hearing aids.'

'Not yet, Ravi, darling,' said Geoffrey. The bubbles in his flute of champagne made him feel young. 'Debbie, stand beside me. We will make our announcement as a twosome; the way they do at the Oscars in Hollywood. I'll go first.'

Geoffrey cleared his throat.

'My wife and I ...' said Geoffrey.

'Propose ...' said Debbie.

'That we ...' said Geoffrey.

'All of us ...' said Debbie.

'Here tonight ...' said Geoffrey.

'Get together ...' said Debbie.

'To organise ...' said Geoffrey.

'A ... reading group!' said Geoffrey and Debbie.

The ensuing silence made Geoffrey and Debbie look at their friends the way you look at a blank television screen; you have switched it on but it does seem to be taking a long time to come to life.

Taking a sledgehammer to crack a nut, Geoffrey said: 'I read somewhere, that if you were to stick a pin into the tail of a diplodocus it would take half an hour before the beast screamed, "ouch!"; you know, for the message to travel from its tail to its tiny brain. Come on folk, feedback. While you're thinking of singing the praises of myself and my, dear wife, I'll fill your glasses.'

'Are you calling me a dinosaur?' said Roger, holding out his glass.

'We ARE dinosaurs,' said Ravi, 'all of us. Last week on the Metro a young woman with a baby in one of those papoose things offered me her seat. I tried to say no but she wouldn't hear of it.'

'You don't look old to me, darling,' said Shirley, patting her husband's hand.

'Give me a kiss. Everyone close their eyes.'

'You never say nice things like that to me, Beryl,' said Roger.

'You don't look old to me …' said Beryl.

'You might sound as if you mean it.'

'One of your faults, Roger is, you never let me finish my sentences. I was going to say, "You don't look old to me … you look like someone I can't believe I ever married".'

'Charming.'

'It's the drink,' said Debbie, 'we all know what drink does to Beryl. Geoffrey, no more drink for Beryl.'

'Yes, dear.'

'In vino veritas,' said Jock.

'Come on,' said Geoffrey, 'hands up, who thinks us all reading a book a month is a good idea? Ravi, are you putting your hand up or wanting a refill?'

'Both.'

'Where will we meet?'

'Will there be wine?'

'Will there be beer?'

'Will there be nibbles?'

'I like olives and those bitesize bits of chicken Debbie does; the ones marinated in a sweet and sour sauce.'

'What day will we meet?'

'Thursday's out. That's my bridge night.'

'Winter nights are best for reading groups.'

'Will we have a holiday from reading in the summer?'

'We'll have a written constitution,' said Debbie. 'It will be democratic. Everyone will have a turn at picking a book. If you fail to read a member's choice you will be fined five pounds. This will be put in a kitty. When it mounts up, which I'm sure it will, we'll have a meeting to decide how it might be spent.'

'How will we know if someone hasn't read the chosen book?' said Roger. 'We're not going to be tested, I hope?'

'No, Roger, you are not going to be tested; you are going to be trusted.'

'Roger will cheat,' said Beryl.

'Beryl, you've been getting at me all night. I don't like it.'

'While alcohol will be allowed,' said Geoffrey, 'Debbie and I do not wish the "reading group" to be an excuse for a booze-up.'

'I'd like to join,' said Flora, 'but … I know this might sound silly but would it be possible for us all to agree not to pick long books?'

'I'll write that into the constitution,' said Debbie.

'I'll open another bottle of Moet,' said Geoffrey.

*******

In the privacy of their own homes the couples discussed the evening the way spies discuss treachery in a 'safe' room.

Geoffrey: I thought that went rather well. We got them all on board.

Debbie: I thought the theatricality we brought to our denouement … superb. Well done, Geoffrey.

Flora: Jock, I hope you didn't mind my mentioning I wanted just to read short books. It didn't sound silly, did it?

Jock: That was a good idea, Flora. As Geoffrey would say, it was 'spot on'. When it comes to my choice I'm thinking of making them read something in the Scot's dialect … a few poems by Burns, perhaps. The English do not have a monopoly on great literature.

Shirley: When I was a druid I wrote a few stories for the Dyfed eisteddfod … it was a long time ago but they were very well received. At Carnarvon I'd two encores … wonder if one can choose one's own work for the reading group?

Ravi: What about something in Sanskrit?

Roger: Beryl, I didn't like the way you went at me tonight.
Beryl: Shut up, Roger.
Roger: Don't you talk to me like that.
Beryl: What are you going to do about it?
Roger: Deny you your conjugal rights.
Beryl: Thank god for that.

*******

They got into the routine of meeting every four weeks on a Wednesday night; mostly at Geoffrey and Debbie's.

On one such night, Ravi said: 'Reading a book a month is like having a dog. What I mean is, if you have a dog, you have to take it for a walk. A book looks after the mind, a dog looks after the body.'

'Just a minute,' said Roger, 'I don't have to read a book a month; not if I don't want to. England is still a free country, Ravi. I'm not living in Putin's Russia, you know. And, if you have a dog, you don't have to take it for a walk.'

'True,' said Ravi, 'but, if you don't, the dog will get fat and die.'

'Of course,' said Beryl, smirking, 'you could always pay a dog-walker to exercise your mutt. I believe they charge ten pound for a thirty minute trot; lampposts not guaranteed.'

'I've not heard of anything so ridiculous in all my years on this planet,' said Roger. 'People with dogs must have plenty of money; that's all I can say.'

'Don't forget, Roger,' said Ravi, 'an unread book will incur a fine.'

'You seem to be forgetting with whom you are dealing. You will be prosecuting a chap who knows a lot about law.'

'When you are found guilty, Roger, you will not be in a court of law. The "Ensemble" will be your judge and your jury. And, let me assure you, evidence of guilt will be much lower than in a court of law.'

'A kangaroo court. Putin's Russia. I will of course appeal.'

*******

Over the ensuing months some choices were liked, others, hated.

Debbie's choice, Hemmingway's 'The Old Man and the Sea', went down well with everyone. It could be read in an afternoon; also its subject: an old man at sea in a boat. They all knew how the 'old man' felt.

At an extraordinary general meeting Geoffrey made it quite clear that an author could not pick her own work, thereby scuppering Shirley's wish of making her choice, her own short stories; of which he'd heard rumours she was planning to do.

'We are not self-publicists,' Geoffrey told the 'Ensemble', 'and they are in Welsh.'

Still determined to support the land of her birth and first language Shirley picked for her choice, 'Portrait of the Artist as a Young Dog,' telling everyone: 'Dylan Thomas is Wales in English.'

This proved to be a popular choice, though Flora didn't like the boys in the story throwing snowballs at cats and worried about the boys, out in the cold singing Christmas carols, all by their young selves, when they should have been in bed reading Enid Blyton.

Beryl picked 'Moby Dick' because she knew Roger, a long time ago, had started to read it but couldn't finish it ... 'Bloody awful book. I hate ships.'

The group thought it too long, that it broke the group's rules about short books.

Geoffrey disagreed. He did not think it too long, though he did think it went on too much about whales.

For his choice he picked 'Pickwick Papers'.

'I seem to remember that's a long book,' said Flora.

'It is very funny,' said Geoffrey.

'That doesn't make it a short book. We agreed … short books.'

'It's no longer than "Moby Dick".'

'Now, I know why you didn't object when Beryl made "Moby Dick" her choice,' said Ravi. 'You're a crafty one, you are, Geoffrey …. Paving the way, were you, for your choice?'

'"Pickwick" made Dickens famous,' said Shirley, 'if only Dickens had been Welsh; "Please, sir; can I have some more" sounds wonderful in Welsh, don't you know?'

'It's still a long book,' said Flora.

'Flora,' said Jock, '"Pickwick" wasn't written as a book. It came out in instalments … like "Coronation Street". Read it a little bit at a time. If I wanted to, I could still do the Great North Run … it would just take me a long time.'

'Like six months,' said Roger.

'No, Roger … three months.'

'Whichever way you look at it,' said Flora, 'it's a lot of pages to read in a month … you know I have a cataract.'

'Why not,' said Geoffrey, 'make my choice a two-month choice? It is summer and none of us wants to be inside reading or, outside reading a book for that matter when we should be out and about, doing active things, like going down to the coast and walking the Long Sands.'

'Lots of nice coffee shops at the coast,' said Shirley. 'There's one Ravi and I love. It's run by a Welshman.'

'His wife is Spanish,' said Ravi.

'We're on first name terms. He's called Owen … speaks Welsh. Ravi is teaching him Urdu. The Welsh love languages.'

'First time I've heard that,' said Roger.

'Which coffee shop are you on about?' said Debbie.

'Does it have a loyalty card?' said Beryl.

While the women discussed coffee shops Geoffrey took the men to his greenhouse to show off his grapevine.

By the end of the evening it was agreed that 'Pickwick' would be allowed but, because it was a 'long book' and it was summer time, it would be a 'two-month' choice.

'It's our summer schedule,' explained Geoffrey, feeling rather pleased with himself; after all, he'd got all his own way. If he'd been flying a Spitfire he'd have done a victory roll. 'In the Lake District they put on more buses in the summer. The Lake District is very popular in summer. In summer we read a book less so we can fill their buses.'

'I'm not planning to go to the Lake District,' said Roger.

'Pedantic twit,' said Beryl.

'The buses run a summer timetable, so why shouldn't we?' said Geoffrey, all beams and smiles.

'Even as a two-month read,' said Flora, '"Pickwick" is still a long read.'

*******

Their get-together broke up at midnight. At Geoffrey and Debbie's front door there was much hugging and kissing.

'Nearly midnight and still light,' said Ravi. 'I love the North's long summer days; so un-Indian.'

'I smell honeysuckle,' said Geoffrey.

'That's my perfume, Geoffrey, darling,' said Shirley, dropping a sprayer shaped like a bullet into her handbag.

'Is that to make you irresistible to Ravi?'

'It is to keep away the midges. I don't need perfume to make my darling Ravi find me attractive; do I, my darling?'

'Ciao!' shouted Geoffrey who was very European.

The human equivalent of the dawn chorus answered his cosmopolitan good night!

'Thank you for a lovely evening.'

'Looking forward to reading "Pickwick".'

'Ciao!'

'Ciao!'

'Hope I'm still here to see the sunrise tomorrow,' said Jock.

'Jock, don't be morbid,' said Flora.

'I'm thinking of buying a house closer to the crem; save time on the final journey.'

'What's he like?'

'Don't forget your stick, Roger,' said Debbie. 'Where's he gone?'

'He's in the cupressus leylandii,' said Ravi. 'Beryl … help him.'

'Silly old fool,' said Beryl, 'drunk at his age. He should know better.'

'Here, let the Scots help,' said Jock; 'it's not often England needs the help of Scotland.'

'Or the Welsh,' said Shirley, grabbing both of Roger's ears while Ravi, Jock and Debbie grabbed the various other bits of Roger they could see sticking out of the evergreen.

'Silly wee man,' said Flora.

'It needed pruning,' said Geoffrey, philosophical about the tree's snapped branches.

'I'll make sure he gets home,' said Ravi.

'Will he be sleeping in the garden shed tonight?' said Flora.

'He can go to hell as far as I'm concerned,' said Beryl.

'I'll take the high road,' sang Jock. 'Everyone follow me.'

'If only you had your bag pipes, Jock,' said Flora.

*******

A front door tells a lot about the people who live therein.

Geoffrey and Debbie's front door was original; circa 1900. Its hinges were stamped: 'Made in Sheffield'.

These days it was a quiet house but, to Geoffrey and Debbie, not an empty one; to them it was a house full of happy memories; memories of their three children, now, all married or living with their partners – the modern version of marriage – in their own homes, far away.

They'd bought the property off a professor of Mechanical Engineering; hence, the front door's brass knocker in the shape of George Stephenson's 'Rocket'; polished every Friday by the couple's 'weekly help'; a fat woman, with a heart of gold who lived in the Byker Wall and who was terrified that the 'bit-on-the-side' she was earning might be found out by the taxman.

Twice a year Geoffrey squirted WD40 into the door's windy keyhole and onto its three sets of Sheffield-made hinges. A methodical man, he logged his maintenance into his e-diary.

The house's long front garden was full of bedding plants and evergreen shrubs. Anyone who knew anything about gardens knew that that lot didn't come cheap.

In one of their lounges – they had two – Geoffrey kept a rocking chair. It had belonged to his maternal grandparents. In the same room, Debbie kept a nest of tables made by a great-uncle who'd made them as a test piece when serving his apprenticeship to be a cabinet maker.

To Geoffrey and Debbie, these items of furniture were as sacred as the busts the ancient Romans kept of their ancestors.

Looking into his shaving mirror the morning after his success at persuading the 'Ensemble' to accept 'Pickwick' as his book 'choice', Geoffrey said to his wife: 'Do you think I should dye my hair?'

'No,' said Debbie, who was in the bathroom with him writing an aide memoire on a note pad, to remind herself that she needed to buy bleach, 'definitely not. If you did, you'd look odd, like Roger and Beryl's plastic front door. Grey hairs go with age … dark hair with youth.'

'Do you really believe that?'

'Yes.'

'Are there not exceptions?'

'No, not even for you, Geoffrey. You will never persuade me that old men who dye their hair look attractive. I believe the expression is, "mutton dressed as lamb".'

'I'm getting shorter. If I live to be a hundred I'll be Tom Thumb.'

'Your grey hair makes you look distinguished.'

'Do you really think so?'

His wife's nodding did not mean she was answering 'yes'. Her head was moving up and down in an attempt to find the best angle to read what she'd written. She sometimes wished she'd stayed with bi-focal lenses, instead of graduated ones.

'Say that again,' said Geoffrey.

'What?'

'That I look distinguished.'

'Darling, you look distinguished.'

'I think I'll wear my red bow tie today.'

'I do hope Roger and Beryl got home alright.'

'They'd not far to go. Interesting though, don't you think?'

'What is?'

'Roger, the Englishman, always rather too full of his Anglo-Saxon heritage having to be helped home by a Scotsman, a Welsh woman and, dear Ravi, a Hindu, born in India under the Raj and now, an adopted Geordie.'

'Symbolic, you mean?'

'Shows the state the country's in. I don't wish to sound boastful but I think last night went rather well. If Beryl hadn't picked "Moby Dick" I'd never have got them to let me have "Pickwick". It is a long book.'

'When are you going to broach your idea of us all going to London to visit Dickens' house in Doughty Street? You know, as a sort of credo to us all having read "Pickwick".'

'First, the "5-Ps"; you know my motto, "Perfect Preparation Prevents Piss Poor Performance". I will introduce my proposal step by step; prepare the ground well beforehand. Jock and Flora will be the easiest to persuade. I'll broach the idea to them, first. You know, I was only up twice last night to use the loo.'

'I know you were. You woke me up. You didn't flush.'

'I didn't want to waken you.'

'You are always forgetting to flush; that is why I'm having to buy bleach.'

'I always lift the seat.'

'You do, my dear, you do.'

*******

Roger and Beryl's front door was a modern, double glazed, black plastic imitation of a Victorian door. Roger thought it 'wonderful'. Every time he put his key into its lock he thought of the bargain deal he'd got off the double glazing firm who'd fitted it at a discount of thirty percent.

'Arty-farty, Geoffrey and his antiques! Listed buildings! Load of crap!'

With sangfroid to the power ten Beryl agreed with her husband that the door was, indeed, 'wonderful'.

She and Roger were never short of things to disagree about. They thrived on sniping at each other. Their marriage was a guerrilla war. Snide remarks and put-downs having long ago replaced kisses and cuddles. If Roger cut his finger he'd claim he was bleeding to death and, if he did bleed to death, it would be Beryl's fault because she'd failed to buy elastoplasts for the medical box when he'd told her Morrisons were selling them, three packs for two.

On the night of the cupressus leylandii incident, Roger slept on the floor at the bottom of his bedroom door like a draught excluder; by mutual agreement they'd had separate bedrooms for years.

'When you realise you've signed up to reading, "Pickwick",' Beryl told the snoring heap on the floor that had once been the love of her life, 'that will sober you up. You only drank so much because it was free. If you weren't so damn big and heavy I'd put you in a wheelbarrow and trundle you onto the Town Moor and leave you out there all night for the foxes to sniff.'

In lieu of not been able to do this, she pinched his nose and called him a silly old sod and a miser.

*******

The marriage of a Welsh siren to a Brahmin Hindu, had produced four daughters, all of whom spoke English, Welsh and Hindi, none of whom now lived at home, and all of whom were stunningly beautiful; exotic products of the Indian lotus and the Welsh leek.

In stained glass Ravi and Shirley's front door depicted the Hindu, elephant god, Ganesha; an idiosyncratic interpretation of that mythical creature, in so much as, in this version, Ganesha's trunk looked very like a leek. The door's knocker was a hand painted piece of lignum vitae in the shape of an elephant's head. Visitors didn't press a doorbell, they pulled a chain as if flushing an old fashioned lavatory. When they pulled it, they heard an elephant trumpet.

After kissing Shirley goodnight three times on the back of her neck, as he did every night, while they were lying side by side, Ravi said: I suppose we'll have to read "Pickwick".'

Shirley: I'm not giving up on my short stories.

Ravi: Geoffrey's up to something.

Shirley: I think he let Beryl have "Moby Dick" to set a precedent.

Ravi: So he could have "Pickwick"?

Shirley: If Geoffrey didn't have us to organise I think he'd die. I get tired of being organised by Geoffrey.

Ravi: But, we are doing "good" when we let him organise us. By letting him organise us we are keeping him alive.

Shirley: So, to keep Geoffrey alive, I have to read, "Pickwick"? If that is the case then, as far as I am concerned, it's a win-win for Geoffrey. He always gets his own way.

Ravi: Have you taken your statin?

Shirley: Damn, no, I forgot.

Ravi: Up you get.

Shirley: Can't be bothered. Missing one will make no difference.

Ravi: You must be "bothered". What is the point of helping to keep Geoffrey alive if you can't be bothered to keep yourself alive? Eins, zwei, drei, up you get.'

Shirley: What is the night coming to? Geoffrey blabbing nonsense in Italian and now you, a Hindu, telling your Welsh wife to get up in German. What is wrong with Welsh? (In Welsh: If I had my way I'd turn Geoffrey into a frog and you, my darling Ravi, into a prince or, should it be a rajah?)

*******

Jock and Flora's front door looked its age. It needed painting. Their gravelled drive was a flowerbed of aggressive dandelions. Bird feeders, full of soil and moss, weighed down the branches of a magnolia. A 'Santa Stop' sign Jock had stuck into the gravel two years ago when his grandchildren had stopped over for Christmas, was putting up a gallant fight against strangulation from out-of-control clumps of wild garlic.

The night Roger fell into the cupressus leylandii, Jock and Flora did not go straight to bed; late though it was. Instead, they drank mugs of green tea. Flora had read green tea was good for the constitution. In the battle to stay fit and healthy one needed all the help one could get.

Flora: I worry, I might not finish "Pickwick" in time. It is a long book.

Jock: You have two months.

Flora: If I don't finish it, Geoffrey will be angry with me. I know he will.

Jock: If you don't finish it in time, blame your cataract.

Flora: I wonder if I could get a doctor's certificate.

Jock: Flora, don't worry about it. It's not important.

Flora: I think Geoffrey uses us. He twists us round his little finger.

Jock: Roger and Beryl … they do argue.

Flora: They always have … Jock, when you've finished your tea will you go under the stairs and get me a new pack of my incontinence pants.

Jock: I don't know why you keep them there.

Flora: You know why … I'm embarrassed. I don't want our children to find them.

Jock: Our children are adults. Angus is a doctor.

Flora: Jock, I am Angus's mum, not his patient. I don't want my son knowing his mother dribbles. Don't forget your statin.

*******

As a first step towards persuading the 'Ensemble' to go on a day trip to London to visit Dickens' house in Doughty Street, Geoffrey rang Jock.

'Hi, Jock, Geoffrey here; you and Flora fancy a coffee at "Gino's"?

'What time?'

'Ten-thirty.'

'We'll be there. You know why?'

'Because it's near Jesmond cemetery.'

'Ever so handy if one of us should pop his clogs.'

'Keep taking the pills.'

\*\*\*\*\*\*\*

Geoffrey liked Gino who owned and ran, 'Gino's'. And, Gino liked Geoffrey. They clicked. When Gino was in a good mood he gave Geoffrey a free brandy with his coffee. Gino was upset about Brexit.

He'd told Geoffrey: 'I have-a lived in the Toon all of-a ma life. This is my home. I wear a black and white scarf when I a-go to the match. Only when England play Italia do I shout for Italia. I shout, "Howay the Bambinos".'

'Gino,' said Geoffrey, 'why are you talking like a stage Italian?'

'I am-a giving the English what-a, they want. They think of me as a foreigner. I do not belong. This is how the English-a expect Italians to speak-a English. I am giving them what they want. I am thinking of going back to Napoli.'

'Please don't.'

'Because of you, Don, I will stay.'

Gino called Geoffrey 'Don' because he thought Geoffrey looked like a mafia don.

'You have style, Geoffrey. You wear a bow tie. You take my bribe of a free brandy; give me a man-hug.'

'The customers will talk.'

'They will know you are my friend.'

'They will think I don't have to pay for my coffee.'

'They will be wrong. Debbie, tell me the truth. If you had known me, Gino Alberti, before you met Geoffrey, tell me true, you'd have married me? True? Say it is true and I'll put an extra shot in your coffee.'

'It is true.'

'Geordies are corruptible ... so like, we Italians. That is why I love the Toon. Geordies are Italians who live in a cold climate.

I love your friends Ravi and Shirley, too. When Shirley speaks Welsh she sounds Italian. Your friends, Jock and Flora … I love them, also. When they call me a "wee bonny Italian" I want to hug them. Of Roger and Beryl, I will say nothing. Mamma Mia! They argue like Neapolitans.'

*******

The morning Geoffrey and Debbie were going to meet Jock and Flora for coffee at 'Gino's', Geoffrey told his wife, just as they were about to sally forth, 'I'm wearing my "lucky" shoes.'

'If you are that keen to persuade the group to go to London, I'm going to wear my "lucky" knickers.'

*******

'You're late,' Flora told Debbie in 'Gino's'.

'I had to change my knickers,' explained Debbie.

'Dribbles?' said Flora.

'No; superstition.'

'Your lucky knickers?'

'Yes; the ones I was wearing when I had to be airlifted out of a cable car on my way down from the top of Mont Blanc.'

'I have a lucky bra; it's the one I was wearing when I anaesthetised my first patient and she didn't die. As a scientist I shouldn't believe in luck; but I do. I'm a silly-billy, aren't I?'

'All of us in the 'Ensemble' are lucky.'

'Because we are still here?'

'Yes, and in good health.'

'But why the need to wear your lucky knickers today? Are you going to the dentist?'

'Geoffrey wants to ask for your support in a venture he has in mind for the 'Ensemble'.

'I have a lucky sporran,' said Jock, who'd been waiting to gate-crash the conversation. 'When I was wearing it on a hike up Glencoe I found a twenty pound note. Roger keeps wanting to borrow it.'

'Have you ordered?' said Geoffrey.

'Service is temporarily suspended,' explained Jock. 'Gino is having a wee ding-dong with his wife.'

'They are rowing in Italian,' said Flora.

'What are they saying, Geoffrey?' said Debbie.

'It's about Brexit; I think.'

'I've never known them argue,' said Flora. 'I do hope they don't come to blows.'

'Kitchens are full of big, sharp knives,' said Jock.

'Jock, don't say things like that; what's he like?'

They listened to the row as if they were listening to Schoenberg; not at all enjoyable. The sound of pans bouncing off walls reminded them of their aches and pains and, in Geoffrey's case, that his denture hurt.

A good fairy, one of Gino's many distant relations, came to their rescue, when, breezing in and strapping on an apron, asked them if they were been served.

'Service has been temporarily suspended,' said Geoffrey.

'It's like the Metro,' said Jock.

Geoffrey placed their order.

'I don't like hearing people argue,' said Flora, 'it upsets me.'

'I can't watch violence on television,' said Debbie. 'To encourage my grandson not to be violent I've hidden his toy gun. I've bought him a toy iron. It heats up ... two A4 batteries. Guess what? He points it at anyone he doesn't like and shouts, "Bang!".'

'Did you not explain its use to him?' said Flora.

'I tried,' said Debbie. 'He told me, "Daddy doesn't iron." Then, he said "Bang!" and shot me. Not wishing to be a spoilsport I pretended to be dead. I got my own back by being dead for rather too long. That scared him. He ran off shouting, "Mam, grandma's dead." Actually I rather liked lying on the floor with my eyes closed. It was very peaceful.'

'Ah, here come the cappuccinos,' said Jock.

Gino's wife, Maria, a brunette from Sicily, waitressed the drinks. Her white apron, streaked with red blotches, made the quartet fear the worst.

'Ketchup,' explained Maria, 'not to worry; not blood. Gino has a headache. He has gone to lie down.'

When she'd gone Geoffrey said, 'In England it's the women who have the headaches.'

'In your case, Geoffrey, it's a few years since I've needed one,' said Debbie.

'You can't have a sex life if you don't have a prostate,' said Geoffrey. 'It's not my fault. Unlike Jean Brodie, I'm not in my prime … Oh, to be young again when women said I looked like a Greek god.'

'Geoffrey, shut up. Sometimes you talk utter rubbish.'

'I'm always getting headaches,' said Flora.

'Flora thinks she has a brain tumour,' said Jock, 'don't you, Flora?'

'I've had a scan.'

'And it showed nothing.'

'I wish to postulate,' said Geoffrey, 'that, Flora's headaches are caused by a lack of adventure. Flora needs a change of scene. We all do.'

'If you think I'm going down the Zambezi in a dug-out canoe with you, Geoffrey, I'm not,' said Jock.

'I was thinking of a trip to London. OPAC,' said Geoffrey.

'OPEC?' said Jock.

'No. OPAC. PAC, as in "pack your bag". I wish you'd get a bloody hearing aid.'

'No need to shout. I was close. PEC, PAC.'

'OPAC!'

'Organisation of Petroleum Exporting Countries; that's what OPEC stands for; never heard of the other one.'

'OPAC, Jock. Organisation of Pensioners' Adventure Clubs.'

'Never heard of it.'

'I'm not surprised. It's a new organisation. I am its founder. We are all going to have membership cards.'

'Who is "we"?'

'The 'Ensemble'. Because we are reading "Pickwick" Debbie and I thought, what a good idea it would be if we, all of us visited Dickens's house in Doughty Street … a day excursion, not overnight.'

'So that is why you picked "Pickwick Papers",' said Flora, 'and Debbie is wearing her lucky knickers.'

'When we go to London,' said Debbie, sounding excited, 'we do what members of the Pickwick Club did.'

'We observe our fellow travellers,' said Geoffrey.

'We make notes about their behaviour,' said Debbie.

'Will we have notebooks?' said Flora.

'Laptops and mobile phones,' said Geoffrey. 'We may be old but we all know how to use modern technology. After all, without our know-how some of the stuff the young drool over today wouldn't have been invented.'

'What if I prefer using a notebook?'

'Up to you; I'm going to call the notes I make: "Ale the Way to Lundun". Whimsy has made me decide to keep a record in the vernacular. I will record everything in the Tyneside dialect; that way, if I write anything risqué, I will not be found out.'

'Like Samuel Pepys?' said Jock.

'Or, the Rosetta stone,' said Geoffrey, determined to have the last word. He wasn't going to let Jock, or anyone else for that matter, hijack his idea.

'If we go,' said Flora, 'I will record using good old fashioned pen and paper. I like to be old fashioned. Last night I went to bed wearing a cardigan my mother knit me.'

'So,' said Geoffrey, pushing to the back of his mind an image of Flora in bed wearing an old cardigan, 'we are all agreed. When I bring up the idea of us all going to London, you'll back me? I mean, if you don't want to throw your hat in the ring, well, that's fine by me.'

*******

In the privacy of their own homes, the two couples talked to each other the way lawyers talk in private about the death penalty; those who love power more than compassion and have a fondness for wearing a black cap being all for it.

Geoffrey: I got the impression Jock wasn't keen about London. Sometimes I think you just can't help people. It would only be a day trip. It would do them good to get out more.'

Debbie: Roger won't want to pay. Have you thought about that?

Geoffrey: If we can persuade the others, Roger will toe the line. He'll not want to be left out. Furthermore, if Beryl thinks he doesn't want to go she will be adamant that she does want to go.

Debbie: Geoffrey, help me off with my shoes, will you? My back is bad today.

*******

Flora: Do you think we should go to London?

Jock: Doesn't matter what we think. Geoffrey always gets his own way.

Flora: He takes advantage of us. I know he does. We are no longer the "force" we were when we worked in Silicon Valley.

Jock: Ah, the "force"; Bob Noyce and the integrated circuit.

Flora: The INTEL way of doing things.

Jock: So un-British.

Flora: The Yanks loved it when I called farts, "botty-burps".

Jock: Do you think Geoffrey and Debbie are the "good Force" or, the "bad Force"?

Flora: They mean well.

Jock: When Geoffrey raises OPAC, or whatever it is he calls it, at the reading group, let's wait and see how the others react.

*******

Later in the afternoon Flora found her husband asleep in his favourite black and white striped deckchair. At his feet, where they'd fallen when he'd nodded off, lay a chisel and a mallet.

In front of him, sunk into a hole in the ground, the digging of which had come close to giving him a heart attack, stood a fifteen foot tree trunk; carving tree trunks into totem poles was his latest hobby.

'I've been thinking,' said Jock, opening his eyes, 'I think we should go to London. Any chance of some Dundee cake … we always have Dundee cake with our afternoon tea.'

*******

Ravi, not privy to any of the above, sitting on a seat, in a bow window, through which sun streamed, put down his paperback copy of 'Pickwick' and, not for the first time, asked himself: Would he ever understand the English? Their island mentality. Shirley was Welsh. Did he understand the Welsh? No. In the early days of their marriage how many times had she told him off when she heard him telling his Indian friends he'd married an English woman. 'Ravi, I'm not English, I'm Welsh.'

He could hear his wife now, on the phone to her brother, who lived in Crymch, speaking Welsh.

When she wanted to turn him on she wore a sari and put a plastic diamond in her belly button. His family in India loved her. His mother, sadly, now in what the Christians he now lived among, called Heaven, had told him, 'She is the wife for you, Ravi. It is not her fault she is a memsahib. No one can have everything.'

The passion in his wife's voice, clicking away in a beautiful Welsh sing-song, reminded him of India.

When Dickens was writing "Pickwick" Great Britain had been a country with an empire. India had been its crown jewel. In those days on a map of the world the colour pink had been everywhere. He remembered his grandfather shouting, with venom, 'Pink is a bloody rash on the world. It spreads and spreads. Who is going to stop it? When will Gandhi get us independence?'

Only last week shopping in Marks and Spencer's a woman had said to him, 'Do you mind?' He hadn't meant to jump the queue but, thinking about Newcastle United's position in the Premier League had made him absentminded.

Her haughty attitude reminded him of how the British had treated his parents and grandparents. The woman was a memsahib. In days of yore she'd have ordered him to carry her bags.

Later over a cup of Darjeeling, Shirley asked her husband if he was enjoying 'Pickwick'.

'It has made me laugh,' said Ravi. 'Dickens's London is like Mumbai. It is full of noise and colour.'

'Like Geoffrey?'

'I wonder why he picked "Pickwick". Geoffrey is devious; no question about it; he'd thrive in India. It takes no imagination for me to see him selling saris in Delhi; with his contacts he'd make a fortune.'

'We all know why you picked "A Passage to India".'

'Do we? I know Roger didn't like it when I told him that reading Forster had reminded me of how snooty the English were and, still are, for that matter.'

'Roger was sticking up for his tribe. He sees things from an Anglo-Saxon point of view. You see things from an Indian point of view; all perfectly natural.'

'Roger is a coelacanth; a prehistoric fish, so rare, that when one is caught it makes the news.'

'We all agreed, only short books. All of us suffer eye strain. A long book takes a long time to read. Before we start reading a long book at our ages, we have to ask, will we live long enough to finish it? I think Geoffrey's up to something.'

*******

Roger and Beryl had their first row of the day going into Newcastle on the Metro.

Roger was of the opinion that 'Pickwick' had hijacked his wife. He was jealous. He'd heard of 'golf widows', well, he was a 'Pickwick widower' and he didn't like it one little bit … bloody, Charles Dickens … bloody, arty-farty, Geoffrey. Who did they think they were, telling him to read a book a month?

To get his wife's attention he kicked her foot.

'Is it a "good read"?' he asked, leering at her over the top of a 'free' newspaper.

'Mr Dickens is wonderful,' she replied, without looking up.

'You're always doing that to me, Beryl.'

'What?' said Beryl, still not looking up.

'Not looking at me when you are talking to me. I'm telling you, I'll not be ignored.'

The more Beryl liked 'Pickwick' the more he hated it. He'd be damned if he'd read it. It was too long. Nor would he pay a fine for not having read it. Why should he? The rules said, 'short books'. End of.

He disliked the Metro. You never knew who you might end up sitting next to; a punk, a communist, a Labour Party supporter? Once he'd sat on a damp seat. What had made the seat damp?

28

He'd sent his trousers off to the dry cleaners and sent the bill to the Metro. He wasn't surprised when he never heard from them. It was the same when he e-mailed letters to newspapers. What did you have to do to get your letters printed? He always gave his name and address. He wasn't ashamed of his views. What was wrong with saying if the Scots were given independence they should be kept out of England by a wall similar to the one Donald Trump wanted to build between America and Mexico? Let the buggers go if that's what they wanted.

As it approached 'Monument' station the train began to brake.

'Our stop,' said Roger, standing up, 'you might not be getting off here, Beryl, but I am.'

'We haven't stopped yet,' said Beryl, still reading 'Pickwick'.

'If you want to stay on until Pelaw, well, that's up to you.'

When the train jerked to a halt, Roger banged his nose on the bare scapula of the young woman standing in front of him.

'Ouch!' he exclaimed, rubbing his nose. 'That hurt.'

'You a dirty old man or something?' said the victim.

She'd a tattoo on her back. It said that she loved 'Ron'. Roger hated tattoos.

'Sorry.'

'That's what my first said when he left me to bring up two kids ... you're a "pervy", aren't you?'

'Young lady, I assure you, I am not a pervert; merely a bit unsteady on my pins.'

'In that case, mate, you need one of those things old people push to stop them falling down ... my gran's got one.'

*******

Roger and Beryl's house had two bathrooms. In the largest one there was also a toilet.

One evening in the latter bathroom when Roger was in the bath and Beryl was sitting on the loo reading 'Pickwick', Roger threw a bar of soap at her.

'I'll not be ignored,' he shouted. 'I've told you, Beryl, I'll not be ignored. It's that bloody book. It's taken you over.'

When he climbed out of the bath, Beryl said to the 'sea-monster': 'When are you going to read Pickwick?'

'I'm not.'

'Roger, it's a funny book. It will make you laugh. You are a member of the "Ensemble". Geoffrey will know you haven't read it. You'll have to pay a fine.'

'No, I won't. And, another thing, Beryl, we're not having turkey for Christmas.'

'I beg your pardon. What on earth are you on about? Christmas is so far away even the turkeys aren't worried.'

'I'm telling you, Beryl, we're not having turkey for Christmas. We're having beef.'

'But, Roger, this is June. Are you mad?'

'You dare ask me if I'm mad, you, the woman on the Metro giggling out loud at that bloody book … people were looking at you, you know. I'm telling you, we're having beef.'

'Why not have turkey and beef?'

'If we have a turkey the piece of beef you'll buy will be small. Small pieces of beef don't taste the same as big pieces of beef. I'm telling you, Beryl, if you buy a turkey I'll throw it out. And, you know I'm not joking. Are you listening?'

'No, I'm doing what you should be doing, I'm reading Pickwick.'

*******

'I'm more nervous than when I gave that presentation in Downing Street,' said Geoffrey. 'And, that was a long time ago.'

'The bunion on my left foot has ached all day,' said Debbie. 'It always does when I'm anxious.'

'What about the one on your right foot?'

'Not a twinge.'

'So, it's a one bunion worry.'

'I suppose that's something.'

The cause of Geoffrey and Debbie's anxiety? This was the night they planned to broach to the 'Ensemble' their idea of a trip to London.

Would Jock and Flora support them? Had it been a good idea in the first place to make them privy to the idea?

In his time Geoffrey had chaired many committees; big, important, committees. The decisions they'd made had affected the lives of thousands of people.

He'd found that when you worked with the Germans, woe betide you if you hadn't done your homework.

When dealing with the Americans he'd learnt not to mention that his hobby was amateur dramatics; hinting instead, that, because he hailed from the north of England, he was forever out on the moors shooting four legged herbivores and drinking whisky with the Duke of Northumberland.

It was Geoffrey's opinion that the 'Ensemble' was a group of flat tyres. They needed blowing up and, he was just the man to do it. His pals needed to be reminded that, while they did not have the energy to dance till two in the morning as they had used to do, they were still more than capable of enjoying themselves by going on a jaunt. The silly old fools were in grave danger of acting their age.

They needed to be reminded they were still young at heart; which was why he and Debbie had gone to all the bother of broaching their idea dressed as Victorians. Presentation counted for a lot in sales. When the 'Ensemble' saw them, seen all the bother they'd gone to, there'd not be a hope in hell of them saying, 'No,' to a day trip to London.

In a Cheval mirror, Geoffrey admired, with a long stare of admiration, his hired, bottle green swallow tail coat and yellow double breasted waistcoat. They were a spot-on fit. He particularly liked his checked black and white trousers which he'd picked as a kind of non sequitur tribute to Newcastle United.

'Don't hog the mirror,' said Debbie.

'Do I look good?'

'You look wonderful. Now, out of the way. I want to check all my ribbons are facing the same way.'

Debbie's dress levitated outwards in all directions from her waist as if someone inside was hard at work with bellows. The dark green material from which it was made, rustled and caught the light as if it were made of mirrors; against this background its dozens of red bows were like the flowers on a camellia. Around her neck she wore what looked like a paper doily.

'I'm serving drinks straight away,' said Geoffrey.

'I thought the club rules stated that alcoholic drinks were to be served after the "meaningful discussion",' said Debbie, 'never, before.'

'I sense opposition to our idea of a trip to London ... I want to get them pissed straight away. It doesn't take much.'

'Jock and Flora will support us.'

'Do you think so? I'm not so sure. I know "Pickwick" is a long book. I broke the rules picking it ... huh, bet none of them will complain when we break the "drinks" rule. They'll moan about "Pickwick" being a long book but, they'll not complain about been offered an extra drink.'

'Roger will ask if he can take his home ... remember, he did that once?'

'I've a miniature whisky for him ... it's a bribe.'

'The older he gets the meaner he gets.'

'Age exacerbates one's traits.'

'If Roger is becoming meaner you, my dear Geoffrey, are becoming more theatrical ... persuading me to dress up like this.

I still can't believe what you did in the King's Arms on Sunday. What on earth possessed you to stand up and say, "with this double cream I bless the pearly head of my rice pudding"?'

'I like rice pudding.'

'I know you do but, to make a speech about anointing its pearly head, with double cream and then, stealing from Burns and calling it the "queen of puddings" was … eccentric. If Jock and Flora had been there … your plagiarism would have horrified them. In their book Robbie Burns is not a poet to be trifled with.'

'I amused the bar staff. I brought a ray of sunshine into their dull lives. A few people clapped.'

'Geoffrey, you were there as a paying customer, not a paid entertainer.'

'I'd had too much wine.'

'And, do stop polishing that glass. If it's not clean now, it never will be. If organising a trip to London is making you this jittery, it's not worth it. And don't spill anything on your costume. It's hired. We have to pay for stains. Have your handkerchief ready in case you drool.'

'I don't drool.'

'Geoffrey, I know you and when I say you "drool", please, believe me. I'm your wife. You, drool.'

*******

Ten minutes before the 'Ensemble' were due to arrive Geoffrey told his wife: 'I'm going to leave the front door open. They can let themselves in. When they are all here we will pop out of hiding and give them a theatrical experience they will remember for the rest of their lives; which, in their case, probably won't be for very long; do not be overawed when they clap and wolf whistle.'

At the door, Geoffrey and Debbie, holding hands, admired their front garden. Geoffrey sniffed the summer air.

'Honeysuckle,' he said. 'I am of the opinion that a sniff of honeysuckle is better for the soul than a sniff of snuff.'

'Geoffrey, you've never taken snuff in your life; there you go again, talking rubbish.'

'I did when I played Sherlock Holmes.'

'When you kept on sneezing because you'd forgotten your lines.'

'My last big part with the "Jesmond Players",' said Geoffrey, looking up into a cloudless blue sky onto which his effortless gift of reliving happy memories had projected an image of himself as a strolling player. 'Moriarty got Sherlock; a touch of amnesia got me. I do hope the "Ensemble" are on time; waiting to "go on" makes me jittery.'

'Where are we going to hide?'

'In the kitchen. I will announce our entrance by banging a pan with a spoon.'

'When they arrive,' said Debbie, 'we'll be putting on a show, won't we?'

'I hope they all arrive together,' said Geoffrey, 'they usually do; they are like sheep.'

'I think they will be impressed.'

'Impressed! If they were younger they'd do somersaults and handstands.'

'I hope Jock and Flora aren't late.'

'Why should they be?'

'Flora told me, Jock hates leaving off carving his totem pole.'

*******

At one minute past eight, Geoffrey and Debbie heard voices.

'Don't let them see you,' said Geoffrey.

The doorbell rang, not once but many times; making it sound like a fire alarm.

'That has to be Ravi,' said Geoffrey, 'he always does that. I think it's because he's from the east. He likes banging gongs, that sort of thing.'

'Ravi's a Hindu not a Buddhist.'

'Coo-eee! Geoffrey, Debbie, where are you?' sang out Shirley.

Through a gap in the door, Debbie watched her guests hang up their coats, take out their copies of 'Pickwick' and file into the lounge where she heard them flop into their usual seats, their various sighs and groans sounding, to her, like an orchestra tuning up.

'Coo-eee!' intoned Shirley. 'Geoffrey and Debbie, where are you. We're coming to get you. The Welsh are here.'

'And the Scots,' shouted Jock.

'And the sub-continent of India,' shouted Ravi. 'Goodness me, dear old England is being invaded.'

In the kitchen Geoffrey said, 'Your hand, Lady Jesmond.'

*******

A star walking out onto a stage expects applause. When Geoffrey and Debbie presented themselves – 'Da-Dar!' to the 'Ensemble – their expectations were 'Archimedean'; which, is to say, they expected Shirley and Ravi, Flora and Jock, Beryl and Roger, to scream with excitement and applaud like maniacs in direct proportion to the amount of effort they themselves had put into the choosing and hiring of the costumes they were wearing.

The ensuing silence reminded Geoffrey of the time he'd lit a dud 'Roman Candle'. How he'd waited and waited, after its fuse had stopped spluttering, for it to explode.

He was not used to failure and took the 'Ensemble's' ennui not so much on the chin, but as a personal insult.

'You might at least clap,' he said; 'when I played with the "Jesmond Players" someone always clapped. I mean to say, Debbie and I have gone to a lot of trouble, dressing up.'

35

'It cost a fortune to hire the costumes,' said Debbie.

'Then,' said Roger, 'you've too much money.'

'If my eyebrows weren't pencil lines,' said Beryl, 'they'd be on the ceiling.'

'If I'd known it was fancy dress,' said Ravi, 'I'd have come as a rajah.'

'I'd have come as a druid,' said Shirley.

'I'd have dug out my kilt,' said Jock.

'Roger could have come as Scrooge,' said Beryl.

'Stop getting at me, Beryl,' said Roger. 'I don't like it. I've told you before, I'm not having it.'

'He wants beef for his Christmas dinner.'

'He's optimistic,' said Shirley; 'at our ages some of us might not see Christmas. I'm on ten tablets a day.'

'I'm on fifteen,' said Jock, 'and Flora's on sixteen …water works, bowels, blood pressure, cholesterol, eye drops, blood thinners, you name it. Young folk want to climb every Munro. My aim's to take as many tablets a day as there are Munros.'

'What do you think?' said Geoffrey.

'About Jock's ambition to take as many tablets a day as there are Munros?' said Ravi.

'No, what do you think about my costume and Debbie's?'

'Who are you supposed to be?'

'Are you characters from "Pickwick"?' said Shirley.

'If they are, I don't recognise them,' said Beryl, 'and, unlike some folk I could name,' glaring at Roger, 'I've read "Pickwick" from cover to cover. I think Mr Dickens is wonderful.'

'If Beryl thinks "Dickens is wonderful",' said Geoffrey, 'why don't we all go to London, I mean, just for the day. Debbie wants to visit Dickens's house in Doughty Street. They have a tearoom and it's not far from King's Cross. While you mull, shall I go and get the drinks.'

'Geoffrey,' said Jock, 'we never serve drinks until after the "discussion".'

'I have lots to say,' said Beryl. 'I've made a list of all the bits that made me laugh.'

'Me too,' said Shirley. 'I thought the humour very Welsh.'

'My mother read it to me when Mumbai was called Bombay,' said Ravi. 'It is very Indian. "Pickwick" is in my DNA.'

'That's cheating,' said Roger. 'If your mother read it to you, that means you didn't have to read it, like we all had to.'

'Roger,' said Flora, 'you sound as if you didn't enjoy reading "Pickwick"?'

'He hasn't read it,' said Beryl.

'Yes, I have,' said Roger. 'I just haven't read every page. It's a long book.'

'Everyone,' said Ravi, 'hands up who thinks Roger should be fined?'

'Get stuffed, all of you,' said Roger. 'I'm not paying. Geoffrey broke the rules picking a "long book". If he can break the rules, why can't I? He's serving drinks before we've had our discussion; that's another rule he's broken. If Geoffrey can get away with breaking rules, why can't I?'

'What if,' said Geoffrey, 'I call this meeting "extraordinary" and, just for this once, all rules are suspended?'

'I won't have to pay a fine?'

'Correct.'

'I'm not in favour of you not paying a fine,' said Flora. 'When you joined the club, Roger, you were told its rules. When I joined my tennis club I knew senior players were only allowed to play in the afternoon between one o'clock and five. Many times I wanted to play in the evening. I knew I couldn't because I'd read the rules.'

'Flora,' said Jock, ever so gently taking hold of his wife's arm, 'Geoffrey is asking what you would like to drink?'

'If going to London means I'm going to get a drink and don't have to talk about that bloody book,' said Roger, 'I'm all for going to London; as long as we don't have to stop the night; there and back, in a day, keep the cost down, agreed?'

'I'm all for it,' said Jock.

'Shall we take a vote?' said Geoffrey. 'Those in favour, hands up. Flora, you haven't voted.'

'In the tennis club rules were rules.'

'Flora,' said Jock, 'it's a rhetorical vote. I told you, if Geoffrey wants to go to London then, we will be going to London; take my word for it; it's a majority decision, we are going to London.'

'Thank you, everyone, for your support,' said Geoffrey. 'Now I know we're going to London I'm going to open a few bottles of the fizzy stuff. Excuse me while I go to the cellar.'

'Can I fire champagne corks at Roger's wallet?' said Beryl. 'Like the proverbial barn door, it's a target too big to miss.'

'If you don't mind,' said Roger, 'I'll crack the jokes.'

*******

When everyone had a glass of fizz in their veined and mottled hands, Geoffrey said, raising his flute, 'Ladies and gentlemen, I give you, "OPAC".'

'OPAC?' said Ravi.

'OPAC?' said Roger. 'Sounds left wing to me. If it's left wing, I'm not drinking to it. You know my views.'

'Not OPEC,' said Jock, 'OPAC … PAC, as in "pack" a bag.'

'We heard what Geoffrey said,' said Roger. 'We know he said "OPAC". We don't need hearing aids. It's you who needs hearing aids.'

'OPAC, 'said Geoffrey. 'Organisation of Pensioners' Adventure Clubs. Members of OPAC, I give you your club.'

'I'll drink to that,' said Roger, 'a lot of silly old sods pretending to be young, sounds about right for us lot.'

'Who will do the organising?' said Shirley. 'I mean, who will book the tickets, that sort of thing?'

'Need you ask?' said Roger.

'Is the sun hot?' said Jock.

'If it's alright with everyone,' said Geoffrey, 'I will do the organising … after all the club was my idea – and Debbie's of course.'

'The earlier we book,' said Roger, 'the better the deal we'll get. Buying tickets on the day costs a fortune.'

'Now I know we're going,' said Flora, 'I think I'm excited.'

'We'll need a trolley for our medicines,' said Jock, 'blood plasma and all that.'

'Don't be silly, Jock,' said Flora, 'your tablets and mine will go in my vanity case.'

'There's no room for Roger's tablets in my handbag,' said Beryl.

'Beryl, I've told you before, I'm not having it … stop picking on me. I have a bad heart. You'll miss me when I'm not here.'

'Beryl,' said Debbie, 'you should be careful Roger doesn't do to you what Dickens did to his wife.'

'What did he do?' said Roger.

'Don't you know?'

'I wouldn't be asking if I knew, would I?'

'He had the family home segregated, doors boarded up, so that he and his missus, though under the same roof, lived separate lives. He tried to get her declared insane.'

'I like the sound of that,' said Roger.

'He had a mistress.'

'He liked the women, did he?' said Beryl.

'Nothing wrong with that,' said Shirley. 'I like men. Yesterday I saw this gorgeous hulk in the Grainger Market carrying a side of beef on his back. He'd lovely eyes; sea-green, they were. When he saw me looking at him, he winked. If only I was fifty years younger.'

'I don't know if you know,' said Geoffrey, 'but Doughty Street is where Dickens wrote "Pickwick" and "Oliver Twist". And, I'll bet you don't know this,' pausing.

'Get on with it, Geoffrey,' said Jock. 'If you don't, your dodgy short-term memory will kick in, then, none of us will know, what you have assumed we do not know.'

'I've forgotten,' said Geoffrey. 'Just joking! … how many of you have spotted the blue plaque in Nelson Street, beside the Café Royal? No one? I knew as much … allow me to enlighten you. The blue plaque tells us Charles Dickens gave a reading in that building when it was a Music Hall. I propose, before boarding our train to London that we meet there for coffee.'

'Every time I go to the Café Royal,' said Ravi, 'I find myself thinking of Oliver Twist.'

'He keeps asking for more,' said Shirley, 'don't you, dear?'

'I do like their croissants.'

'Let's talk dates,' said Geoffrey, whipping out his mobile to check his diary. 'Now, if I may suggest …'

*******

The day for the trip to London dawned bright and sunny. Like bees from different hives but, nevertheless bees all heading for the same bed of flowers, each couple in the 'Ensemble' made its own way to the Café Royal; apart, that is, from Flora and Jock who, because they were coming back from a funeral in Edinburgh would be met up with when their train, the train on which Geoffrey had booked seats for the 'Ensemble', stopped at Newcastle.

Initially, Geoffrey had rolled out the idea that they all meet at his house and then, 'we can all walk into town together. It's not far'.

'I know it's not far,' Roger had snapped back, 'but some of us don't like walking as much as you do.'

Geoffrey knew a red-line when he heard one and had not pressed the point. A good leader knew when to back off.

Roger and Beryl were being driven to the Café Royal by their grandson.

Ravi and Shirley were getting the Metro.

Geoffrey and Debbie were walking.

'I feel virtuous, walking,' said Debbie.

'We are doing our bit to combat global warming,' said Geoffrey; 'more than can be said of that diesel car, over there.'

'If everyone had as small a carbon footprint as we have the ice-caps wouldn't be melting. Roger is so lazy.'

'And mean.'

'He hates walking.'

'They are missing a delightful walk,' said Geoffrey, 'it's their loss.'

'I can taste diesel.'

'Is that a chaffinch?'

'That's a budgerigar; dear me, escaped from its cage. If I see a note in the newsagents asking if anyone has seen a lost and missing – owners of missing pets always put "lost and missing" – budgerigar, I'll let them know.'

'This morning, Debbie, we are like that budgerigar, don't you think? We have escaped our cage, at least for a day. I wonder for how long it will survive out, alone, in the wicked world?'

'Not long if a hawk sees it.'

'Jesmond is so rural.'

'How Roger dare ask his grandson to drive him and Beryl into town, I don't know.'

'It's because he can't use his Metro pass until half past nine. He hates walking and he refuses to pay full fare. Ravi and Shirley are getting the Metro but paying doesn't bother them.'

'Be lucky if they're on time.'

'The Metro has only broken down twice this week.'

'Amazing how we accept incompetence. It is so easy to get used to the third rate.'

'It's good of Flora and Jock to come back early from their relative's funeral in Edinburgh. They wouldn't miss our jaunt for the world. I know they wouldn't. Jock loves our company. I liked his text: "Four weddings and a funeral!! My kilt's done one wedding and ten funerals!" Edinburgh to King's Cross. I always think that has a ring to it. Edinburgh to King's Cross. It rolls off the tongue. It's like saying, "Abracadabra". The Flying Scotsman. You have the tickets?'

'No, dear, you have the tickets.'

'Do I?'

*******

'Where are they?' said Roger, looking at his sundial-large wristwatch and, at the same time, shooing away a cooing pigeon with his walking stick; he and Beryl were outside the Café Royal. 'Just because we are first here, Beryl, I hope that doesn't mean we have to buy the coffees.'

'You'll get your loyalty card stamped,' said Beryl.

'Beryl, you're doing it again; not looking at me when you are talking to me.'

'I was looking at the blue plaque Geoffrey told us to look out for; to think, all those years ago, Mr Dickens was in Newcastle; right here. I know this might sound silly but I think I can feel his "presence".'

'If you tell Shirley that she'll agree with you. The Welsh are superstitious. Where the hell is everyone? I don't like to be kept waiting.'

'Co-ee!' shouted Shirley, as she and Ravi spotted Roger and Beryl.

'Bloody Siamese twins, those two,' said Roger, commenting on the way Ravi and Shirley had come into Nelson Street, linking arms.

'Bore da,' said Shirley, 'Isn't this exciting? I feel like singing, "Land of my Fathers".'

'Glad we're not first here,' said Ravi, 'that will save us a few bob.'

'What do you mean?' said Roger.

'Didn't Geoffrey mention, "First in the queue, first to pay"?'

'I didn't pay a fine for not reading "Pickwick" and I am not buying everyone a coffee, so there.'

'Ravi, stop teasing,' said Beryl. 'If we were jaunting off to Lourdes where miracles are as common as sparrows, Roger would have bought us a coffee, I know he would; but, as we are off to London, why expect him to?'

'Scrooge changed,' said Ravi.

'I never cared for Scrooge, after he mended his ways,' said Roger. 'Anyway, Geoffrey said we were having a kitty which, he will confirm, when he gets here; if, he ever does. And, stop picking on me. And where are Jock and Flora? They are always on time.'

'They are in Edinburgh,' said Shirley.

'What! Are they not coming?'

'Did Ravi not text you? Ravi?'

'I forgot ... sorry, Roger.'

'Am I part of the "Ensemble", or, am I not?'

'Of course you are, Roger. My fault. I apologise. Geoffrey sent me a text telling me that Jock and Flora have had to go to Edinburgh for a funeral. They'll be on the train Geoffrey has booked us on. He did tell me to tell you.'

'You losing your memory, Ravi?'

'If you are trying to find out if I've forgotten you owe me for those tickets Shirley and I bought you and Beryl for "Peter Grimes", then the answer is "no".'

'I don't like opera.'

'You might have liked it.'

'But, I didn't.'

'So, I have to pay for you to find out what you like and what you don't like, is that what you are saying?'

'It was a long time ago.'

'So was the First World War but we still "remember".'

'That's why we have Poppy Day,' said Shirley.

'At least it's not raining,' said Beryl. 'I'll text Debbie; find out where she is.'

'I'll text Geoffrey,' said Ravi. 'I hope they haven't forgotten.'

'I'm sitting down,' said Roger, flopping into an aluminium chair provided by the Café Royal for its al fresco customers.

Taking their cue from Roger the others too, sat down; standing for too long made their backs and legs ache.

'These are for the smokers,' said Ravi.

'Because none of us smoke, we shouldn't be sitting here, is that what you are saying?' said Beryl.

'Of course he's not saying that,' said Roger. 'Where the hell are they? We're going to miss our train. If we miss the train I'm not paying "on the day" prices. I'm telling you that, now. And I mean it.'

'I think we are doing good sitting here,' said Shirley. 'If these seats are for smokers and we are sitting here that means we are stopping people smoking and that is a good thing.'

'In Sainsbury's car park I've seen perfectly fit people park in the spaces reserved for the disabled,' said Beryl.

'Rules are there to be broken,' said Roger. 'Geoffrey knows all about that.'

'Roger,' said Ravi, 'you are an iconoclast.'

'The last time you used that word,' said Shirley, 'Jock thought you'd said "Elastoplast" ...remember?'

'Jock needs hearing aids.'

'Debbie's in Northumberland Street,' said Beryl, reading a text off her phone. 'Geoffrey's forgotten the tickets. He's had to go back home for them.'

'Geoffrey's got Alzheimer's,' said Roger.

Reading a text off his phone, Ravi said, 'Geoffrey says: "Debbie forgot tickets. Go inside. I want an Americano, hot milk on the side and a Danish. Be there in ten minutes."'

'Where is he now?' said Shirley.

'On the back of a tandem.'

'A what?' said Roger.

'You know, a bicycle for two people.'

'I know what a "tandem" is. I haven't got Alzheimer's. What's he doing on a tandem?'

'A neighbour is bringing him in.'

'Geoffrey should have given us our tickets. He treats us like children. In you go, Ravi, old man, the one first through the door pays.'

'What will Debbie want?' said Ravi.

'She'll have the same as Geoffrey,' said Shirley. 'They always have the same.'

*******

So they could keep an eye out for Geoffrey and Debbie, the 'Ensemble' sat close to a window.

'It's not cheap,' said Roger, looking at the menu.

'For once in your life, Roger,' said Ravi, 'forget about money.'

'Are you paying?'

'No. Geoffrey said we're having a kitty; that's what you said.'

'If I have a coffee and Geoffrey has a coffee and a Danish, that means I'm subsidising him. I'm not a fan of subsidies. They don't work. If we're having a kitty I'll have a bacon sandwich and a coffee.'

'I'll have a cup of tea,' said Beryl.

'You get a nice pot of tea here,' said Shirley. 'Ravi, I'll come to the counter with you, I want to look at the cakes. They are expensive but, who cares? We're on a jaunt. I'm glad Geoffrey persuaded us to do this … it's made me feel young, like I did when

I was sixty. Such a pity we're not stopping in London overnight. A strange bedroom and a bed with clean sheets makes me randy.'

'Don't you go getting any ideas, Roger,' said Beryl, 'we're "Pickwickians", not sex maniacs.'

'It was different when I was in my prime and you wanted babies.'

*******

When Ravi and Shirley were away at the counter, ordering, Roger said to Beryl: 'I thought Ravi might have forgotten about the money I owe him for the opera tickets. It was thirty years ago.'

'I seem to remember enjoying "Peter Grimes".'

'I didn't.'

'You were the only one in our row who didn't clap.'

'We're number fifty-five,' said Shirley coming back to the table waving a silver tube with a round base and the number, fifty-five, at its tip.

'It reminds me,' she said, 'of those holiday couriers who hold up a hat on the end of a stick so the group they are leading don't get lost. Years ago Ravi got lost in Amsterdam; didn't you, darling? He ended up in the red light district. I found him looking into a window full of naked women. He said, "You would think they would know they can be seen". I told him, "Ravi, my darling, you are in the red light district". "I didn't know", he said.'

'Did you believe him?' said Beryl.

'I gave him the benefit of the doubt.'

*******

While they waited for their order and for Debbie and Geoffrey to arrive, Roger twitched. He kept looking at his sundial and, like a swimmer in a rough sea, kept bobbing up and down to look out of the window.

Ravi reminded them not to get 'too comfy'.

'When Geoffrey gets here, as sure as India is too hot in the summer, he will suggest we move to a different table; that is what he always does.'

'Where are they?' said Roger.

'Roger, deep breath,' said Shirley, 'that's what I did when I'd to stand up in front of two-thousand of my countrymen at the eisteddfod and recite my poems. It stopped my agitation dead in its tracks.'

'I am not becoming agitated.'

'Yes, you are,' said Beryl.

*******

A short while later, Debbie arrived.

'I'm exhausted,' she sighed, flopping into a chair. 'Geoffrey's blaming me for forgetting the tickets. I didn't. He forgot them because he was fussing about drying his hair.'

For a man of his age – for a man of any age – Geoffrey had a lot of hair. Old age had turned it into the colour of the winter plumage of the ptarmigan.

'After showering to make sure it keeps its shape,' continued, Debbie, by way of explanation, 'he wears a shower cap for half an hour. He wears it while eating his toast and marmalade. He always has two slices of toast and two cups of tea. When he's eaten those he knows his hair will be dry, that it will retain its shape when he removes the shower cap. He calls the time it takes him to eat his toast and marmalade, his "hair timer". This morning the elastic in the shower cap broke. There was hell on. You'd think the government had stopped our winter fuel allowance; that's why he forgot the tickets.'

'If the government stopped my winter fuel allowance,' said Roger, 'I'd commit suicide.'

'Geoffrey's lucky to have hair,' said Ravi, who had very little. 'Having hair makes you look young. Geoffrey's older than me but, because he has hair, he looks younger. And ... no one has noticed.'

'Noticed what?' said Roger.

'That, I've had my hair cut. To look smart for our trip to London I've been to the barbers.'

'You have no hair to cut,' said Roger. 'Pay for a polish, did you? How much?'

'Ten pound.'

'You've been robbed.'

'The barber was a young man with a lot of chat. I like chatting to barbers. You learn a lot, chatting to barbers. He'd a pony tail. On his forearm a tattoo said: 'I love Marilyn'. "Girlfriend or wife?" I asked him. "Labrador," he told me. "I loved that dog. You impersonating a hobbit, sir?" drawing my attention to the fuzz brewing on the tops of my ears. "Aural cavities, sir? Hairs growing in earholes is like grass growing in gutters. It shouldn't be there, sir. Now, let's be honest, sir; it, shouldn't, should it? When it grows in gutters grass is trespassing. Trespassers should be shot, that's what I think. Starboard gutter first, do you think?" "Nautical man, are you?" "Not allowed to comment, sir. Official Secrets Act, if you know what I mean. This is like looking at seaweed underwater, sir. Where's my wet suit? If I don't come up for air in five minutes, close the shop and send for the police. Eyebrows? Fisherman, are you, sir? That's a beach-caster, if ever I saw one. Take that down to the Longsands on a windy night and you'll catch more than cold. I don't like to mention this, sir ... nostril hair ... you have a lot of it ... permission granted, I'm assuming." Snip. Snip. "I have hairy hands," I told him. "I don't do hands, sir. I'm strictly ENT – ears, nose and tips of ears ... that'll be nine-fifty, ten pound if you leave a tip which most of my customers do ... leastways the ones with a sense of humour do. Have you a sense of humour, sir?" It goes without saying I gave him ten pound.'

'I'd have done the same,' said Roger. 'Money means nothing to me.'

'I do hope Geoffrey's not going to be much longer,' said Debbie.

'Do you think,' said Beryl, 'as we get older we are becoming impatient?'

'When it's winter,' said Ravi, 'I can't wait to cuddle up in bed.'

'We like to cuddle up, don't we?' said Shirley.

'Number fifty-five?' said a waiter.

'And here comes Geoffrey,' said Debbie, looking out of the window, 'our order and Geoffrey arriving at the same time … thank goodness, now he can't complain his coffee is cold.'

*******

Geoffrey's arrival on a tandem caused heads to turn. While not in the same league as a penny-farthing; it came a close second.

Geoffrey sat on its back seat; not in the least out of breath because he'd let his 'driver' as he called Magnus – a big lad, at least six-foot four, the son of a neighbour – do all the pedalling.

'Well done, Magnus,' said Geoffrey, 'hold the bike steady for me, will you, so I can get off; years since I've been on a bike. Oh! Bloody hell' (getting off the bike) 'that made my crotch ache. Lock up the velocipede and come in for a coffee, will you? You'll recognise most of us: all neighbours; that is, unless you don't like being with old people. A lot of people don't, you know. I think I'm chaffed.'

'I use Vaseline.'

'Do you?'

'On a cycle ride I always carry a spare inner tube, two spanners a pump and Vaseline for my undercarriage. And, no, I don't mind being with old people. I always tell my "Pops" … that's what I call my grandfather … I wouldn't be here if your sperm hadn't been an Olympic swimmer.'

'Quite,' said Geoffrey, 'so, you will come and join us for a coffee?'

'Espresso, two shots with a glass of water and ice in the aqua. I expect your pals are all Tories.'

'Not quite,' said Geoffrey, ever so slightly bending his knees to ease the discomfort he could feel in his crotch, 'we are of the Social Democrat ilk, all, that is, except one; there is always an exception.'

'And, "Brexit"?'

'We try not to talk about it.'

'I like to meet Tories. It helps me get to know what the enemy is thinking. Off you toddle. Espresso. Two shots with a glass of water and ice in the aqua. I'll lock up the bike. You can't trust anyone these days.'

*******

Geoffrey ambled into the Café Royal, repeating, 'Espresso. Two shots with a glass of water and, ice in the aqua'. He did not want to forget the order. If he'd to go back to Magnus, cap in hand and say he'd forgotten, he'd lose, what he believed was called, 'street cred'. A man had his pride.

In the doorway of the Café Royal, repeating Magnus' order to himself he stopped to remove his bicycle clips and to comb his hair.

'Excuse me,' said a young woman pushing a double buggy, whose entrance into the Café Royal he was blocking.

'Careful,' said Geoffrey.

'If you weren't blocking the doorway,' she said, 'I'd be able to get in. I go to a hairdresser's when I want my hair done. I don't stand in the middle of a doorway, getting in everyone's way. You're a fire hazard, you are.'

'I'm going to London.'

'Bully for you … now, if you wouldn't mind.'

'Sorry.'

'By the way you've got egg on your chin.'

'Have I?' said Geoffrey, rubbing his chin.

'Your fly's open,' said the young women, shaking her head and smiling.

Geoffrey pulled up his zip. What had she been doing looking at his crotch? He shrugged, what the hell. These things happened; even to young people.

Despite the hitch over the tickets there was still time for coffee and a slow walk to the Central Station. A good organiser always left slack in the schedule ... rendezvous with Jock and Flora. Everything was sailing along pretty well, as planned.

'Morning, all,' said Geoffrey, hugging and kissing everyone the way a bee visits every flower in a garden.

When he hugged Ravi, Ravi whispered: 'We are in the same sampan. I had the egg on my chin yesterday ... you are not alone.'

To show he was more than worthy of being the leader of the 'Ensemble', he touched his bow-tie and flounced the red and white spotted handkerchief drizzling out of the top pocket of his off-white linen jacket the way a dog owner at a show, flounces the tail of her champion Pekingese. He admired his brogues – hand-made by a cobbler in Gateshead – and, just for good measure, checked he was zipped up.

'Sorry about the delay. We forgot the tickets.'

'You forgot the tickets,' said Debbie. 'You were fussing about your hair.'

'It wouldn't have happened to Ravi,' said Shirley.

'Ravi, unlike my good-self, is not blessed with flowing locks. Ravi, I know you won't believe this but, having lots of hair is a problem. It's like having a dog. You have to look after it. You have to take it for "walkies"; even when it's raining.'

'Husbands are like that,' said Beryl. 'Cats can look after themselves but dogs can't ... husbands are like dogs. If I didn't make Roger change his underpants, he'd be a smelly old man.'

'Are we alright, sitting here?' said Ravi.

'What's wrong with here?'

'Not too close to the door?' said Beryl.

'The sun in your eyes?' said Shirley.

'Draughty,' suggested Ravi, 'we are close to the door?'

'If everyone is happy I'm in favour of staying put. Ah! Here comes the man of the moment; my saviour, Magnus. I'm sure you'll recognise him; my neighbour's son. You'll have seen him around.'

Because Magnus was wearing cycling shoes with grips on their soles, he approached the 'Ensemble' with the clip-clop musicality of a well-shod horse.

Shirley eyed his bulging crotch, made prominent by a tight fitting one piece cyclist's leotard, very similar to those worn by male ballet dancers.

'I think you know everyone,' said Geoffrey, 'familiar faces, more or less, eh? I'll get your order.'

'Espresso, two shots with a glass of water and ice in the aqua, remember, Geoffrey?'

'Thank you for reminding me but I had remembered.'

Hi! Everyone.'

At the counter, Geoffrey found himself standing behind the woman with the twin buggy.

'Twins?' he said.

'Yes.'

'I don't suppose you know this, but I'm a twin.'

'You mean there's another one like you?'

'My brother's not like me.'

'Thank god for that.'

'I've been married for fifty years.'

'I'll remember that for the pub quiz. There's always a trivia question.'

'Your babies are smiling at me. I think they like me.'

'Mister... they have wind.'

Geoffrey had a vague memory of his own children when, very young, suffering from wind. In fact, thinking about it, Debbie had blamed 'wind' for all their children's screaming bouts. It was like now, when he went to the doctors, no matter which doctor he saw, no matter the ailment he was asking advice about, they all said the same thing – 'at your age you have to expect a few aches and pains'.

The woman paid contactless, the way all young people paid these days.

Geoffrey knew all about the technology. It worked because of principles he himself had discovered. How things had moved on since he'd retired.

'I still use cash,' he said.

'I'd be surprised if you didn't. You're like my mum ... she's in a mental home.'

'That is sad; very sad. Espresso, two shots with a glass of water and, ice in the aqua, please,' he told the young lady serving behind the counter.

'Hi! For an old man that's a trendy drink... there's hope for you yet.'

'It's not for me, it's for my chauffeur, the young chap who is waving at me.'

'He's not waving at you, mate; he's waving at me. I know him. Magnus and I are members of Momentum. Hi! Magnus. How come Magnus is your chauffeur when I know he doesn't own a car?'

'He owns a tandem.'

'You came here on Magnus's tandem?'

'All the way from Jesmond. I confess, he did most of the pedalling. Magnus is my neighbour.'

'Magnus talks a lot about an old geezer who's his neighbour. You are not, by any chance the "Geoffrey" he is always going on about, are you?'

Geoffrey nodding, paying with cash, picked up his order number ... 71 ... he'd do anything to be seventy-one again. Seventy-one was young.

'Magnus thinks you're wonderful,' whereupon, without warning, she kissed Geoffrey on both cheeks.

'Wow!' said Geoffrey. 'Do that again.'

And she did and might have done it a third time if one of the twins hadn't started to cry.

The kisses so went to Geoffrey's head that he'd no recollection of walking back to re-join the 'Ensemble' but knew he must have done because, he could hear Roger asking him: 'what was all that about?'

'Women like me,' said Geoffrey. 'I've always been popular with the ladies.'

'She's called Michelle,' said Magnus. 'Until three years ago she was called "Michael". The Americans did the operation. In her groin she always knew she was a woman. Wonderful what the Americans can do. They have the technology.'

'They've put men on the moon,' said Ravi.

'And changed a man into a woman, have they?' said Geoffrey suddenly looking like a rubber dinghy with a leak and as if what he'd just been told was threatening to make him sink under the table.

'Gender fluidity is the name of the game, these days,' said Magnus.

'I don't know why anyone would want to be a woman,' said Beryl, 'I really don't.'

'Did he, I mean, "she", give birth to the twins?' said Roger.

'Good heavens, no,' said, Magnus, 'they are adopted. The Americans are good, but not that good.'

'Maybe, when the Americans can put a man on Mars, they will have the technology to allow men to give birth.'

'If they do,' said Beryl, 'it will come too late to help me. I had a caesarean and a breech birth.'

'We're both members of Momentum,' said Magnus. 'The twins are called Catkin and Acorn.'

'What nice names,' said Beryl.

'Espresso and water?' said a waitress.

'Hi! Chantel,' said Magnus, 'it's for me. Ice in the aqua?'

'Use your eyes, big boy. Seeing is believing.'

'If the wind is in the east.'

'And the west wind doesn't blow.'

'Ciao.'

'Ciao.'

'What a delightful young lady,' said Debbie. 'At least she didn't kiss you, Geoffrey.'

'You know,' said Geoffrey, 'in my time I've been kissed by a horse, a cat, a dog, a woman and, once, on stage, I had a pretend kiss with a man but, that's the first time my flesh has parried with … what do you call it, Magnus?'

'Gender fluidity.'

'We will talk more of this in Doughty Street.'

'Do you have a job, young man?' Roger asked Magnus.

'Activist.'

'Do you remember me?'

'Of course I do. You're the old geezer who threw a pan of water over me when I knocked on your door and told you I was from the Labour party.'

'No, I did not.'

'But, that's what you wanted to do.'

'Maybe, but, I didn't. I have self-control; more than can be said for some of your people.'

'You'll be wanting to bring back the birch?'

'And capital punishment. Why do you wear your baseball cap back to front? I've always wanted to ask someone like you, that question.'

'I'm making a statement, aren't I? Same as you, wearing that tie. My dad went to that school, so did I. They chucked me out.'

'Magnus is an independent spirit,' said Debbie. 'He is a gifted mathematician, which is why he and Geoffrey get on so well.'

'On the way here,' said Geoffrey, 'we shouted numbers at each other.'

'The question we had to answer was, is it a prime number?' said Magnus, adjusting his baseball cap so it fitted better over his pony tail.

'Made me feel young,' said Geoffrey, 'at least seventy.'

'Why don't you get a job?' said Roger. 'Contribute to the economy.'

'Magnus has a job,' said Debbie. 'When he's not canvassing for the Labour party, or taking his turn to feed the deserving poor at the food bank, he is a part time maths lecturer at the Open University.'

'I'm going to the toilet,' said Roger. 'Out of my way, young man, this is an emergency.'

'Want me to put a flashing blue light on your head?'

'My husband has prostate problems,' said Beryl. 'Roger, don't forget to do your fly up.'

'I know a good joke about men who have prostate problems,' said Magnus. 'It's one of my mum's. We were watching the last Olympic Games with my dad and one of his pals; both have had their prostates out. We were watching the rowing. When they came into the room Mum said, "Here come the coxless pair"; cruel, I know, but rather witty. When she's not too busy pretending to breastfeed the twins Michelle is always saying witty things. I sometimes think the operation has made her wittier than when she was a man.'

*******

Roger left the Café Royal's marbled loo, shaking his hands dry and with a bar of its soap in his pocket.

Much to his disappointment he found the 'Ensemble' had not missed him; there they all were clucking away as excited as battery hens let out for a stroll in a field.

'Magnus has gone,' Beryl told her husband, 'and do stop impersonating a shag drying its wings. Why didn't you dry your hands in the loo? That's what normal people do.'

'How many times do I have to tell you? I don't like using those hot air machines.'

'Roger hates competition,' said Beryl, 'don't you?'

'Beryl, you are doing it again. I'm telling you, I'm not having it. And, another thing, Geoffrey; I hope you are not going to charge the coffee you bought Magnus to the kitty. He's not part of our group. He's young. I hate the young.'

'No, you don't,' said Beryl, 'Magnus is just one young man. He is not ALL young men … just because you don't like Magnus and Magnus is young, doesn't mean you dislike young people.'

'Don't you question my logic,' said Roger, 'I went to a grammar school.'

'My husband went to a grammar school,' said Beryl, 'therefore he cannot be such a bigot as to believe in capital punishment, bringing back the birch and using nuclear weapons on North Korea.'

'Watch it … it's not my fault you failed your eleven plus.'

'Ah!' said Ravi. 'In England you have the eleven plus … in India we have the caste system.'

'That Magnus,' said Roger, narrowing his eyes, 'came knocking on my door wanting to know if I'd vote for Jeremy Corbyn. Like hell I would. Corbyn's a pacifist. He won't press the nuclear trigger. Nor would Geoffrey; pacifists, I hate them. The sooner grammar schools make a come-back, the better; that's what I think.'

'Have you had an MRI scan?' said Geoffrey.

'You know I have. We all have. We wouldn't be here if we hadn't.'

'Do you know who pioneered its invention?'

'Some brainy boffin you knew at Cambridge.'

'He was Peter Mansfield and he failed his eleven plus.'

'Bollocks!' said Roger.

'You might have sold him a second-hand car,' said Shirley.

'I'm not ashamed of being a businessman ... nothing wrong with making money.'

'I just wish you'd spend it,' said Beryl.

'Let me explain,' said Geoffrey, changing the subject in a clumsy but necessary attempt to defuse, what was rapidly becoming, an overheated conversation, 'the seating arrangements I've booked for us on the train.'

'Just a minute,' said Roger. 'I've heard whispers about a kitty. I don't mind contributing but I'm not paying for Magnus's coffee and iced water. Coffee and iced water! He must think he's in Paris. Newcastle is not Paris and, another thing, I don't like the French.'

'Roger, please,' said Geoffrey, 'one thing at a time; it's not our fault you went to a grammar school and we are not fit to clean your shoes; let me explain about the tickets. We are not all sitting together.'

'If that means I'll not be sitting next to Roger,' said Beryl, 'that, suits me fine.'

'There are eight of us,' said Shirley. 'It can't have been easy getting eight seats all together.'

'It wasn't that,' said Debbie. 'It was my idea that we should spread ourselves ... that way we will meet more people. When we all come together in London we'll have more to talk about. Our encounters will have been more varied. I thought it very "Pickwickian". It's what Mr Dickens would have done.'

'A most splendid idea,' said Ravi; 'after all, it's not as if we are going to London for pleasure. We are OPAC. We are a club. Our mission is the same as the Pickwick club ... to meet interesting people. To find out more about the country we call home.'

'Some of us will be travelling first class and some second,' said Geoffrey.

All reacted as if they'd been told they were going to be shot at dawn.

'In first class you get free coffee and biscuits,' said Roger.

'In first class they'll be serving the full English,' said Shirley.

'I don't mind going second class,' said Beryl, 'just so long as I don't have to sit next to Roger. I think Mr Dickens would have thought second class more fun. In that film about the Titanic steerage had more fun than first class.'

'More steerage passengers died than first class,' said Shirley.

'In first class you get free crisps,' said Ravi, 'English poppadoms! I so much like crisps.'

'Let me explain,' said Geoffrey; 'there are eight of us. I have booked five seats in first class and three in second. Believe me; that was all that was available. Not my fault. At an agreed point, perhaps at York, a convenient halfway point, don't you think? We'll swap seats.'

'Who gets to sit in the first class seats first?' said Roger.

'We draw lots. For years I was in the Boy Scouts. I have come prepared.'

From a jacket pocket Geoffrey produced an envelope, out of which he tipped eight pieces of folded paper.

'On each piece of paper, 'he said, 'there is written "First" or "Second" … everyone, take your pick. I will pick for Flora and Jock.'

In some cases husbands were not sitting with their wives. In some cases this suited the wives. In some cases it suited the husbands.

'It's like when we were invited for dinner with that judge you know, Shirley,' said Ravi. 'Northumberland pick and mix. No one allowed to sit next to their partners. I never saw you all night.'

'That's because his sister took a fancy to you. I rescued you by reminding her I was your wife, that I was Welsh and, that in my youth, I'd been a druid. I told her in voluble Welsh to take her thieving hands off you. I wouldn't have objected to sharing my crème brûlée with her, but I'm not sharing you with anyone.'

*******

Rejuvenated by the Café Royal's excellent coffee and food, and more than ready to fight another day, or, in their case, the train journey to London, the 'Ensemble', strolled into the morning sunshine of Nelson Street.

'Just a moment,' said Geoffrey, 'everyone put a brake on their momentum.'

'Don't mention "Momentum" to me,' said, Roger, 'bunch of left-wing lunatics.'

'Gather round, please; everyone. And that includes you, Roger; under the "Blue Plaque", if you please. I have something to say.'

'You're not going to make a speech,' said Roger, 'make a fool of yourself and us, in the middle of Nelson Street, I hope? If my stockbroker sees me he'll think I've lost my marbles and try to sell me "Penny Shares".'

'Roger, shut up,' said Beryl. 'Geoffrey is trying to get us all in the right mood for our jaunt; the "Pickwickian" mood. I know he is; carry on, Geoffrey, I'm listening.'

Standing under the 'Blue Plaque' and pointing at it, Geoffrey said: 'A ship is launched by having a bottle of champagne smashed across its bow. I wish to launch our pilgrimage to Doughty Street with a paean of praise to the "Inimitable". Thank you, Mr Dickens, for all the laughter you have given us. Thank you, Mr Dickens, for visiting the "Toon" in eighteen fifty-four. I could go on; indeed, I want to go on but, if I did, we'd miss our train and we don't want that, do we? In homage to the "inimitable", I bow.'

'And curtsey,' said Debbie.

'Everyone blow the "Blue Plaque" a kiss,' said Geoffrey. 'It is not mandatory but, I think it shows respect.'

'I'll blow it a kiss,' said Beryl, doing just that.

'Beryl,' said Roger, 'you're giving that plaque more than you ever give me these days.'

'Roger's jealous of a "Blue Plaque",' said Shirley.

'Silly old fool,' said Beryl.

'Onward,' said Geoffrey, leading off, 'next stop, Doughty Street.'

'For tea and cakes,' said Ravi.

'As long as they're not too dear,' said Roger.

*******

At the end of Nelson Street, a swarthy fellow, who needed a shave, pestered the 'Ensemble' to buy a 'Big Issue'. His smile showed him to be missing many front teeth. A pug dog, with bulging eyes, peeked out, like a joey, from a sling made from a bed sheet, hanging round his neck.

'"Big Issue", sir?'

'You must be kidding,' said Roger.

'Yes, please,' said Debbie. 'Geoffrey, your wallet. We are "Pickwickians"; ergo, philanthropists.'

'I've nothing smaller than a twenty.'

'Debit the kitty.'

'Keep the change,' said Geoffrey.

'Bless you, sir. You is a good man … a good man. Budapest, say thank you to the good man.'

The dog barked.

'What a loud bark for such a little dog,' said Shirley. 'I'll make a note of that. It is just the sort of idiosyncrasy Dickens' "Pickwickians" would have made a note of and spoken about at their AGM.'

'It's like Doctor Who's Tardis,' said Ravi. 'Is that what you are saying, my love? That its external measurements are no clue as to how big it is inside. From a little dog you expect a little bark. Is that what the love of my life is saying?'

'When you said, "keep, the change", Geoffrey,' said Beryl, 'you did just what I imagine Mr Pickwick, would have done. Well done, you. Where's Roger?'

'He's fainted,' said Debbie.

'I haven't fainted,' said Roger, 'I'm speechless; twenty pound for a Big Issue. I've never heard of anything so ridiculous in all my life. Twenty pounds for a Big Issue. My mouth's gone dry.'

*******

On its way down Grainger Street, the 'Ensemble' was asked three more times to buy a 'Big Issue'. Roger, who'd claimed possession of the copy Geoffrey had bought, courtesy of the 'Ensemble's' kitty for twenty pounds, showed it to these would-be sellers as an excuse not to have buy another one.

'Sorry, mate, but I've already bought one.'

The more he brooded on Geoffrey handing over twenty pounds for a "Big Issue" the more he concluded, not for the first time in his long life, that 'kitties', like old age, were not for the faint hearted.

'I always feel awful not buying one,' said Shirley.

'Onward,' said Geoffrey, 'tempus fugit.'

*******

In Newcastle's Central Station the 'Ensemble,' studied the 'Arrivals' and 'Departures' board.

'Our train's on time,' said Ravi, 'that's bad news. It's like when Newcastle are two-nil up at half-time and you think they are home and dry and then they lose. The poppadum is not food until it is in your belly; is what my mother used to tell me.'

'I do hope Jock and Flora are on it,' said Beryl. 'I think I need the loo.'

'I wonder if that board is telling the truth,' said Shirley. 'It might be a post-truth arrivals and departures board.'

'Only when the train is in will we know,' said Ravi, 'or, as we say in India: there is water in the well but there's a hole in the bucket.'

'Ravi, my darling,' said Shirley, 'a little optimism wouldn't come amiss.'

'I am a pessimist because I was born under the Raj. All Indians born under the Raj are pessimists. The Raj gave us no hope. The only hope we had was to get rid of the British.'

'My darling, you know I understand. Never forget, I am Welsh. The Welsh are still under British rule. You were a baby when Grande Britannia ruled India. It was all a long time ago. Do cheer up. You have a British passport. You have a season ticket for Newcastle United. You will live to see them win the Premier League, I know you will.'

'I will not live forever; no one lives forever.'

'That's why he's a pessimist,' said Geoffrey, 'it's because the "Toon's" not doing well.'

'For Christ's sake,' said Roger, 'Ravi's blubbing. Pull yourself together, man.'

'You alright, old son?' asked Geoffrey.

'It's railway stations,' said Shirley, 'they always do this to him. They bring back memories … deep breaths, my love. When the British partitioned India, Ravi's family had to flee, by train, to a Hindu part of India. They were lucky to survive. Railway stations remind him of all the horrors he saw.'

'People with gouged out eyes, slit noses, cut off ears … people without heads, slit throats. I see it all,' said Ravi.

'Deep breaths, Ravi … in … out.'

'I'm a bit like that every time I see a Labrador,' said Roger. 'Beryl and I had our Labrador, Gin, for ten years, didn't we,

Beryl? You remember her, Ravi? She was part of the family. Beryl and I still miss her. Every time Beryl and I see a Labrador, we hold hands, don't we, Beryl? Or, at least, we used to. What I'm trying to say, Ravi, is, I know how you feel, so does Beryl; don't you, Beryl?'

'Have a barley sugar, Ravi,' said Beryl. 'I bought them for the train.'

'Platform eleven,' said Geoffrey.

'Platform ten,' corrected Debbie. 'Geoffrey, you must wear your spectacles.'

'When I were a lad,' said Geoffrey, 'to get onto the platform a ticket inspector clicked your ticket. I seem to remember they were all fat; now, it's all machines … robots.'

'You can't argue with a robot,' said Roger. 'I think all robots should be called Beryl … know, what I mean?'

'When a robot goes AWOL,' said Geoffrey, 'you don't argue with it, you give it a kick … that's how I repair my freezer. I give its motor a kick … never fails.'

'Don't you even think about kicking me, Roger,' said Beryl. 'One text from me and our sons will lay you out like a carpet.'

'Excuse me,' said a railway employee wearing a cap with a prodigious amount of scrambled egg on its peak and a well-cut, plum coloured suit, also with lashings of scrambled egg. 'I couldn't help overhearing your comments about robots. I'm Charles,' drawing the "Ensemble's" attention to his name pin, 'customer services. My job? To humanise the traveller's experience; to put a smile on the face of every passenger it is my privilege to help; to put, sir, a human face on them robots what I overheard you saying you hates.'

'You'd put a smile on my face,' said Roger, 'in fact, I'd be hysterical if you knocked twenty pound off the price of my ticket. I'm a pensioner. I have to count the pennies.'

'Your request, sir, is above my pay grade; believe me, sir, I would if I could but I can't. What I can do for you all is open this little gate with my "open sesame" card and let you access the platform without using the "robots".'

'Like, VIPs?' said Debbie. 'Geoffrey, we are VIPs.'

Before Charles had time to use his 'open sesame' card he was attacked by a middle-aged Oriental woman wielding an umbrella. Her language, full of high-pitched vowel sounds, made her sound agitated; with her were three delightful looking teenage girls; all with enchanting moon-shaped faces and melt-in-the-mouth, Oriental, brown eyes.

Debbie told Charles: 'The woman is Chinese. She wishes to know the time of the next train to King's Cross.'

'I thought she was going to murder me. I watched a "Fu Manchu" film last night. This is a first for me; a Chinese who speaks Chinese but, no English.'

'She is speaking Mandarin,' said Debbie.

'Which you speak?'

'Yes.'

'But, you're not Chinese.'

'You do not have to be Chinese to speak Mandarin.'

'Get away.'

'It is like someone who lives in Sunderland supporting Newcastle United; highly unlikely but possible.'

'Got it,' said Charles, tapping the top of his railway cap with a timetable as big as an old fashioned bible, 'received and understood.'

Charles was no slouch when it came to dealing with Joe Public.

*******

In the ensuing conversations between the Chinese and Debbie, many bows, hugs and handshakes were exchanged. They insisted on Debbie photographing them standing beside Charles.

'They love your uniform,' Debbie explained to him. 'They think it looks Chinese.'

Finding someone who can speak your language when you are in a foreign country comes as a relief to the traveller who is struggling to make herself understood. The gratitude of the Chinese knew no bounds.

'They want to know where to get tickets,' said Debbie.

'Follow me,' said, Charles.

'I'll go with you, you'll need an interpreter.'

'We'll wait for you here,' said Geoffrey.

'We shouldn't split the "Ensemble",' said, Roger, leaning on his walking stick like Charlie Chaplin. 'A good general never splits his force. You stick together … that's how battles are won … by sticking together.'

'You are getting anxious,' said Shirley, 'deep breath.'

'Shirley, don't you start telling me what to do … and, Beryl, we're having beef for Christmas.'

'Of course we are, dear'.

'And, stop whispering to Shirley. I know you are talking about me … women … they should never have had the vote.'

'I'm going to have a look in W H Smith's,' said Ravi.

'I'll come with you,' said Roger.

In W H Smith's Ravi picked up a copy of 'Scientific American'; Roger, a 'Daily Telegraph'.

'Put that on your bill,' Roger told Ravi, 'it's only coppers. You can afford it. I mean, what are friends for?'

*******

Returning to the concourse after having made their purchases, Ravi and Roger panicked when they could see no sign of Geoffrey, Beryl or Shirley.

'Where are they?' said Ravi. 'I hate railway stations.'

'We're going to miss the train,' said Roger, 'I know we are … and if we do we won't get our money back. It will be our fault if we miss it. Where the fuck are they?'

The station was busy.

'We should be wearing luminous bibs,' said Roger.

'Or,' said Ravi, 'orange survival suits so, when you fall in the water, the lifeboat man can see you.'

'Ravi, we're not in the bloody North Sea, we're in Newcastle Central Station. I was thinking more on the lines of what those children, over there, are wearing; so their teachers don't lose them; the way we've lost our wives and Geoffrey; where are they?'

Ravi, ever the connoisseur of the female form, thought the woman leading the crocodile of young children, to whom Roger had drawn his attention, rather 'dishy'. All of her charges were wearing green bibs. They were walking in twos but, unlike drilled soldiers, not in step. There were many deviations in the symmetry of their line. They approached the two yellow and mottled cabbage leaves, called Ravi and Roger, like a large and potentially dangerous caterpillar.

Bringing up the rear was a fat woman in a black trouser suit.

'Jennifer,' shouted the fat woman in the black trouser suit, 'WALK ... no skipping if you don't mind ... thank you very much ... Bernadette, watch the old gentleman with the walking stick.'

'You Charlie Chaplin, mister?' a boy with a Mohican haircut asked Roger.

'Sorry about that,' said the adult in the black trouser suit, 'it's the way you are leaning on your walking stick. We know all about Charlie Chaplin, don't we, Dylan? Dylan, stop doing that. We are taking the children to see a medley of Charlie Chaplin films at the Tyneside Cinema ... silent movies, gentlemen ... your era? Dylan, keep in line.'

'I didn't like the way that brat spoke to me,' said Roger. 'And, that adult, the fat one – I suppose she was a teacher – was chewing.'

'Stress,' said Ravi.

'She looked more like a football manager than a teacher ... you know, the ones who come on television, chewing?'

*******

The reason Geoffrey, Shirley and Beryl had moved from where Ravi and Roger had left them was Geoffrey's curiosity about a 'Blue Plaque'.

'At last we've found you,' said Roger. 'You shouldn't have gone wandering off. I thought you might have been murdered.'

'I think Debbie speaking Mandarin really impressed the Chinese ladies,' said Shirley. 'If only there were as many Welsh speakers on our planet as there are Chinese … if there were, Wales would be a big fish in the sea and Cardiff would be as important as London.'

'Whales are mammals,' said Roger. 'Ha! Ha!'

'Roger, your knowledge of natural history never ceases to amaze me … twit.'

'Mr Pickwick would have taken out his notebook and made a full transcription of what is written on the blue plaque,' said Geoffrey.

'I've photographed it,' said Shirley.

'The station was built in eighteen …' began Geoffrey.

'I can read,' said Roger, 'and, I can also tell the time.'

'Quite,' said Geoffrey, looking at his watch and then, at the station clock. 'I agree, time IS getting on. I do hope Debbie has not forgotten about us. When she starts speaking Mandarin she goes oriental … time doesn't matter. Tell you what … I'll wait here for her, you guys go through onto the platform.'

*******

Where was his wife? His hearing was not good. To locate sound you need two ears. Geoffrey had only one and that one wasn't very good, either. Was someone shouting his name? It sounded like Debbie. If so, where was she?

To his surprise she was on the other side of the barrier. How'd she get there? Her Chinese pals were waving at him as if he was an old friend. He checked his watch; time to get a move on if, or he'd miss the train.

While waiting for his wife, anxiety had made him pummel his railway ticket into a ball.

'Don't even think about it, sir,' said a railway employee, with the eye of a hawk, who'd been watching him.

She opened the gate for him.

'Thank you,' said Geoffrey. 'We don't want to upset the robots, do we?'

By the time he reached Debbie the Chinese had left his wife.

'I've been waiting for you under the clock,' said Geoffrey. 'How'd you get through the ticket barrier without me seeing you?'

'Charles opened a gate for us.'

'Clever Charles.'

'The Chinese think you're wonderful.'

'Do they really?'

'It's your bow tie. They think you look like a movie star.'

'I've always liked the Chinese.'

*******

On the train from Edinburgh to Newcastle, Flora and Jock cuddled up to each other in airline seats. When the train turned a bend, Jock leaned against his wife.

'What are you like?' said Flora.

They squeezed hands.

Flora was wearing a lightweight tartan trouser suit, made for her by a bespoke tailor in Jesmond. Jock, despite the warm weather, was wearing a heather coloured Harris Tweed jacket, tartan trousers, a checked Barbour shirt and a Newcastle University tie.

'I enjoyed the funeral,' said Jock.

'The pipes made you cry,' said Flora.

'I don't think the vicar got my joke about my being so old it would save time if I stayed at the crematorium.'

'She was a very polite young woman. She did not wish to offend you. It was like when you were in hospital and that nice young lady asked you if you wished to be 'resuscitated' but, because she thought you might be an ignoramus and might not know what the word meant, waffled on about, if you went to sleep, did you want to be woken up.'

'And, I said, "It all depends on what's for breakfast. If it's porridge with cream and a gargle of Grouse, wake me. If it's two slices of white cut-loaf, smeared with margarine, don't bother".'

'Then, you asked her, "Are we talking about 'resuscitation'?".'

'She did smile.'

'I seem to remember that by the end of your consultation she and you were quite matey.'

'She came from Fife. She could quote Robbie Burns. She told me she drank too much wine. I told her I drank too much whisky; a clever wee lassie; knew when to bend the rules and when to break them. Rose Macdonald was her name. I, of course, called her "Resurrection". Difficult shouting "Resurrection" across a ward when you have a tube up your nose.'

'Yet, in a way, "Resuscitation" and "Resurrection" are, what you might call, "hollering" words. The sort of words you'd shout in a cave because they'd make a lot of echoes.'

'Aye, and "death" is a very short word; but, it means forever and ever, amen ... our lives but a hiccup between two eternities.'

'Look ... Bass Rock.'

'The home of the gannets ... they have hard heads, gannets. If we hit the water as hard as they do when they are diving for food we'd have concussion.'

'Roger would make a good gannet.'

'Indeed he would.'

'And Shirley would like "Resuscitation" and "Resurrection", because she's Welsh and the Welsh like long words. What will happen to your cousin's dogs?'

'And cats.'

The sun pouring into the carriage made them sleepy. They used each other as pillows; their intimacy, helping them forget their aches and pains.

'A text from Geoffrey,' said Jock, swiping his mobile open, as they passed Morpeth. 'Apparently when we change seats at Newcastle we're not sitting together. Geoffrey has split our group up. Some of us will be in first class; some of us in second. At York … we all swap seats … second class to first and vice versa.'

'I hope I'm not sitting next to Roger,' said Flora.

*******

As they approached Newcastle, passengers began to take down their luggage whereupon, the train, as if telling these optimists not to count their chickens, stopped.

'I wonder if we are First class to York or, Second,' said Flora.

'Does it matter?'

'Come on, Jock, think about it. In first class breakfast and lunch are gratis.'

'Geoffrey said he's going to pay for everything on his credit card. At the end of our jaunt he's going to divide what he's spent by four.'

'Should he not divide by eight? Not all married couples share their money the way we do. Roger and Beryl have separate bank accounts. Beryl told me Roger is paranoid about keeping thirty thousand in his current account. When it goes below, he cadges off her. "It's your turn to buy the coffees" … that sort of thing. Even when she knows it's not her turn and he knows it's not her turn, she doesn't say anything. She told me it's better to pay than watch him sulk; but, she always gets her own back. She has a little black book in which she writes down his peccadilloes.'

'Sad. I hope they don't come to blows; if they did, well, that would spoil our jaunt … a text from Geoffrey.'

Geoffrey: Where are you?

Jock: On a train.

Geoffrey: I know you are on a train, dear thing, but where is the fucking train? Alnmouth? Morpeth?

Jock: Byker Bridge.

Geoffrey: Get out. Walk.

Jock: Door's locked.

Geoffrey: Roger says you more than fifteen minutes late you get refund.

'Funny, isn't it?' said Jock, closing down his phone, 'Geoffrey never swears except when he's texting.'

As the train had not moved for five minutes, a young man, whose seat had been across the aisle from Flora and Jock's and who'd stood up to get off, sat back down again.

He'd bright blue eyes and ginger hair, which Flora thought made him look like Loch Rannoch in October when, on a sunny day, its black water reflected blue sky and the reds of autumn leaves. A leather man-bag strapped across his chest – it looked like a saddle bag – gave him the aura of a mountain man or, a pony express rider. Flora imagined him getting off the train at Newcastle and, not hailing a taxi, but jumping onto a horse.

Her eyebrows knitted when she saw him put a cigarette in his mouth.

'Don't worry,' he told her, 'I am not going to light it.'

His accent told Flora that he was from the Highlands. Flora, the most gentle and demure of women, loved the Highlands because they were wild and were all the things she was not.

'Would you like some chewing gum?' said Flora. 'I always carry a packet. I don't chew myself, but I know it helps.'

'When I watch Newcastle play I'm never without a packet,' said Jock. 'Once, a long time ago, at a penalty shoot-out I went through two packets.'

'Thank you, that's very kind,' said the young man, taking a stick. 'I have an interview in half an hour. If this train doesn't get going, I'll be late for it.'

Because she was used to Jock doing silly things, Flora was not in the least surprised when the young man put the gum into his mouth without removing its foil wrapper. Unlike Jock, though, he was quick to realise his mistake.

'I'm always doing things like that,' said Jock.

'Like what?' said the young man, who for the umpteenth time looked at his watch.

'You know ...'

'No, I don't know.'

'You know ... like forgetting to take the wrapper off the chewing gum my wife gave you.'

'Did I?'

'Yes, I'm afraid you did but, not to worry, I'm always doing silly things like that. This morning I put a tea bag in the coffee percolator.'

'And the other morning you put milk in the teapot,' said Flora.

'It's easily done.'

'Is it?' said the young man.

'It is when you are as old as I am ... you a geneticist?'

'As a matter of fact, yes. How'd you know?'

'I wish I could say it's because I'm Sherlock Holmes, but I've been reading the tag on your bag, "Hamish Sinclair. St Andrew's University. Department of Genetics". May I be rude – believe me, I don't mean to be – but the interview for which you are so anxious to be on time, is it to do with genetics? Is it at the "Centre for Life"? With whom is your interview?'

When the young man had answered these questions, Jock said,' Leave this to me,' and rang a number on his mobile.

'Reg ... Jock here. I know I'm retired. Where am I? I'm on a train stuck on Byker Bridge. Guess who's with me? No, not Gordon Brown ... a wee laddie from St Andrew's. You're interviewing him this morning. He's worried he's going to be late. If he is, it's not his fault ... would you have a word?' –handing Hamish the mobile– 'Reg wants to have a word with you.'

'Yes, Prof ... no, Prof,' said the young man.

After the phone call Hamish looked at Jock the way a curate looks at a bishop.

'I didn't know, you were that "Jock",' he said. 'I have one of your books in my bag. May I shake your hand, sir? I thought you were dead.'

'Aye,' said Jock, shaking the young man's hand, 'I'm still here.'

'He sleeps a lot,' said Flora.

The sound of bagpipes tuning up like a herd of elephants with bad arthritis trying to stand up after wallowing in mud, cut short Jock and Hamish's erudite gossip about developments in genetics.

'It's a pipe band on their way to a gig in a cellar under the Tyne Bridge,' said a standing passenger. 'They're in an ugly mood. They've been drinking.'

The sound of the pipe band playing 'Auld Lang Syne' made Jock's eyes water as if he'd been peeling onions.

'It's the pipes,' Flora told Hamish.

'And what he's playing,' said Jock. 'We should have taken Andrew's bloodhound. He was fond of that dog.'

'Andrew's bloodhound is a family pet,' Flora told Hamish. 'Andrew was Jock's cousin. We've been to his funeral. That's why we are on the train. We're coming back from Andrew's funeral. I've known him since he was a puppy. He has a red leather collar with five spikes on it. I don't think a bloodhound should have a soppy collar, do you?'

Hamish found it difficult to empathise with Flora's rambling. To him, a hale and hearty young fellow, the land of the very old was a foreign country he'd no wish to visit.

'Tissue?' said Jock.

'I have one in my bag. I can't open my bag. Your blubbing makes my hands go all shaky.'

'Please,' said the young man, 'take my handkerchief. It's clean. A stick of chewing gum for a handkerchief, seems fair to me.'

'Thank you,' said Jock, 'very kind of you, I'm sure.'

Jock checked that the tartan handkerchief was clean. He knew a lot about germs. You couldn't be too careful. You could catch awful things from a handkerchief given to you by a total stranger.

As it looked OK, he blew into it, with much determination and vigour, the contents of his large nose.

The desecration of his handkerchief made Hamish look as if he was trying to pass a gall stone.

He knew one thing; when he was old, he would never, ever, fill a stranger's handkerchief with snot.

'The Stuart tartan,' said Jock, looking at the handkerchief and its contents. 'It's very green. A healthy colour, I'm thinking. My grandmother was a Stuart. I don't tell many people this but, I'm related to Bonnie Prince Charlie.'

'In that case,' said a passenger standing in the aisle, 'you'll be like me, you'll be for an independent Scotland. When's this bloody train going to move?'

'We didn't have a vote,' said Flora. 'We live in Newcastle.'

'Roses and thistles grow on both sides of the border,' said Jock.

'Traitors,' said the man, 'bloody, traitors; that's what you are.'

After ten minutes the train moved; to celebrate its resuscitation, the pipe band played 'Scotland the Brave'.

Once again passengers stood up and began a slow exodus towards an exit.

When Jock offered to return the borrowed handkerchief, Hamish, ever so politely, said, 'Please, keep it. I think your need is greater than mine. I can't believe you are still alive.'

'Sometimes,' said Jock, 'nor, can I; give my regards to Reg.'

'I wonder if Geoffrey is going to put us in First class or Second class,' said Flora. 'Do you think we should tell them about Hamish?'

'Definitely … we'll call it, "The Adventure of the Dirty Handkerchief".'

*******

The train pulled into Newcastle Central ten minutes late; by British standards this meant it was on time; the glass being, as it were, half full, rather than, half empty.

'Can you see them?' said Flora.

'There they are.'

'I didn't see them. Are you sure it was them?'

'Of course I'm sure. I've just blown my nose; that always helps me see better.'

'Did they see us?'

'I don't know, probably not. I've got the bag. We'll get off … find them on the platform.'

The rendezvous of a Soyuz space capsule with the International Space Station was easy-peezey-lemon-squeezey compared to Jock and Flora's rendezvous with the 'Ensemble'.

'Can't see them,' said Flora. 'Why are young people so tall? This is like been in a maze. I don't like it.'

Phones rang. Texts were sent. Before they'd even met up Flora was on her phone telling Debbie all about Hamish; to assist their rendezvous, Geoffrey streamed, Jock a real-time video.

'I can see you on my screen,' said Geoffrey, 'can you not see me waving?'

'I can see you,' said Jock, 'this way, Flora. We have visual contact.'

*******

When they met up, Geoffrey, made it quite clear to everyone that there was no time for the usual 'kisses and cuddles'.

'Here are your tickets. Jock, you are in First class ... till York. Flora, it's your lucky day, you are with me and Roger, in Second class ... all the way to York. Coach F, for Second class ... coach G, for First class. Follow me. Where is coach F?'

A whistle blew. A railway employee, holding open a carriage door, gestured that they'd better board now; not in the next fifteen minutes or whenever they fancied.

'Where's coach F?' said Geoffrey.

'Next to the engine.'

'Have we time ...?'

'No, sir, you have not,' said the railway employee who made it clear to Geoffrey that further discussion was out of the question by shouting, 'All aboard!' and blowing a whistle.

'Everyone, get in,' said Geoffrey, 'if we don't, I fear the willow-warbler may smack us with that thing in his hand that looks like a table tennis bat. I wonder what it's called.'

*******

The 'Ensemble' found making its way to their carriages, akin to negotiating an obstacle course.

Geoffrey had to keep saying, 'Excuse, me, please', like a vinyl record stuck in a groove. 'Excuse me, please.'

'You want a machete?' said Jock.

'Gangway,' said Roger, prodding a passenger with his stick.

'Watch it, mate! Vicious old sod.'

They climbed over suitcases, folded prams and people sitting on the floor with their legs sticking out.

'This is India,' said Ravi. 'I feel at home.'

'Don't exaggerate,' said Shirley, 'no one is hanging out of windows ... Ravi, deep breaths ... don't you go having one of your wobbles, here.'

'This reminds me of the Cairngorms,' said Jock, straddling a suitcase blocking the aisle, 'I should have brought my ice-axe.'

'Nil desperandum,' said Geoffrey.

\* \* \* \* \* \* \* \* \* \*

It pleased Flora that the First and Second class coaches the group were in were next to each other. She did not like the idea of Jock being too far away from her. If he wasn't close by he couldn't look after her.

She worried that if she had to go to see him in an emergency, she'd have to pass where the two coaches joined. Since childhood she'd never liked the way coaches swayed and rattled where they joined. She feared they might come apart.

\* \* \* \* \* \* \*

The three seats Geoffrey had booked in second class shared a table.

'Would you like a window seat, Flora?' said Geoffrey.

Flora said she would. Geoffrey was such a gentleman, unlike Roger, who had taken, as if it was his god-given right, the other window seat.

Roger was so selfish. He didn't deserve Beryl. How Beryl put up with his sulks she couldn't imagine.

'How was your journey down, Flora?' said Geoffrey.

'We're moving,' said Roger.

'No, we are not,' said Geoffrey. 'It's the other train that is moving … optical illusion, Roger.'

'I wouldn't have been fooled like that when I was young. A good job Beryl's not here. She's started keeping a record of the silly things I do. I think she's planning to have me sectioned. I'm not having that. It's all go!' Whereupon, curling up like a cat, he closed his eyes and went to sleep.

'You'll miss going over the river,' said Geoffrey. 'It's always exciting seeing the bridges.'

'Seen them before.'

'We're off,' said Geoffrey, sounding all excited, 'modern electric trains have amazing acceleration.'

'It's a diesel engine pulling us,' said Roger, eyes closed. 'You can smell it.'

'Steam engines,' said Geoffrey, 'took ages to get going. I suppose all of us in the 'Ensemble' are steam engines … out of date … slow to get a move on.'

'It takes me ages to get going in the morning,' said Flora. 'If I jump out of bed I go all dizzy. Before I stand up, I sit on the edge of the bed and name ten English counties.'

'Wouldn't it be wonderful if society treated its old people the way rail enthusiasts treat steam engines? We'd be polished and kept in heated sheds and brought out for jaunts.'

'People would wave at us and think we were the bees-knees.'

'We'd be treated like trophies. I wonder when Newcastle are going to win a trophy.'

'We are crossing the river. What a wonderful sight. The sun has turned it into a ribbon of gold. It's lovely.'

'When we were young,' said Geoffrey, 'it used to smell of rotten eggs but, not now. I don't know if you know this, Roger, but it was cleaned up courtesy of a grant from the EU; new sewers, new sewage plants to make dirty water clean, all paid for by Brussels.'

Geoffrey did not know if this was true; he just thought it might be; so many lies had been told about the benefits of leaving the EU, did it matter if he threw in a porky on the 'remain' side?

'To keep the peace we agreed not to talk about the EU,' said Roger, opening his eyes. 'You know my views … the sooner we are out the better.'

'Anyone want a barley sugar?' said Flora.

A long time ago her bag would have been filled with lipsticks and the contraceptive pill; now it was chewing gum, sweets and incontinence pads.

*******

In first class Beryl, Debbie and Shirley sat together. On their shared table were four upturned mugs, their rims resting on paper doilies.

'In Wales,' said Shirley, pointing at the doilies, 'they would have been ironed.'

'Love the hygiene,' said Debbie.

'The mugs are the sort you find in a "greasy spoon".'

'Not silver service,' said Beryl. 'Roger hates drinking out of a mug. At home he insists on having a cup and saucer.'

Shirley, checking the reserved label on the unoccupied fourth seat, said, 'It's booked from Darlington to York. I hope he's tall, dark and handsome.'

'Your children would be shocked if they heard you talking like that,' said Debbie. 'We are old. The young assume we are no longer interested in the opposite sex.'

'Wouldn't it be absolutely fascinating if it was someone famous,' said Beryl; 'after all, we are travelling first class.'

*******

Across the aisle Jock and Ravi sat opposite each other at a table for two.

'The river's looking nice,' said Jock. 'One of the finest salmon rivers in England, the Tyne. The best of course are in Scotland.'

'When I die,' said Ravi, 'I wish for my ashes to be scattered on the Tyne. All rivers lead to the sea. One day the waters of Tyne will meet the waters of the mighty Ganges. Water will take me back to the land of my ancestors.'

'Getting old is not for the faint hearted,' said Jock. 'Coming down from Edinburgh, I'd an attack of the "blubbers". I know it upsets Flora but I couldn't help myself.'

'I did not feel well in the station.'

'Your memories?'

Ravi nodded.

'I wish we weren't old,' said Jock. 'It upsets me I can't walk as far as I used to. I wonder if I will live long enough to finish my totem pole.'

'That is why in their infinite wisdom and mercy the government has given us bus passes,' said Ravi.

'Roger keeps a record of how much money his bus pass has saved him. He says it makes him feel better about all the tax he pays.'

'Never forget, my dear Jock,' said Ravi, waxing philosophical, 'Mother Nature abhors the vacuum. In my case she has replaced "infirmity" with "cunning". Did I tell you about last week? Last week a chap rang my doorbell. I was having my afternoon snooze. Shirley was out at her bridge club. I don't know if you know but I've changed my bell-sound from one elephant, to a herd. Even I can hear it now which is how I came to answer the door to this chap selling raffle tickets. He'd a blue rosette pinned to his jumper and wanted me to put a poster in my window to say I supported the Conservative party. I warned him I was hard of hearing. "Wax," I told him, putting a finger in an ear and giving it a good waggle, as you do when you go wax hunting.

'"I'm fund raising money for the Conservative party," he said.

'"What?" I said.

'"The Conservative party."

'"What?"

'"The Conservative party."

'"The Communist party?"

'What pleased me so very much was that I could see he was getting annoyed. To help me he put one of the raffle tickets he was trying to persuade me to buy, under my nose. I nearly fainted when I saw the price. Roger would have died.

'"What are they?" I said, "I can't see without my glasses."

'"Raffle tickets."

'"What?"

'Under the Raj he'd have had me whipped.

'"Never mind," he said.

'When he was walking away I heard him mutter: "Fucking deaf old sod." I was not having that.

"You can fuck the Tory party as well," I told him.'

'You did provoke him,' said Jock.

'Scratch a Tory ... what do you expect?'

'Tories are like scratch cards. They promise more than they deliver.'

'We wouldn't talk like this if Roger was here.'

'Ravi,' said Shirley, leaning across the aisle, 'are you having the full English?'

\* \* \* \* \* \* \* \* \* \*

'Think I'll go and check on the others,' said Geoffrey, 'see if they've settled in. I do hope they are not being naughty. When Debbie gets with Shirley and Beryl she can be risqué.'

'It's all go,' said Roger. 'Let them look after themselves. I don't know how you can be bothered. It's all go.'

\* \* \* \* \* \* \*

In first class Geoffrey sat down in the empty seat next to Shirley, Debbie and Beryl.

'The coffee smells good.'

'Have a sip of mine,' said Debbie. 'First class is not what it used to be ... remember the Pullman? White tablecloths, proper cutlery. How times have changed.'

'May I have a piece of toast?'

'Geoffrey, this is a First class carriage, not a food bank.'

'Tickets from Newcastle, please ... have your tickets ready, please.'

The man's badge said, 'Gordon' and that he was a 'Carriage Care Assistant'. Geoffrey thought, damn it, the fellow's a ticket inspector. Nothing wrong with that. Next thing, passengers on Jumbo jets would be called ... astronauts.

His uniform was full of pockets, loops and holsters; for phones, notepads, pens, timetables and his ticket clippers. Geoffrey wondered if the ticket clippers would be any good for cutting toenails.

To Geoffrey, Gordon's largest piece of kit, a ticket machine the size of a football, looked like a ray gun. Gordon was 'Flash Gordon'. Anyone who'd not paid, Gordon would fire his ray gun at them.

Why, Geoffrey pondered, did everyone these days need so much 'stuff' to do the simplest things? Take, Marcus, a lovely young man, but, why did he need so much 'stuff' to ride a bicycle? A helmet, cyclist's shoes and, a one piece that made him look as if he was wearing one of Henry the eighth's codpieces.

When he, Geoffrey, went for a walk, he strolled out of his front door like the free spirit he was, giving not a thought to his footwear. Some of the people he knew, when they went for a walk, MUST have walking shoes; MUST have their GPS app on their mobile to tell them how many steps they'd done and how fast their heart was beating and, their blood pressure.

'Tickets please. All tickets from Newcastle, please; thank you, sir.'

Gordon was not an athlete. He'd baggy eyes, lardy skin and a paunch.

'You are in the wrong coach, sir,' said Gordon, 'this is First class ... your ticket is second class.'

'But, Geoffrey looks First class, doesn't he?' said Shirley.

'You mean, the bow tie?' said Gordon. 'I'll grant you do look First class, sir. But, what I wants to know, sir, is, what are we going to do about it?'

'He's my husband,' said Debbie.

'Makes no difference, madam … even if he was the Pope … him that's inaffable … you cannot sit in First class if you have a Second class ticket.'

'We have First class tickets,' chorused Shirley and Beryl, 'and, so has Debbie.'

'Ladies,' said Gordon, his raised eyebrows folding his brow into ells of flesh, 'the railways does not do, "buy two and get one free". The railways is not a supermarket.'

'Are you going to lock my husband up?' said Debbie.

'No, madam, I am not. You have three choices, sir.'

'Do I?' said Geoffrey.

'Give Geoffrey a choice and he will dither,' said Debbie. 'He's my husband, you see; I know what he's like.'

'You have three choices, sir … you go ever so quietly back to your seat in Second class … or, you pays for an upgrade which I will work out the price of, to the farthing, on my 5G Hewlett-Packard computerised ticket machine or …'

'We don't use farthings anymore,' said Shirley.

'I seem to remember they had a robin on them,' said Beryl.

'I know we don't use farthings anymore,' said Gordon, 'it was my little way of trying to make you lot feel, well … comfy.'

'You were trying to take us back to a time when we did use farthings?' said Debbie.

'Because you think that is the era to which we belong?' said Shirley.

'Yes, madam, I was. I do believe I have what is called a "heart of gold".'

'Do we look that old?' said Beryl.

'Put it this way,' said Gordon, 'if you lot don't know about farthings, I'll eat one of those sandwiches, wrapped in plastic, you passengers are daft enough to pay four quid for.'

'Geoffrey,' said Debbie, 'is always saying that he and I were born in the age of steam, aren't you, dear?'

'But not, thank goodness,' said Geoffrey, 'in the age of the Penny-farthing bicycle. Now, young man, what is my third option?'

'Your third option, sir, is what might be called the nasty option. You argues the toss with me, sir, until the train stops at Durham, whereupon a nice big policeman will escort you off the train.'

'Durham has a jail,' said Shirley.

'And a cathedral,' said Beryl.

Leaning across the aisle Ravi said, with feeling, 'If you go to jail, Geoffrey, I'll visit you.'

'So will I,' said Jock, 'but only if visiting day is not a Friday … on Friday I play chess.'

'As I said earlier, sir, you does look First class … I don't get many bow ties in Second. In fact, come to think about it, I don't get many bow ties in First. You might think I'm rambling on a bit, sir, but there's purpose behind it. I'm giving you time to think. On my training course we was told give the passenger time. Now, let me see,' punching numbers into his 'ray gun', 'I can upgrade you for … eighty-five pounds.'

'That won't be necessary, 'said Geoffrey. 'I will return to my Second class seat.'

'Thank you, sir. If I may say so, sir, a very wise move.'

'Take a doggy bag with you, Geoffrey,' said Jock, dropping a sausage onto a serviette and handing it to Geoffrey.

'Thank you,' said Geoffrey, 'it's at times like this one finds out one's real friends.'

'Have a slice of my bacon,' said Ravi, 'I've just removed its rind.'

'Thank you, Ravi, very kind.'

'Make a sandwich,' said Beryl, 'here's a slice of my toast.'

*******

Back in Second class, Roger said, eyeing Geoffrey's bacon, sausage and toast, 'Where'd you get that?'

'First class are having breakfast … they indulged me.'

'What's Beryl having?'

'The full English.'

'And I'm sat here with nothing. I hope she chokes.'

'Roger, that's an awful thing to say,' said Flora. 'Beryl's your wife.'

'She hates me.'

'If you are hungry,' said Geoffrey, 'there's a trolley service.'

'I'll have to pay if I buy off the trolley … it's free in first class.'

'Your turn will …' munch … munch … 'come when we change at York … something to look forward too. You know,' licking fat off his fingers, 'that was rather tasty. Anyone got a tissue?'

'On your bike,' said Roger.

'I hope Jock is having the full English?' said Flora. 'He needs building up. When he's eating he can't cry.'

'It's all go,' said Roger.

*******

In first class, Shirley told her husband, 'I'm off to the loo. You haven't been since we left home. Do you not need to go?'

'No.'

'I've not been married to you all these years without knowing when you need the loo.'

'I don't need to go.'

'Are you sure? You've had two coffees since we left Newcastle. Coffee is a diuretic. It makes you pee.'

'I know what "diuretic" means.'

'Dear me, I think I'm going to wet myself. It's all your fault, Ravi, keeping me talking. The loo's engaged. I can see the sign; someone's using it. Ravi, I need you to come with me? Ever since I got locked in a loo in the Vatican,' she explained to Debbie and Beryl, 'I don't like locking toilet doors. When I started to panic a priest whispered through the key hole that I should pray. I told him to get a fucking locksmith. I don't normally use the F word but I was desperate.'

Standing outside the occupied loo, Shirley did the sort of war dance children do when they want to let their parents know they are 'desperate'.

'Good luck,' the woman who came out of the toilet told Shirley.

'I see what she meant,' said Shirley, looking into the cubicle, 'it smells; there's no loo paper.'

From a pocket Ravi produced a packet of tissues.

'Ravi, my darling, you are wonderful. When you do things like that, I know why I married you.'

Standing guard outside the unlocked toilet door Ravi wondered what his mother would have thought of her son, a Brahmin, standing guard outside a loo on a train while his wife, a Welsh memsahib, did what was necessary.

'Excuse me,' said a short fat man with a waterfall tummy, 'I need to use the loo … for those in peril on the sea … make way for the needy.'

'My wife is using the toilet,' said Ravi.

'You sure? The sign says FREE.'

'I assure you it is ENGAGED.'

'Why doesn't she lock the door? What's the prob?'

'She doesn't like being locked in.'

'Women!' said the short fat man. 'I'm not being personal, mate, don't get me wrong but when she … your good lady comes out, do I take it you will not be wanting to use the necessaries?'

'When my good lady comes out; the facilities will be all yours.'

'Thank god for that. When I have to go, I have to go. Will she be long?'

Ravi shrugged.

'Women,' said the short fat man, 'if I had a penny for every minute my wife's kept me waiting outside a toilet, you know what? I'd be a rich man. Do you know how many handbags she has? Have a guess.'

'Thirty-five.'

'Put a nothing on the end and you'll be close. How long's your good lady going to be?'

Ravi shrugged.

'I'm a locksmith by trade. I'm not telling you that to show off. I mean, it's not as if I'm boasting, like me saying, I've met the Queen, no, I'm telling you … Christ! I'm going to piss myself. I'm telling you because talking takes my mind off … how long's she going to be?'

'She's not been in there that long.'

'Easy for you to say that.'

'If it helps to take your mind off your desperate need to go for a pee,' said Ravi, trying to be helpful – after all, everyone in the 'Ensemble' knew about the urgency of having to go for a pee – 'tell me about your job as a locksmith.'

'Master locksmith, if you don't mind.'

'Self-employed?'

'The only way to make money … I'm dribbling … I know I am.'

'Concentrate on your trade; you were saying, you are a master locksmith.'

'The tales I could tell you. I most enjoy it when people ring me to tell me they've locked themselves out … talk about panic … think it was the end of the world. They'll pay anything to get back in. You have them over a barrel … a seller's market … charge them what you like, but, you always makes sure you gets your money before you lets them back into their comfy nests … that's the golden rule, that is … get your money afore you lets them back in. How long's she going to be?'

Ravi shrugged.

'If it's raining and I sees, they are that bit keener to get back inside I tell them my call out charge is a hundred quid. If it's winter, heavy frost on the ground, a freezing wind coming off the North Pole my call-out is one hundred and fifty.'

'In the cold your van will use more fuel. You have every right to charge more.'

'Me and you are on the same wavelength, mate. You in business? How long's she going to be? Once you let them back into their homes, they'll tell you to "Fuck off", if you'll excuse my French. They'll tell you, "It took you two seconds to open my door, I'm not paying a hundred quid for that." One guy worked it out I was on seven thousand an hour; wish I was. Is she finished yet? What about you telling her I'm an urgent case, that, if this was Accident and Emergency, I'd be wheeled straight in.'

Ravi tapped ever so gently on the toilet door.

'Who's there?' shouted Shirley. 'Ravi, is that you?'

'It's me, dear. There's a man outside desperate for the loo.'

'He'll have to wait. I'm not finished.'

'What are you doing?'

'I beg your pardon?'

'The gentleman has the same problem as Geoffrey.'

'Don't we all? Tell him, I'll be out in a jiffy.'

'She won't be long,' Ravi told the locksmith.

'Like, half an hour?'

'What about reciting the alphabet backwards … that'll take your mind off, you know what; or, I could teach you how to say, "I need the loo" in Hindi.'

'What about you telling your wife to just bloody well hurry up.'

'I think she might be putting on her "face".'

'If I piss myself, I won't be able to look anyone in the "face".'

'Ravi,' said Shirley, popping her head round the door, 'go and ask Roger for soap, will you? When we came on the train he made a point of dashing off to the loo ... this loo.'

Everyone in the 'ensemble' knew, Roger collected 'freebies' ... soap, shower caps, shoe cleaning cloths, sachets of shower gel; provided free in hotels, he took them all.

'Do you mind?' Shirley told the short, fat man, who was standing on tip-toe to leer at her over Ravi's shoulder, 'I'm having a private conversation with my husband.'

'He's a locksmith,' said Ravi.

'He's a nosey parker?'

'He's bursting.'

'Bursting?'

'As in, if you don't hurry up, missus,' said the indignant master locksmith, 'I'm going to wet myself.'

'Don't be silly,' said Shirley, 'that's what little boys do. Ravi, go and get the soap. I'm not leaving the loo without washing my hands. In my long life, necessity has forced me to abandon many of my cherished principles. I am Welsh. The Welsh are a hygienic people. In my youth, "Mr Locksmith", I have skinny-dipped in Llyn Cau. In my autumn years I refuse to leave a public loo without washing my hands and, what is more, leaving it cleaner than I found it. If only I had my marigolds and a Brillo-pad. Ravi, you won't believe this but someone has written "shit", with shit, on the mirror; off you go and get me some soap, please.'

'I thought I was supposed to be standing guard?'

'Hygiene is more important than my phobia ... tell the locksmith to stand guard ... and tell him to take his foot out of the door.'

'Would you mind taking your foot out of the door?' Ravi told the locksmith. 'It appears you are on guard duty.'

'Who wears the trousers in your house?'

'My wife.'

'Are you a man or a mouse?'

'A mouse!' said Ravi, proudly; doing his best to make his wife's dominance over him sound like an achievement; the way the British, when they talked about Dunkirk, made that disaster sound like a victory. 'Now, if you'll excuse me.'

*******

His wife wanted soap, did she? Shirley was not a typical Indian wife. She was Welsh. When she called him 'Darling', he melted. He always had and supposed he always would. Had she forgotten he was a Brahmin? Did she think he was a coolie? Next, she'd have him delivering parcels round Jesmond dressed as a Deliveroo man ... thank goodness he was too old for that caper.

If Shirley was right about Roger helping himself to soap in the train's toilet, which, in his heart of hearts he knew she was, getting him to admit it ... getting him to hand over part of his loot would be like pulling teeth without anaesthetic, the way they had in his youth in Mumbai.

His wife wanted soap, did she? Roger was a prat. 'Prat' was an English surname. Ah! The English ... their love of hygiene ... cleanliness is next to godliness. What price, shit? Eating shitty germs boosted one's immune system ... who should know that better than him ... the outstanding work he'd done in that field ... that is, if they didn't kill you first ... there was always a proviso.

*******

'It's me,' said Ravi, addressing Flora, Geoffrey and Roger.

'I can see that,' said Roger. 'I had my cataracts done last year; you forgetting that? What do you want? When First class visits Second class it means First class wants something. When a duke knocks on a peasant's door it means his car's broken down and he wants someone to give him a push-start.'

'Did you see the "Angel of the North"?' said Flora.

'I glimpsed it … it came and went very quickly,' said Ravi.

'I thought it looked … lovely. On the border between England and Scotland I think we should have a thistle as big as the "Angel of the North".'

'If we do that,' said Roger, 'we'll have to have a rose as big as the "Angel of the North" on the English side; fair do's, that's all the English ask for; fair do's. It's all go.'

'What do you want?' said Geoffrey, 'not your slice of bacon back, I hope? I've eaten it … very tasty it was too.'

'Lucky you,' said Roger, 'apart from Geoffrey, us poor things in Second haven't had a bite to eat. I've never thought of Geoffrey as a scrounger, that is, up till now. If you see any of these on your travels,' waving a free Metro newspaper at Ravi, 'be a good chap and snatch them up. There's a coupon inside offering twenty pence off a bottle of bleach. When your kitchen sink gets blocked you need bleach. Do you know how much a plumber charges to unblock a sink? Bleach isn't cheap either. It's all go.'

'Roger,' said Ravi, 'when we boarded the train you went to the loo?'

'Eh? Might have done … why?'

'Yes, you did,' said Flora, 'didn't he, Geoffrey?'

'Roger,' said Ravi, 'when you went to the loo did you help yourself to loo paper and soap?'

'They are "freebies", aren't they? I've paid for them … all that money the franchise running the East Coast line makes is tax payers' money … my, money; tax-payers money.'

'You don't pay tax … your accountant sees to that.'

'I'm thinking of the people who do; but, that's me all over, isn't it? Thinking of others. Roger, the "Good Samaritan", that's me.'

'Shirley is in the loo … she needs soap to wash her hands.'

'Oh, is she indeed; as she is one of "us" I'm more than happy to oblige; mind, I hope she's not too proud to accept help from an Anglo-Saxon. You can have a choice. I have "Brown Windsor", from the train or this bar of "Dove Beauty Cream" from the Café Royal; which do you think she'd prefer?'

'Roger,' said Ravi, shaking his head, 'have you no shame?'

'No,' said Roger. 'End-of.'

*******

Ravi found his return journey to the toilet, clutching a slippery bar of 'Brown Windsor,' while the train lurched and swayed, difficult. His balance was not as good as it had used to be when he was young.

He reminded himself that he was the proud owner of a British passport; ipso facto, that he must adopt the 'Bull dog' spirit of war-time Britain; which Roger, the petty thief, was always harping on about.

He arrived back at the toilet without having dropped the 'Brown Windsor', which he accounted a minor miracle. At every lurch of the train the soap had wanted to fly his grip the way India had wanted to leave the Raj and become an independent country.

The sign on the toilet door's handle said, 'Engaged'. And where was the master locksmith? He'd promised to stand guard.

'It's me,' said Ravi, knocking on the door, 'I've got the soap.'

'Piss off!' shouted a male voice from inside the toilet.

'Ravi, darling,' said Shirley, coming up behind her husband, 'I'm not in the loo. The locksmith is in the loo. When he started wetting himself he gave me no choice … I had to let him in. I mean, look at the mess he's made.'

Yes, there was water on the floor outside the toilet door; not a pool but as much as if an ice-cube had melted.

*******

'Look there's Durham cathedral,' said Flora.

93

'Norman power,' said Roger. 'I like the Normans. No messing with them. When they built that cathedral they were telling the Saxons to get stuffed … don't get any ideas, mates … we are here to stay.'

'If you stole soap off the Normans, they'd put you in the stocks or send you to Australia in a prison ship.'

'The Normans didn't know Australia existed.'

'I know that.'

'Why'd you say it then?'

'I forgot. I get anxious when I'm not with Jock.'

'I'll tell you something … I'll bet Beryl is not missing me.'

'Lots of people on the platform,' said Geoffrey.

'And the train's already full,' said Flora.

'I hope those bloody kids aren't coming in here,' said Roger.

*******

But, of course, they were. As a cat will be determined to sit on the knee of a person who is terrified of cats, children wearing bibs, in this case, yellow ones, seemed predestined to head Roger's way. After what had happened to him in Newcastle's Central Station, the sight of a child wearing a bib put him on his guard; clutching his stick, he prepared to rebel boarders.

Why were they making so much noise? Why were they all pushing and shoving? Who was in charge? Was anyone in charge? Had they escaped from a lunatic asylum? When his prep school had taken him on a visit he'd worn a collar and tie and had, always, been well behaved; if he hadn't he'd have been given a clip round the earhole.

'Miss, will we have to stand?'

'Miss, Dylan's standing on me foot.'

'You sit there, Anthony … next to the nice old gentleman with the walking stick. I want you where I can see you. If you are going to be sick, Anthony, tell me. Anthony always thinks he's going to be sick on trains,' this female, who appeared to be in charge, explained to Roger. 'He says he's always sick on trains ... but,' glaring at Anthony, 'not today, Anthony, not today. Anthony, look at me! Promise Tracey you are not going to be sick over the nice gentleman who is letting you share his seat. Promise?'

'If I'm not sick will I get something?'

Roger knew what he'd give him. And the child's haircut; shaved at the sides, with a lot left on top. At his prep school everyone had had a centre parting. What was wrong with Brylcreem and a centre parting?

'I'll give you a gold star. You already have three,' said Tracey. 'One more and Mrs Dickenson will give you a good behaviour certificate in assembly.'

'If you promise not to be sick over my friend Roger,' said Flora, 'I'll give you a sweet. I call them my "sucky" sweets. I'm a grandmother. I have five grandchildren. Are you this nice little boy's teacher?'

'I'm a CSW,' said Tracey, holding out her name tag.

'Geoffrey, what's it say?' said Flora. 'My spectacles are in my bag.'

Geoffrey bringing the spectacles hanging on a chain round his neck up to his eyes, said, 'Tracey Wallop ... CSW.'

'CSW,' said Roger, 'is she something to do with co-op?'

'Not "CWS",' said Flora, '"CSW".'

'CSW,' said Tracey, '"Child Support Worker". I look after Anthony, don't I, Anthony? Anthony has problems, don't you, Anthony?'

Anthony shrugged. If he shit his pants instead of going to the loo, so what?

'You said I could have a sweet.'

'You know the rules, Anthony ... never ... never take sweets off a stranger.'

'Do not talk to strangers,' said Anthony, 'tell a policeman ... tell a policeman ... tell a policeman.'

'Very good, Anthony … we heard you the first time … no need to keep repeating … we heard you … we heard you. The children have been watching a video about what to do if a strange man … it's usually a man,' looking at Roger and Geoffrey, 'offers you a sweet or a lift home in his car. Anthony, you have remembered all about the video … well done, you! What a good memory you have when you try. Well done you!'

'Do I tell a policeman about her,' pointing at Flora, 'offering me a sweet?'

'No.'

'Why not?'

'Because you have told me.'

'You're not a policeman.'

'I know that; I am your CSW.'

'When my friend Flora offered you one of her "sucky" sweets,' said Roger, 'she was trying to be kind. She wasn't trying to poison you.'

When Anthony donned a baseball cap back to front Roger wished Flora's sweet HAD been a 'poison' sweet; a sweet, as full of poison, as one of those capsules secret agents carried and swallowed when they knew the game was up and to stop them spilling the beans when they were tortured, killed themselves.

The fashion irritated Roger, no end. And, why was he wearing a hat when he was inside? There was no need to wear a hat when you were inside. It was like putting up an umbrella when it wasn't raining or, a parasol when it wasn't sunny.

'If you wore your underpants like that,' said Roger, eyeballing Anthony the way a wizard might look at a prince before turning him into a frog, 'you won't be able to go for a pee.'

'Eh?' said, Anthony.

'Would you take your hat off if you went into a church?'

'Eh? Why would he do that?' said Tracey.

'Because,' said Geoffrey, 'that's what you do when you go into a church.'

'Women keep their hats on, men take their hats off,' explained Flora.

'Never been in a church,' said Anthony. 'There's one at the end of our street. It's falling down. I smashed one of its windows. I like the colours its glass makes. When you look through its red glass, you sees blood. I've been to a police station. I've had my fingerprints taken … bet you haven't?'

'Shop-lifting or drugs?' said Roger, 'and give me back my vouchers. They are mine.'

'You a "bleach" sniffer, mister?'

'You don't ask old people questions like that,' said Tracey. 'Anthony, tell the gentleman why you were in a police station.'

'Visit,' said Anthony.

'The school takes its children on visits,' explained Tracey. 'Today, we are off to Darlington to see George Stephenson's Rocket; last week we visited a police station. They gave us coffee and biscuits and fizzy drinks for the children.'

'They took my fingerprints,' said Anthony. 'Look!' bringing his hands close-up to Roger's face. 'You can still see the ink. Miss, why's what we are going to see called "The Rocket"?'

'Because it went fast.'

'Like a space rocket, Miss?'

'Not that fast; it could go faster than a stage coach but not as fast as the train we are on now.'

'What's a stage coach?'

'A box on wheels,' said Geoffrey, 'pulled by horses.'

'What's a "horses"?'

'Anthony!' said Tracey. 'You know what a horse is.'

'No, I don't. I wouldn't say I didn't know, if I did.'

'Of course you wouldn't, Anthony; you are not a liar.'

'Tracey, I am going to tell me mam you called me a liar. You'll get wrong for saying that, Miss. I knows you will. You shouldn't call people liars when they're not.'

'Anthony,' said Flora, 'do you know what a dog looks like?'

'Course, I do; seen lots of shite machines.'

'A horse is like a very big dog.'

'Does it bark?'

'No, it neighs. Geoffrey, you are good at impersonations.'

'Neigh! Neigh! Neigh!' neighed Geoffrey.

'It's all go,' said Roger.

'Oh, them; I knows what you mean now. I've seen them on the telly. I've never seen a real one, though. Are they real? Did this thing the hosses pulled; did it carry people?'

'Six inside and as many again sitting outside on its roof,' said Geoffrey.

'Did the people sitting on the roof, not fall off?'

'I'm sure they did, sometimes.'

'Are yee "posh"?'

'Me?' said Geoffrey, 'good heavens, no … whatever put that idea into your head?'

'Because you've got a propeller under your chins.'

'Ah! My bow-tie. That's a good description of a bow-tie, Anthony. Your metaphor will make my wife laugh.'

'Is she not your wife?' pointing at Flora.

'Flora is a dear friend but not my wife. My wife is on the train but in another carriage.'

'Is that because you don't like her?'

'Certainly not. The reason my wife is not sitting beside me is a long story.'

'My dad said that when I asked him how he'd got a black eye.'

'You know who George Stephenson is?' said Roger.

'He built "The Rocket". It went faster than a stage coach but not as fast as this train.'

'Well done, you,' said Tracey.

'But,' said Roger, 'do you know who Winston Churchill was?'

'Tracey, Miss, who was Winston Churchill?'

'I'm not a walking encyclopaedia, Anthony … no one can know everything.'

'Was he George Stephenson's friend?' said Anthony.

'No, he didn't know George Stephenson,' said Roger.

'Did you know George Stephenson?'

'I used to play football with him.'

'Anthony, the man's telling lies. You may be old, mister, but you're not that old ... I'm not daft. Anthony, when you write your story about your visit to Darlington to see George Stephenson's Rocket, do not say you met a man who played football with George Stephenson ... you'll lose marks. You, mister, could be the cause of our school becoming a "failing school". I could lose my job.'

*******

At Darlington, Beryl, in First class, scanned the platform to see who had booked the window seat she'd sat in since leaving Newcastle. It was booked from Darlington to York. She liked having a window seat. Roger would never let her have a window seat ... having a window seat was a novelty. She hoped whoever had booked it wouldn't make a fuss about wanting it.

Looking out of the window she said, 'What is Roger doing on the platform?'

'Does he think he's at Kings Cross?' said Debbie.

'Dementia?' said Shirley.

'With Roger,' sighed Beryl, 'anything is possible. How I wish euthanasia was legal.'

'What's going on?' said Ravi.

'Am I missing something?' said Jock.

'Roger's having an argument with a woman on the platform,' said Beryl. 'A boy wearing a baseball cap, back to front, is making V-signs at him.'

'The woman he's arguing with,' said Jock, 'is she a big woman or a little woman?'

'What difference does that make?' said Shirley.

'If she's a big woman I'll not go to his rescue … if she's a little woman, I will.'

'She's medium,' said Debbie.

'In that case,' said Jock, 'I don't know what to do.'

'I'm going to see what's going on,' said Ravi. 'Come on, Jock, Roger needs our help.'

'The guard's blowing his whistle,' said Debbie.

'Roger's going to miss the train,' said Shirley.

'He can't do that,' said Beryl, 'he's got my King's Cross spending money in his money belt. I'll kill him if he misses the train.'

'It's one for all and all for one,' said Debbie. 'Come on, girls; you as well, Beryl; he's your husband.'

'Dear me,' said Shirley, 'I thought we were OPAC, not the three musketeers.'

*******

At the scene of the disturbance the 'Ensemble' found Flora and Geoffrey pleading with Roger to board the train.

'On or off?' a railway employee was asking Roger. 'Or, do I have to call the police?'

'On,' said Geoffrey from inside the train. 'Roger, get on the train. Get on the bloody train, Roger.'

'That child told me to fuck off,' said Roger. 'I'll not be spoken to like that … I won't.'

'Tell us about it on the train … remember, we are "OPAC" … put it in your notebook. That is why we are here; to observe and make notes of what we see.'

'On, or, off?'

'On,' said Ravi manhandling his cantankerous old pal onto the train.

'I will not, repeat, not, have a child tell me to "Fuck Off"', said Roger as the train pulled out of Darlington station. 'Not to have done something would have been appeasement; and we all know where that landed us in thirty-nine. It was bad enough him making faces at me. If that's all he'd done I'd have turned a blind eye. When he told me to "Fuck Off" ... well, that was too much.'

'You don't know for certain that's what he said,' said Flora.

'I can lip read.'

'But,' said Geoffrey, 'think of it as a plus. When we get to London, we'll have lots to talk about. It is grist to the mill. Dickens would have loved Anthony.'

'Roger, the child wasn't normal,' pleaded Flora, 'he had problems.'

'That's what they said about that murderer they released last week. It was in the "Daily Mail"; he's killed again. If I had my way he wouldn't have killed again. Do you know why?' I'll tell you why ... because if I was in charge of crime and punishment in this country, I'd have had him executed ... dead simple, a dead man can't hurt anyone. In this country we are as soft as muck.'

'Roger,' said Flora, 'have a "sucky" sweet. I think it's my last one but you can have it.'

'The sooner we get to York and I'm in first class and don't have to mix with shite like that brat, the better.'

*******

Arriving back in First class, Beryl, Debbie and Shirley found a, young man looking at their seats. He was wearing a blue suit, a white shirt, a plain red tie and a matching red pocket handkerchief.

'Quite the dandy,' thought Shirley.

'A professional man,' thought Debbie.

'Bet he's a lawyer,' thought Beryl, 'that's what he looks like to me; and I should know.'

'The window seat is my seat,' he said. 'My secretary always books me a window seat. Whoever is sitting there, would they please remove their debris?'

'I'm the culprit,' said Beryl. 'I do apologise.'

'Just be good enough to remove your rubbish. I have work to do. If you don't hurry up about it, I'll call the guard.'

'He's called Gordon,' said Debbie.

'And, he's not called a "Guard", he's a "Carriage Care Assistant"; a "CCA",' said Shirley.

'Just remove your rubbish, will you, please. I'm in no mood for a lecture on railway nomenclature.'

'For a young man, you are very impatient,' said Beryl.

To this comment the young man made no reply; with hooded eyes and an unsmiling face he watched Beryl clear her 'debris' with all the hidden glee of the bully, who, by his power has forced a teetotaller to knock back a double whisky.

When they were all sat down, Shirley, Beryl and Debbie exchanged what are called 'knowing glances'. The signal for their revenge began with a wink from Shirley.

'My neighbour,' she said in her beautiful Welsh sing song, as loud as if declaiming one of her poems at an eisteddfod, 'never puts my wheelie-bin away. Ravi always puts hers away but she never puts ours away. I mean, how long do we keep putting hers away if she never puts ours away?'

'Why do you put hers away?' said Debbie.

'I try to be a good neighbour. It makes me feel good.'

'A gin and tonic makes me feel good.'

'I've started liking flavoured tonics with my gin ... the liquorice one is my favourite. Have you tried them?'

'Let's have a "gin and flavoured tonic" party.'

'What a good idea,' said Beryl, 'and ... we'll put all our empty bottles in your neighbour's wheelie-bin.'

'Do you have a wheelie-bin?' Debbie asked the professional man with the red tie and matching red handkerchief poking out of his jacket's breast pocket. 'I'm asking you because I don't want you to feel left out of the conversation.'

'He's working,' said Shirley, 'never disturb a man when he's working ... that's what my father used to say. He never had a wheelie-bin ... he had a dustbin. Do you remember dustbins? My brothers, sadly now all with the angels, used them as shields. After they'd seen "Ivanhoe" ... three times in one week ... they made my life hell ... wanted me to throw bricks at their shields. It was to test their manliness.'

'He's not working,' said Beryl, peeking at the man's screen, 'he's playing "Dungeons and Dragons".'

'My grandson likes computer games,' said Debbie.

'Children spend too much time watching television and "gaming" ... I think that's what they call it,' said Shirley. 'The young man will know ... excuse me, are you "gaming"?'

'I think we're intruding,' said Debbie. 'Are we intruding?'

'We've been watching you,' said Shirley, 'you are very highly strung.'

'You keep biting your biro,' said Beryl.

'Violently, sometimes,' said Debbie.

'Bloody old busy bodies.'

'Are you talking to "Dragons and Dungeons" or us?' said Shirley.

'It's not our fault we are old,' continued Shirley. 'One day you will be old.'

'If he lives that long,' said Debbie. 'Highly strung people are not long livers.'

'If you say "sorry" for calling us "bloody old busy bodies" we won't e-mail your boss and tell him you were watching porn.'

'I was not watching porn,' said the young man, for the first time, looking his tormentors in the eye, 'and, furthermore, you do not know who I am or, for whom I work.'

'Yes we do,' said Beryl, 'you are called Hugo, you are a lawyer and you work for Green, Brown and Pink.'

'That,' said Shirley, 'explains the red tie and matching handkerchief.'

'You're not a partner, are you?' said Debbie. 'But, you'd like to be. I surmise you dream of a law firm called "Green, Brown, Pink and Red".'

'Utter rubbish.'

'That's what MPs say when they are asked if they want to be prime minister. "Denial through bluster", I call it.'

'And, bluster, young man, is not an argument,' said Shirley. 'I expect better from a lawyer; don't we, girls?'

The three women nodded.

'Of course,' said Beryl, 'if you let me have the window seat I will delete the photograph I took of the papers you were incautious enough to let me see.'

'That's blackmail.'

'The deal you are working on involves millions of pounds?'

'Mind your own business. I have a schedule to write for a client. I must have it ready before York.'

'If it was that urgent,' said Debbie, 'why were you wasting time playing games on your laptop?'

'Playing games helps me think. When I'm not thinking about what I'm supposed to be thinking about, ideas pop into my head.'

'Mozart was like that,' said Shirley, 'his best tunes popped into his head in a stagecoach.'

'I wonder if potholes played a part,' said Beryl, 'you know... bump ... bump ... and we have "Figaro here ... Figaro there".'

'Potholes sound more like Beethoven,' said Debbie.

'If you don't mind, ladies, we'll be in York in fifteen minutes. I have work to do. If I have been brusque, I apologise.'

He typed with a pen in his mouth. When he'd a good idea, the pen moved like an old fashioned typewriter carriage from one side of his mouth to the other.

Shirley, looking across the aisle at her husband, said: 'Ravi nearly fell down the stairs this morning; didn't you, my darling?'

'Drunk?' said Beryl.

'Ravi's not a boozer; are you, darling? Unlike some people I could name. He'd forgotten to tie his shoelaces.'

'I had tied one,' said Ravi.

'Yes, dear, but you have two feet. Instead of tying the other one you began to cut your nails. I've been telling him for years,' talking to Debbie and Shirley, 'finish the job you are doing before you start something new. When we were first married he was into Land Rovers. We had a Land Rover chassis in our front garden for five years. The neighbours didn't like it. They didn't say anything, but, I know they didn't like it. I mean, who could blame them? The front garden looked like a scrapyard. He loved that chassis. I sometimes think he loved it more than he loved me. He called it, "Bertha". "When are you going to put some clothes on Bertha?" I'd say to him. How's your totem pole coming along, Jock?'

'I'm having trouble deciding how many feathers to put on the eagle's wings.'

'Problems. Problems, life is full of them.'

'Roger went through a phase of collecting money belts,' said Beryl, 'then it was guns and knives. Now, it's banana labels; you know, the stickers you find on hands of bananas.'

'What's he "carrying" today?' said Debbie.

'You won't believe this, but his walking stick is a "sword" stick.'

'Geoffrey once had a passion for fishing … now, it's opera. He can't understand anyone not liking opera. He's tried to convert me, but I can't say I'm a fan.'

'Don't you think it strange,' said Beryl, 'that when someone takes up a hobby and becomes obsessed by it, they think that everyone should be as enthusiastic about it as they are?'

'When I was a druid,' said Shirley, 'I thought everyone should be one.'

'Do you still believe?' said Debbie.

'I have a recurrent dream. I'm on top of a monolith holding a cross ... a Welsh dragon breaths fire on it ... melts it ... as if it was wax. Ravi likes interpreting my dreams; don't you, my darling? He says it is the way I was brought up ... Welsh chapel ... don't read the paper on a Sunday or buy a loaf of bread. He says my dreams are telling me I am a chapel girl. Sometimes in bed, when he's asleep, Ravi talks to himself in Hindi; don't you, my darling? When he's homesick for Mumbai he puts a chair in the passage and sits and stares at Ganesha.'

'The Hindu elephant god you and Ravi have in stained glass on your front door,' said Debbie. 'I've always liked it. When the English see stained glass they expect to see blokes with saucers on their heads ... not an elephant with a trunk that looks like a leek.'

'Dear Ravi,' said Shirley, looking across the aisle at her husband of many decades who, along with Jock, sat opposite him, was nodding off. 'I hope our trip to London is not going to be too much for him.'

'York,' said Debbie. 'I love York ... its city walls ... its shops. If Newcastle had kept its city walls Geordies would have something more to offer tourists than bridges and Brown Ale.'

'I like the Minster,' said Beryl. 'Roger wouldn't pay to go in but I did. When I came out he was furious. I'd kept him waiting two hours. I could have stayed longer. Inside, I found peace. It made me forget I was married to Roger.'

'That's why I have a shed,' said Debbie. 'When Geoffrey is getting on my nerves I go to my shed and shut the door. Geoffrey put electricity in for me. If it had a loo, it would be perfect.'

'Excuse me,' said the young man, 'if it's not too much trouble, I want out.'

'The train hasn't stopped, yet,' said Beryl.

'The kind young man is giving you plenty of time, Beryl, for you to stand up and get out of his way because you are old. Isn't that right?' said Debbie.

'Say "excuse me",' said Beryl.

'Excuse me.'

'That's more like it.'

'Don't forget your "debris",' said Debbie.

When he'd gone, Beryl said, 'I don't think he liked us.'

'Do you think it was because we are old? We are not the "men magnates" we were when we were young. Pompous ass.'

'Didn't Geoffrey say we change seats at York?' said Shirley.

*******

As the train pulled into York station, Roger erupted like Vesuvius.

'What's the rush?' said Flora.

'This is where we change seats; Second class to First class … First class to Second. I'm going back to where I belong; no more brats are going to tell me to F-off. A good job I didn't get my hands on that youngster. If I had, I'd have given him a smack.'

'Roger, you know as well as I do, corporal punishment is no longer allowed.'

'And, I'll tell you something; that young twerp knows it as well. He wasn't as daft as he made out. "I can do and say anything I like; you can't touch me"; that was his attitude. When he's older he'll scrounge every penny he can get off the state.'

'Roger, it is funny, isn't it?' said Flora.

'What is?'

'If I tell you, you promise not to shout at me?'

'I promise but, I probably will.'

'You are a … contradiction.'

'Me?'

'When you are angry and full of busy you never say, "It's all go". You only ever say, "It's all go" when you are doing nothing and are going to sleep.'

'I do that, Flora, to give amateur psychologists like you, something to talk about. I've told you, I am Roger the "Good Samaritan". When you and Beryl get together you can organise

107

a seminar on the subject. Where are my vouchers? I've got ten, you know; that's a pound off a bottle of bleach. I was brought up during the war. I don't like waste.'

'I have memories of York,' said Geoffrey, talking to his window reflection, a far-away look on his face.

'Ouch!' said Roger.

'What's wrong?' said Flora. 'Roger, are you alright?'

'My money belt is digging into my belly button. I don't know if you know this but, I have a funny belly button. Geoffrey, come on, stop talking to yourself … we have to move. If you want to daydream, that's up to you. I'm off to First; for the "full English," lots of leg room and a window seat … got to have a window seat.'

*******

Roger fumed; did the silly bitch blocking his way to First class not know his need to get there was urgent? That she was playing a dangerous game coming between a man and free sausage, bacon and egg? He wondered if the breakfast included baked beans and black pudding. If it did he'd have them. He liked a bit of black pudding and the beans would make him fart which would annoy Beryl.

'I do apologise,' the woman, who was tall and tres elegant, told Roger, 'it's my case … it is rather heavy … would you mind … perhaps not … you do look more Methuselah than Mr Universe … and do stop whacking me with your stick … I am not a cow to be prodded into a pen.'

'Roger, do step aside,' said Geoffrey, 'there's a good chap. The lady needs help with her case.'

'Ah!' said the lady, 'a gentleman. I thought they all went down with the Titanic.'

'Allow me,' said Geoffrey.

'It's the handle … it is stuck.'

'You press this little button,' said Geoffrey, 'see … and up pops the handle … shall I wheel it for you or will you?'

'If I grant you the pleasure of "wheeling" will it please you?'

Geoffrey knew a fellow thespian when he saw one.

'My lady,' he said, bowing, 'if you will be Queen Elizabeth, numero one, I will be your Sir Walter Raleigh. I do not have a cloak to throw over a puddle to stop your feet getting wet but, with your permission, may I trundle your suitcase?'

'Retired are you … from the stage?'

'Never, sadly, in a professional capacity.'

'An amateur?'

'I have trodden the boards.'

'I am an opera singer.'

'I love opera,' said Geoffrey. 'What about …' touching his bow tie, 'if I trundle while you sing?'

'An aria for a porter … what a lovely idea … I like it.'

Thus it was, much to Roger's disgust, that Geoffrey trundled the opera singer's suitcase – she was a mezzo-soprano – off the coach and onto the platform at York station while she, keeping to her part of the bargain, sang, at full belt, 'One fine day' from 'Madam Butterfly'.

Roger hated opera, having never fully recovered from watching Aida in Verona's open air theatre in the pouring rain … not to mention the price of the tickets. And that he owed Ravi money for 'Peter Grimes'. Ravi had a memory like an elephant. That elephant Ravi had in stained glass on his front door wasn't a joke.

*******

Before the train left York the 'Ensemble' had a pow-wow.

'We have a problem,' said Geoffrey.

'I know what you are going to say,' said Jock, 'five of us in first class and three of us in second class, it doesn't work out, does it?'

'Ravi and I volunteer to stay in first class,' said Shirley.

109

'That, Shirley, is not the OPAC spirit. The aim of our jaunt, in case you are forgetting, is to meet as many different types of people as possible. We are artists and like all artists we must suffer for our art.'

'Geoffrey?'

'Yes?'

'Sometimes, your pomposity overwhelms me.'

'That's as maybe … as far as I'm concerned, we are thermometers … the purpose of our jaunt is to take the temperature of England.'

'And Wales … don't forget Wales.'

'And Scotland,' said Jock.

'I was thinking about Scotland,' said Flora, 'I was a wee bit scared to speak up.'

'That didn't stop you having a go at me,' said Roger, 'about saying, "It's all go"; you can be courageous when you want to be; you're a dark horse, you are, Flora.'

'I apologise,' said Geoffrey, 'I should have said, to, "take the temperature of our dear, precious, United Kingdom".'

'What about the Raj?' said Ravi, 'don't forget the Raj … the jewel in the crown of the British Empire.'

'Great Britain no longer has an empire,' said Debbie.

'It is as dead and buried,' said Geoffrey, 'as the half-a-crown I dropped, by accident, into the River Tyne in nineteen fifty nine. In those days, I was so young, I couldn't handle alcohol. I seem to remember I'd had two pints at the Crown Posada and was feeling merry.'

'The old money,' said Roger, 'when it was no longer legal tender, I'd to take my whisky bottle full of loose change to the bank. I was lucky to get my money back; gave me quite a scare, I can tell you. Old money and the Raj, all gone.'

'I am not so sure about the Raj,' said Ravi. 'Last week, in Marks and Spencer's … I was in a queue waiting to pay for underpants.'

'Y-fronts or boxer shorts?' said Beryl.

'Beryl,' said Flora, 'you are making me blush.'

'Y-fronts,' said Shirley, speaking up for her husband, 'Ravi likes to have his undercarriage tucked in ... don't you, dear?'

'Roger's ... boxer shorts,' said Beryl.

'Do you mind,' said Ravi, 'I am telling my story of what it is like to be an Indian in a post-Raj, United Kingdom ... as I was saying ... I was in this queue ... I have lived in this green and pleasant land long enough to know how to queue ... when the man in front of me ... he looked to be about seventy ... a mere child of nature ... said, "You," meaning me, "hold that", handing me his crutch while he took out his purse and paid for a custard trifle in a plastic tub. Worse ... after completing his transaction he clicked his fingers to let me know he wished to have his crutch back.'

'Interesting,' said Roger, 'about him having a purse, I mean. I was thinking of getting one for my loose change. This money belt is giving me hell. I don't care who gets to sit in First all the way, as long as yours truly gets a seat in First, a window seat and the full English.'

'In the spirit of OPAC,' said Debbie, 'I am happy to go to Second class.'

'If Flora doesn't mind,' said Jock, 'in the spirit of OPAC I volunteer to go to Second as well. Let the Welsh, the English and the Indian subcontinent know it's not true what they say about the Scots being mean. Aye, it's a wee myth told by the English after they'd cleared the Highlands and the poor folk they'd left alive had no porridge to offer their visitors; the poor folk weren't being mean, they were starving.'

*******

The 'Ensemble's' pow-wow, beside a door, was testing the patience of passengers wishing to leave and board the train.

When, at last, they disbanded and headed to their seats a man carrying a pair of skis told them: 'Not before bloody time, either; bloody baby-boomers.'

'I do apologise,' said Geoffrey.

'It's not your fault you are old and useless, mate. My mother committed suicide when she was your age.'

'I'll willingly step aside, to let you by,' said Geoffrey, touching his bowtie, 'but I refuse, point blank, to kill myself.'

*******

In First class Geoffrey stretched out his legs. He'd opted to sit at the two-seater table, hitherto occupied by Jock and Ravi. He'd been eighteen when His Majesty's Government had sent him a letter ordering him to report to Fulford Barracks, York. National Service. What a jolly time he'd had. The corporal with bad breath who hated Geordies. The man's spitefulness … how, on a whim, he'd torn up his weekend pass … how the horrible little man had described having sex with his wife … all, a long time ago. A different world. No computers, no mobile phones.

Ravi, Shirley, Flora and Roger were sitting across the aisle from him.

'More leg room in First class,' said Flora.

'When we come to working out who pays for what,' said Roger, from his window seat, 'you two,' pointing at Ravi and Shirley, 'should pay more … while Flora and I have been squashed up in Second class you have had the luxury of First class … hi!' leaning across Flora to grab the arm of a tall young man, wearing a dark blue waistcoat, a white shirt and a badge, 'Coffee and the "Full English".'

'Eh?' said the tall young man brought to a shuddering halt, by Roger's scrawny hand, the way fighter planes are 'arrested' by trip wires when they land on aircraft carriers.

'Coffee and the "Full English",' repeated Roger.

In days of yore when he'd dined on Pullmans, all expenses paid, the fellow would have called him, 'sir'. God-dam-it, there was enough muck in the fellow's nails to grow cabbages. His cuff-links were ceramic replicas of female breasts.

'How many sausages, sir?' said the tall young man, winking at Shirley.

'How many can I have?' said Roger. This was more like it … a la carte … individual service … a little deference wouldn't come amiss but, all in all, things were looking up.

'Roger …' said Flora.

'They come in packs of twenty,' said the tall young man, taking out an imaginary notepad and licking the tip of an imaginary pencil.

'What you doing?' said Roger.

'Roger …' said Flora.

'I'm taking your order, mate.'

'But you haven't got a notebook … or, a pen,' said Roger. 'And, do not call me "mate". I am a paying passenger. You call me "sir".'

'Roger …' said Flora, 'the nice young man is not a waiter … he is the same as you and me. He is a passenger. I think you should say "Sorry".'

'Why?'

'Because you have made a mistake.'

'I never make mistakes.'

'God doesn't like people who tell lies.'

'There is no god.'

'A theological dispute,' said the tall young man who seemed to be finding the situation he now found himself in, to be thoroughly amusing and enjoyable. 'I don't think we should go down that route.'

'It's your fault,' said, Roger, pointing an accusatory finger at him, 'you are dressed like a waiter.'

'It's because he's old,' said Flora, in an heroic attempt to blame Roger's belligerence on advanced years.

'Age has nothing to do with it,' said Roger. 'It was a mistake anyone could have made; even a teenager.'

'Oh dear,' said Flora, 'I find it hard to remember when I was a teenager. I think I wore a mini-skirt.'

'By your lovely accent and the plaid you are wearing,' said the tall young man, unfazed by Roger's attack and addressing Flora, 'I'm guessing you're a Scot.'

'I am that,' said Flora, coming to life like a Steradent tablet dropped into water.

'In that case we are kin,' pointing at himself, 'born and bred in Mallaig … family still live there.'

'Would you be speaking the Gaelic?' said Flora.

Roger thanked god they'd no bagpipes. Anyone could have mistaken the young twerp for a waiter. He looked like a waiter. And Flora trying to say he'd made the mistake because he was old. If Beryl had said that, he'd have told her to shut her mouth. Furthermore the ensuing conversation, in Gaelic, between Flora and the tall young man – a language, in Roger's opinion, full of guttural sounds like water going down a plug hole – irritated him, like eczema. This was a fucking English train.

He'd never known Flora have so much to say; never seen her so animated. Speaking in her native wood-notes-wild, took years off her. She could be seventy. He'd never fancied Flora before but he did now … at least for a fleeting second.

'Hoy!' he said, as full of himself as a Manichaean preaching, 'English, good; Gaelic, bad; this is an English train; on an English train you speak, English.'

'Wrong,' said the tall young man, 'the train is not English, it is owned by Deutsche Bahn.'

'No matter who owns the wheels, this is an English train … in England …going through Yorkshire at eighty miles an hour …

well, at least ten ... in England we speak English. Flora ... what's he saying? I know you are talking about me ... what's he saying?'

'He is saying,' said Flora, flustered and embarrassed, 'he is saying ...'

'Spit it out, Flora ... spit it out.'

'He is saying you are a ... a very nice young man.'

'I don't believe you.'

'Oh dear, I'm no good at telling lies ... he says, to mistake him for a waiter you must be ...'

'Yes?'

'Losing your marbles ... Oh dear ... I wish Jock was here to hold my hand.'

'And, what else ... I know there's more.'

'And ... to tell you ... Roger, prepare yourself for bad news ... when I tell you ... you will think it is the end of the world but it isn't ... not really; I mean, the end of the world but, the nice young man has just told me, hot breakfasts are no longer being served.'

'The ovens have packed in,' said the tall young man. 'I've been to the galley to ask about my,' winking at Flora, '"Full Scottish". Instead of kippers and two slices of toast and marmalade, I'm having a croissant ... that is if chef can find a way of defrosting it. He's from Poland, resourceful bloke. He's placed my croissant on a sunny window ledge; nice to have met you all, well, most of you.'

'What a nice young man,' said Flora. 'Roger, would you like one of my "sucky" sweets? I think I have one left but I'm not sure.'

'Roger is in shock,' said Ravi. 'Roger, put your head between your knees.'

'He is grieving for the "full English",' said Shirley. 'He is grieving the way we will one day grieve when we lose our partners.'

'Is it best to have loved and lost or never to have loved, at all?' said Ravi.

'I hope I die before you, Ravi, my darling,' said Shirley.

Roger disliked people talking about him as if he was four months old and hadn't a clue what they were on about. They'd done that to him in the hospital; all those medics talking about his innards, as if he couldn't understand what they were saying. He wasn't having it. If only Beryl was with him; he'd have had a real 'go' at her.

What does a drummer do when he has no drum to beat? If he is an old drummer like Roger he closes his eyes and goes to sleep; which is what Roger did, muttering, 'It's all go' and 'Bollocks'.

'Roger reminds me of a starving polar bear I saw die in a BBC natural history programme,' said Ravi. 'It just curled up on the ice waiting to die. No fuss. No bother.'

'Roger's not starving,' said Flora.

'Ah ... but, he thinks he is.'

'I can't see Roger dying without making a fuss,' said Shirley.

'It's all go,' muttered Roger, to let them know he was listening. He knew the rules of the game; show these wise-cracks they were getting at you and you'd make their day. Well, he wasn't going to make anyone's 'day'. Stuff the lot of them. 'Bollocks! It's all go.'

The strong sunlight pouring into the carriage was making orange curtains of his closed eyelids. Sometimes, no matter how hard you tried, you just couldn't shut out the wicked world; not one hundred per cent, you couldn't.

*******

Meanwhile, Geoffrey, sitting in the seat across the aisle, was taking a stroll down memory lane.

Why had his elder brother died at such a young age? Had his mother loved his brother more than she'd loved him? When would he die? How long you lived was a lottery. His brother used to share out sweets in the manner of all older brothers ... one for you ... two for me.

He was vaguely aware of the boo-how going on with Roger. On the Roger Richter Scale of happenings it barely registered as a tremor. He'd long ago ceased to be surprised by Roger. The man who'd sat down opposite him, on the other hand, intrigued him.

In between pretending to be more asleep than he was, he studied the new passenger with whom he was now having to share a table. Would the fellow take more than his half? Debbie always took more than her half of their double bed; sharing a table wasn't as intimate as sharing a bed but, it was a little bit like that. The fellow had already taken up more than his fair share of leg room.

He'd a shaven head, this fellow and a scar ran like a motorway from the top of his right ear to the corner of his right lip. Razor slash? Machete? Had he fallen through a window and cut himself? The cicatrix made Geoffrey feel like a lepidopterist who'd seen a rare butterfly. This was what OPAC was all about. There were just as many characters around today as there had been in Dickens' time; no doubt about that.

The fellow's black and white pin-stripe suit was 'loud'; its stripes as wide as those on a Newcastle United strip. The uniform of a professional man? A barrister? A judge? A hedge fund manager? Maybe a Harley Street surgeon. It was just the sort of suit you'd expect to find a chap wearing in First class.

Geoffrey had worn a suit just like that when he'd played Mr Toad. 'Wind in the Willows'; they were the days. The applause. Three curtain calls, he remembered.

The man's tie? Guard's regiment? A Cambridge college? Trouble was the white shirt was dirty. Its collar needed ironing. He knew about ironing because Debbie was a stickler about removing creases.

Perhaps the man was fond of the shirt. Geoffrey had shirts he was fond of. It annoyed him when Debbie threw them out. When Debbie was in the grip of one of her cleaning out manias there was no stopping her … these days he didn't argue. What was the point? She always won.

Every so often, Geoffrey caught a whiff of an 'air-raid' shelter smell.

The sun streaming into the carriage made him feel sleepy. He wanted to nod off. The cut-it-with-a-knife pong coming off the man now sitting opposite him, made this impossible; no doubt about it, the fellow, reading the 'Financial Times' upside down, was a phoney; at the debrief, that's what he'd call him, the 'Phoney'.

The cigar poking out of his breast pocket was … chocolate. His shirt cuffs flapped like jib sheets between tacks.

What kind of shoes was he wearing? You could tell a lot about a man by looking at his shoes. An old guy wearing shoes with Velcro fastenings told you he couldn't fasten his laces. Geoffrey always wore leather brogues with leather laces. He was proud of the fact that he could still tie his own shoelaces.

To take a peek at the 'Phoney's' footwear, Geoffrey, pretending he'd an itch, ducked under the table to give an ankle a good scratch.

The 'Phoney's' shoes were shiny, cheap, black plastic; their rubber soles were worn and one shoe was missing a lace. In lieu of socks the man had painted his ankles black.

While he pondered this, Geoffrey took a piece of folded newspaper out of his wallet.

'Shirley,' he said, bending across the aisle and handing Shirley the newspaper cutting, 'which one in that photograph do you think is me?'

'Was that taken when you were in the army?' said Ravi, looking at the photograph with his wife.

'Which one do you think looks like me?' said Geoffrey.

Shirley and Ravi scrutinised the photograph.

'That one,' said Shirley.

'Wrong,' said Geoffrey.

'Let me have a look,' said Flora. 'I've seen baby photographs of Geoffrey. That one … I've known Geoffrey for so long I'd pick him out easy.'

'That's the one I thought looked like me,' said Geoffrey.

'I knew I'd recognise you,' said Flora.

'Trouble is, it's not me.'

'Which one is?' said Shirley.

'None of them.'

'None of them!' said Ravi. 'If you are not on the photograph, why are you showing it to us?'

'Because I thought I looked like the soldier Flora thought looked like me. He does look like me, doesn't he?'

'A little bit,' said Ravi, 'I suppose.'

'I'm wondering if I have a double.'

'The thought of two Geoffreys is too much for anyone to contemplate,' said Shirley.

'Do you know any of the soldiers in the photograph?' said Ravi.

'I've no idea who they are. I found the cutting in a library book. I thought it strange I looked like the soldier you thought I looked like … as if someone was sending me a message. The book I found it in was called, "Great Mystics of the East" … all I'm saying is, it makes you wonder.'

'It makes me wonder about you, Geoffrey,' said Ravi. 'I'm the mystic from the east, not you. I can understand Geordies going metaphysical about Newcastle winning the premier league, but … Geoffrey, I am worried about you.'

'Geoffrey's eccentric,' said Shirley.

'Excuse me,' said Geoffrey to the 'Phoney', 'you don't know me, do you?'

'I beg your pardon?'

'You don't know me?'

'Should I?'

'No.'

119

'You're not selling anything, are you? This is first class, don't you know? Not a beach in Turkey where conmen in pyjamas try to sell a chap a Rolex watch made by a tinsmith with a hammer in Timbuktu. There's many a Rolex made out of a recycled hookah, don't you know?'

The man's fanciful protestations and the way in which he'd expressed them made Geoffrey pause for thought; the fellow was a thespian, just like himself; in spite of the radioactive pong coming off him, Geoffrey, recognising a fellow eccentric, warmed to him.

'My dear fellow,' said Geoffrey, 'would you do me the favour of looking at this photograph?'

'No, I'm doing the crossword ... see.'

'May I?' said Geoffrey, taking the newspaper.

The answers Geoffrey read were ... dear me ... ehfijggssr.

'What a clever fellow you are,' said Geoffrey, 'writing your answers in code.'

'I try to make it interesting ... otherwise it's too easy.'

'Quite ... by the way, twenty-five across is "Cincinnatus".'

'Clever bugger, aren't you?'

'I'm good at crosswords. I think it's because I'm related to Isaac Newton.'

'Who's he?'

'Tickets, please, all passengers from York, tickets, please.'

'Ah! The return of the Jedi,' said Geoffrey. 'Fear not, Gordon, no need for the handcuffs. I have a First class ticket.'

Only when he took out his wallet, to get his ticket, did he remember that, what with all the kerfuffle at York, the 'Ensemble' had changed seats but, not tickets. Not to worry ... Gordon was a reasonable man.

'Tickets, please ... all passengers from York. Your ticket, please, sir,' Gordon asked the 'Phoney.'

'Dear me, dear me,' said the 'Phoney' beginning a pantomime search of pockets real and imaginary.

To show he had money he placed on the table, for all to see, a wallet stuffed full of monopoly money.

While Geoffrey rehearsed the explanation he was planning to give Gordon, of why he, Roger and Flora did not have First class tickets, he, Flora, Ravi and Shirley (Roger was asleep) watched the 'Phoney's' vaudeville act, with raised eyebrows. They'd have so much to talk about when they had tea and cake in Doughty Street.

'Nope,' said the 'Phoney', 'it isn't there … now … where might it be? Ah!' pulling out from a trouser pocket a soiled handkerchief and a rosary, at the sight of which, crossing himself, he exclaimed, 'In the sacred name of Mary, blessed mother of our Lord and saviour, Jesus Christ … where might it be?'

'Is it in your shoe?' said Flora. 'When I worked in the Far East … a long time ago now, I sometimes hid money in my shoe … always my right shoe … you see I'd a bunion on my left foot.'

'Ah!' exclaimed the 'Phoney', 'thank you, madam'; you have reminded me of my secret hiding place,' whereupon, instead of removing a shoe for inspection, he removed his toupee – a toupee, so good, no one had thought it was a toupee.

Its removal revealed a red and scarred head.

'Ah! You stinker,' said the 'Phoney', 'that's Greek, by the way … my ticket,' handing Gordon a railway ticket.

Gordon thought he'd seen it all … wrong! The ticket under the toupee … that was a new one … wait until he got back to the canteen … tell his mates.

'I'm sorry, sir,' said Gordon, 'this is a ticket from Derby to Leicester.'

'Derby to Leicester?'

'Yes, sir … Derby to Leicester.'

'Is this train not going to Leicester?'

'No, sir … King's Cross … next stop, Doncaster … (where you, *mate, will be on your bike*) … this ticket, sir, it is dated, January … we are now in the month of June.'

'But it is a rail ticket?'

'Yes, sir.'

'So, we are, as one might say, "getting warm"?'

'Except, sir, we are not playing "Hunt the Thimble".'

'Try your shoe,' said Flora.

'While the gentleman finds his ticket,' said Geoffrey, 'I wish to explain to your good self why I and this lady,' making a sweeping gesture across the aisle towards Flora, 'and the gentleman asleep in the corner seat are enjoying all the comforts of First class on Second class tickets; all I and my friends need to prove to you that we have every right to be sitting in First class is … a teeny-weeny bit of your time and patience. First of all I and my friends did not board at York.'

'I know you didn't, sir. You and your friends boarded at Newcastle and, when you did you were second class. Once again, sir, do you wish to be upgraded?'

'You have remembered me from our previous contretemps. I am flattered. No one likes to be forgotten. Gordon, I assure you … my friends and I have first class tickets.'

'Show them to me, sir, that's all I'm asking.'

'Our problem is this … our friends have them and they are in second class. We swapped seats at York, you see.'

'I have the right ticket,' said Ravi, looking rather pleased with himself.

'And, so do I,' said Shirley.

'I know you do, sir … madam … you was checked at Newcastle.'

'We're good boys and girls, we are.'

'I think,' said Ravi, pointing at Geoffrey and winking, 'he needs to be kept an eye on.'

'Look,' said Geoffrey, standing up, 'while this gentleman,' nodding at the 'phoney', 'is trying to find his ticket why don't you and I saunter to the next carriage where, as in the last act of a play, all will be revealed; wake up Roger.'

'I know how to wake up Roger,' said Ravi, 'you touch his money belt.'

When Ravi did just that, Roger reacted like a Ninja. The force and speed with which he bent back Ravi's little finger, made Ravi exclaim, 'Roger … It's me … Ravi.'

'Who's after my money?' said Roger, opening his eyes. 'Oh, it's you, is it? You'll have to be quicker than that, Ravi, to get my money. I may be old but I'm still quick … still pack a punch.'

'Roger,' said Geoffrey, 'give me your Second class ticket and … you, Flora.' Turning to Gordon, 'Gordon, why don't you and I saunter to the next carriage where my three friends in Second class will give me, voluntarily, of their own free will, three First class tickets for three Second class tickets.'

'Why would they do that?' said Gordon. 'That's like giving someone three fivers for a ten pound note?'

'Let me explain.'

'I wish you would, sir. Mallard! Mallard!' Gordon intoned into his mobile phone. 'I'll be back,' he told the 'Phoney'.

On their way to Second class to find Debbie, Beryl and Jock, Geoffrey asked Gordon, 'Am I correct in thinking "mallard" is a code word?'

'Staff-only information, that, sir, my lips is sealed.'

'I'd wager a tortoiseshell butterfly on the back of a ladybird with an extra spot that you were asking for "back-up"; like they do in the movies. Have no fear, Gordon, Geoffrey and his OPAC friends are on hand to help. If that fellow with the scar doesn't find his ticket and, I personally don't think he will but, of course, I may be wrong … you have more experience of dealing with the public than I have … if he doesn't find it you can rely on me and my friends to restrain him, should he become violent.'

'It's not the gentleman with the scar I'm worried about, sir. I've had to deal with plenty like him in my time … though the ticket under the toupee was new … I'll put that down to experience … no, sir, it's not him I'm worried about.'

'Who, then?'

'Think about it, sir.'

'Oh!' said Geoffrey.

* * * * * * *

On reaching Second class, with a chastened Geoffrey in tow, Gordon found himself having to deal with a domestic.

'This is my seat,' a middle-aged woman with two black eyes was shouting at Beryl. 'I know you want my seat, but you can't have it because it's my seat.'

'Gladys,' said Gordon, 'what you doing in second class? You always travel first.'

'I wants a drink of water.'

'Gladys will be getting off at Doncaster,' said Gordon. 'She's one of my regulars. York to Doncaster every day. Give Gordon your ticket, Gladys; remember, I stopped you eating dog biscuits, last week. I am here to help.'

'I wants a drink of water. Where's my water?'

'This is Second class, Gladys … you don't get waiter service in Second class. You should be in First. You know that. Let me show you to your seat.'

'Will I get a glass of water?'

'Of course you will.'

'In a plastic bottle with a red top?'

Gordon nodded.

'That woman,' making a fist at Beryl, 'she's in my seat.'

'Come on, Gladys; you be a good girl and behave. You follow Gordon back to where you should be.'

'What about our tickets?' said Geoffrey, 'do you not want to see them?'

'Don't you worry, sir, I haven't forgotten you. It's a question of priorities, isn't it? Come on, Gladys, you be a good girl and follow Gordon back to First class, where you belong.'

'Phew!' said Beryl, when they'd gone. 'And I thought dealing with Roger was bad; silly old me.'

Geoffrey explained to Beryl, Debbie and Jock why he needed their First class tickets.

'I shall make a note of what has just happened in my notebook,' said Beryl. 'We'll have a lot to talk about when we get to Doughty Street, won't we?'

*******

In First class Gordon put Gladys in a single seat, with its own table.

'I wants my water,' said Gladys, in a voice loud enough for everyone, in the carriage, to hear.

Geoffrey, who'd followed Gordon and Gladys back to First class explained, to the 'Ensemble' what had happened to Beryl.

'I wants my glass of water,' shouted Gladys.

'What about me?' said Roger, 'I wants the "full English" … but, I know I'm not going to get it unless, that is, Ravi and Shirley are like those birds who feed their young by regurgitating half-digested food.'

'Don't be disgusting, Roger,' said Shirley.

'At least I'm not making a fuss about not having the "full English" the way that woman is going on about wanting a glass of water.'

'The poor woman has mental health problems,' said Shirley.

'Gordon!' shouted Geoffrey, 'I have my First class ticket. I am legitimate. You can cancel, "mallard".

'Later, sir, if you don't mind. If I don't get Gladys her water she'll pull the emergency cord.'

'I wonder if Gladys would like a "sucky" sweet,' said Flora. 'I'd give her one but I don't think I have any left.'

'Where's the fellow with the scar who couldn't find his ticket?' said Geoffrey.

'Hiding in the loo, I think,' said Shirley.

'We don't think he had a ticket,' said Ravi.

A few minutes later Gladys approached the 'Ensemble' in an aggressive manner; the way a seagull attacks you when you are sitting on the fish quay eating al fresco fish and chips.

'What's your name?' she asked Flora.

'Hello,' said Flora.

In case the 'mad' woman turned violent, Roger grabbed his walking stick. He'd never hit a woman before, but, if he had to, he would.

Much to everyone's relief Gladys did not wait for Flora to reply. Her question had been rhetorical.

Returning to her seat as quickly as she'd left it, Gladys kept herself busy by counting her loose change. Judging by the sound the coins made when she spilled them out of her purse she had lots of copper and silver.

'Someone hit the jackpot?' said Roger.

Gladys counted the coins more than once. If Roger could have seen her, he'd have empathised.

*******

'Gordon,' said Geoffrey, after Gordon had returned and given Gladys her bottle of water, 'our tickets.'

Gordon clicked them, mechanically. His hands trembled. He looked tired. Gladys had taken a lot out of him. At Newcastle he'd been a bouncy castle full of air; not now.

'Gordon, if that water's free,' said Roger, 'I'll have two bottles.'

'It's been a long day, sir,' said Gordon, 'but, I'll do my best.'

*******

Fifteen minutes later a voice on the carriage's loudspeaker system announced: 'Next stop, Durham … I mean, Doncaster.'

'That sounded like Gordon,' said Roger, 'I think he's in a bit of a state. I hope he's not forgotten about my bottles of water. If I can't have the "full English" surely I can have a glass of water. It's not much to ask, is it? "It's been a long day, sir" what's he mean by that?'

'Doncaster,' said Ravi.

'Looks busy,' said Shirley.

'I used to know someone from Doncaster,' said Roger, 'always called it, "good old Donny"; can't say it turns me on.'

'Can you commute?'

'To where?'

'To London ... early train down in the morning, late train back at night.'

'Wouldn't fancy doing that ... the cost ... put a hole in my wallet as big as the one made by that meteorite ... the one that wiped out the dinosaurs ... I hope Gordon doesn't forget my water. It's all go.'

'Do you think it's true,' said Flora, 'that Londoners think Doncaster is in Scotland? Look ... there's a McDonald's ... surprise, surprise.'

'If they think that,' said Geoffrey, leaning across the aisle to join in the conversation, 'I blame prejudice. When I lived in Reading for a spell, my landlady, knowing I came from Newcastle, wouldn't believe me when I told her my parents' house had an inside toilet and a back garden. To make her trust me ... I wanted her to know she could rely on me to pay my rent every week ... I told her that of course I was joking. "We have, Mrs Sloane ...", she was called, Sloane, I remember ...'

'Was she a "Sloane Ranger"?' said Shirley.

'No, definitely not ... a landlady offering a postgrad student B and B accommodation does not wear green wellies and go to gymkhanas ...no, no, as I was saying ... to put the woman at ease ...'

'Like giving her a diazepam,' said Flora. 'I sometimes take one when Jock forgets to put out the wheelie bin and I have to do it myself.'

'Will everyone stop interrupting me,' said Geoffrey, 'I am telling a story.'

'You have started so you will finish,' said Roger.

'My grandchildren are always saying that,' said Flora. 'They get me to say it fast hoping I'll say "farted" instead of "started". If I've had a small sherry I'll sometimes say "farted" on purpose ... just to make them laugh ... I love to hear my grandchildren laugh.'

'Well?' said Shirley.

'Geoffrey's taken the huff,' said Roger. 'If anyone has the right to take the huff, it's me ... no "full English" and, so far, not even a bottle of water. I hope Gordon has a good memory. I will of course be writing a letter.'

'Come on, Geoffrey,' said Ravi, 'we want to hear your story ... no more interruptions anyone.'

'As I was saying,' said Geoffrey, 'to keep the poor woman happy, I pandered to her prejudices ... yes ... pandered. "Mrs Sloane," I told her ... remember, at the time I was big into amateur theatricals ... close to turning professional in fact ... "Mrs Sloane," I told her, "you are quite right ... I am ashamed to admit it ... my parents' "loo" as you call it ... up North we call it a "netty" ... is at the bottom of a long back yard full of potholes. We use this utility only in fine weather ... when it's raining and cold in the winter we use a piss pot ... nobody likes going for a number two when it's raining and there's frost on the ground ... not to mention April coming in like a lion and never going out like a lamb." She knew this was more like it ... what she was hearing had the ring of truth. I knew I had her on my side when she asked, "Is there a pit heap at the bottom of the yard?" "Of, course." "You poor thing ... do you know how to flush a toilet?" "Bucket?" "In Reading, you pull a chain ... let me show you, then I'll make you a nice cup of tea." The South has lots of strange ideas about the North.'

'If southerners think Doncaster is north,' said Flora, 'where do they think Newcastle is?'

'I have a theory' said Ravi, 'and remember I come from the mystic East and speak as an adopted Geordie. I postulate ... to the good folk of southern England, Newcastle is Atlantis, a city of myth and legend.'

'You mean we once had a football team?' said Roger. 'If we get relegated I'm not sure I want to renew my season ticket ... when the team goes down they don't bring the price down ... they didn't last time.'

'I mean,' said Ravi, 'Newcastle is like us. It is past its sell-by date. It is looking around for something to replace its glory days when Britain had an empire and my daddy in Mumbai used to clean the boots of a British major with a waxed moustache. Who would believe ... looking at us ... at us old folk ... the contribution we have made to the way the young live today ... likewise my adopted city, Newcastle. How many in London know or care that London Bridge is opened and closed by hydraulics built and designed on Tyneside?'

'Geordies built ships and guns,' said Shirley, '"alms for oblivion" as the bard said in one of his plays.'

'When London wanted coal, they knew where we were,' said Roger, 'now, London treats the north-east the way Beryl treats me ... if she's not ignoring me she's telling me I'm useless and should get my finger out ... sees a weed in the garden and she's at me ... she still trusts me with her money though,' patting his money belt, 'she knows her money is safe with me.'

*******

At Doncaster, Flora said, 'Look! 'Look! He's handcuffed to a policeman.'

129

'And, he's lost his wig,' said Shirley.

'Goodness me,' exclaimed Ravi. 'Gladys is wearing the 'Phoney's' toupee.'

'He wasn't wearing socks,' said Geoffrey, 'did anyone notice that? What looked like socks was black paint.'

'Since I had my hips done,' said Ravi, 'Shirley has to help me put on my socks.'

'Ravi, darling,' said Shirley, 'protocol; on jaunts, we do not talk about our weaknesses or politics. Our "weaknesses" make us weep; "politics" make us come to blows.'

'If Jock was here,' said Flora, 'you'd set him off about his prostate.'

The train began to move.

'It's all go,' said Roger, closing his eyes.

*******

'This seat free?' said a fat man, wearing a union jack waistcoat. Before Geoffrey had time to reply the man, sat down.

'I'm sure we'll come to an agreement as to how we share the leg room. You are not one of those people who put a newspaper on a seat to make those of us who are looking for a seat think the seat's taken, I hope,' removing the 'Phoney's' copy of the Financial Times off the seat.

'It belonged to the gentleman who got off the train at Doncaster,' explained Geoffrey.

'I thought you might be like those Germans who put a towel on a sun lounger; very possessive, the Germans.'

On the man's shoulder, like an epaulette, drivelling pearls of saliva, lay a white bulldog with eyes the colour of apple blossom and a red tongue; trembling all the time as if it had Parkinson's disease.

'I'll bet you and me are the same age,' tapping Geoffrey's foot under the table to make sure he had Geoffrey's attention, 'just by looking at you I can tell we have the same values. We come from the same era. You don't mind Brexit?' stroking his dog.

'Your dog is called Brexit?'

'After the "cause"; to make Britain free; to stop the "Frogs" and the "Krauts" telling us what to do; isn't that right, Brexit? Give Daddy a kiss.'

'He loves you.'

'It's the marmite … loves marmite. Before I takes him out I puts marmite on my lobes … keeps him happy and makes me smell nice. You'd never believe the people who've asked for the name of my aftershave. If you don't mind my saying so, you talk funny … not a foreigner, are you? Not one of those Romanians, are you … come here to scrounge?'

'I'm from Tyneside.'

'A Geordie.'

'I'm half Viking. My grandmother was Norwegian.'

'So, you are … wait for it, Brexit … steady in the trenches … so you are … you ready, Brexit, an, IMMIGRANT.'

On cue, Brexit whimpered.

'Howls like a wolf; doesn't he? Good dog! Good dog! Trained him to do that … every very time he hears the, you know, the "I" word I've trained him to let rip. Good dog! Good dog! He hates foreigners more than what I do … and that's saying something. Bloody scroungers.'

'Off to Crufts, are you?'

'Crufts? You must be bloody joking. You taking the piss or what? All those poncey foreign dogs. Brexit would fight them in their pens … wouldn't you, Brexit? He'd fight them in their owner's arms. He'd fight them in their furry little dog baskets … Good dog! Good dog!'

'You don't mind his saliva soaking your collar?'

'Why? Should I? Not a dog man, are you?'

'I like dogs but I've never had one as a pet.'

'You're a cat man, aren't you?'

'Actually, yes. My wife and I have two cats, Poppy and Daisy.'

'Poppy and Daisy. I knew it. Ever since I sat down next to you Brexit's nose has been working overtime. Good dog! Good dog! Brexit hates cats, don't you, Brexit?'

'What a surprise you'd get if he answered, "yes".'

'No, I wouldn't ... know, why? Bulldogs can do anything. Bulldogs are British. Once they get their teeth into something they won't let go. If Brexit got his teeth into "talking", he'd learn, because he wouldn't let go until he had. Good dog! Good dog! Because you've told me where you are from, I'll tell you where I'm from. I'm proud of where I come from ... unlike you Geordies I have something to be proud about and, I don't have an accent. I talks the Queen's English. I'm from Spalding.'

'Would that be near Doncaster?'

'What makes you think that?'

'You boarded the train at Doncaster.'

'I work there, that's all. I wasn't born there. Never forget the village of your birth; that's what I say. I came into the world in Spalding; lived there all of my life until last year when I had to leave to find work. I'm not work-shy like what these foreigners is.'

'Spalding,' said Geoffrey, 'you have, I believe, a cauliflower festival.'

'We have,' said the man, leaning aggressively across the table, 'a ... flower festival.'

'Sorry,' said Geoffrey, 'when a chap gets on in years the memory plays tricks, you know.'

'It comes to us all, I'm sure.'

'Up North we have leek shows.'

'Maybe that's the difference between the north and the south. You have "leek shows", we have "flower shows". Chalk and cheese when you think about it. Cauliflowers, indeed! Good dog! Good dog!'

'Brexit is licking your collar.'

'It's because he's run out of Marmite. No more for you, my lad until we gets to London. I'm not giving him anymore; know why? When we gets to London I wants him hungry. If he's not hungry he won't growl when we're marching.'

'Marching?'

'PFB – "Pooches for Brexit". You want a sticker? Show you my badge.'

To show Geoffrey the badge, the man lifted the dog off his shoulder.

'Good god!' exclaimed Geoffrey. 'Your dog only has three legs.'

'Nothing wrong with that, is there? He's still a bulldog. Lost it in a fight. Here's me badge ... see? "PFB". It's enamel, can't afford giving out enamel badges to non-members, especially cat lovers. Too expensive. Stickers is different though ... stickers is affordable.'

From an inside pocket he pulled out a roll of 'PFB' stickers.

'They're like tea bags,' he explained, tearing one off the roll, 'perforated ... bloody perforations ... here, it's your lucky day, you can have one and a half. I'll only charge you for one.'

'They are not free?'

'You don't want to make a donation?'

'No, I do not.'

'You're a "Remainer", aren't you?'

'I might be.'

'Cat lovers is always "Remainers". And them what reads the "Guardian" and wears bowties. Good job I'm saving my ammo for the march; otherwise, I'd let rip. Good dog! Good dog!'

'I'll make a donation,' said Roger, piping up from across the aisle. 'How much? What's the minimum?'

'Two pound.'

'I'm a pensioner, you know, not one of those millionaires who donate thousands to the Tory party. I was thinking more like ... ten pence. My wife has my money. She's in the next carriage.'

'You don't get the sticker until you've paid.'

'Fair enough. I don't want something for nothing.'

'You're not going to get something for nothing, either, mate. Good dog! Good dog! What's with the missus and you travelling in separate carriages? Had a row or something? I'm thinking, Brexit might be able to help ... has a history of helping in matrimonial disputes ... don't you? Good dog! Good dog! It's because he's missing a leg. When the parties sees he's missing a leg, they feel so sorry for him they forgets their own troubles. He's up for hire. All you have to do is say the word. It'll cost you, mind. If you think he's dear ... try a lawyer.'

'How does Brexit manage on three legs?' said Geoffrey.

'He's a tripod, isn't he? Tripods don't fall over so, why should he? Good dog! Good dog! You want back on Daddy's shoulder, don't you? I can read him like a book.'

*******

In Second class Debbie told Beryl and Jock, 'I'm off to the loo.'

A billy-do stuck on the door of the first toilet she came to, said, 'OUT OF ORDER'.

The queue outside the next one was longer than the queue she'd stood in when, as a teenager, she'd queued to see the 'Beatles'.

Undaunted she pressed on down the train's congested aisles. Was it too much to ask for a working loo, without a queue on a modern, high-speed train?

To stiffen her resolve she hummed, 'Onward Christian Soldiers'.

The train's swaying was doing its best to lift her off her feet. It wanted to dump her onto the lap of a seated passenger, the way you drop an egg into a frying pan. It banged her up against standing passengers. She'd to climb over suitcases. Searching for the Holy Grail was not for wimps. She was too old for trekking.

All this for a wee. Was it worth it? She was sure her need was more psychological than physical. She'd a strong, retentive bladder; all of her mother's side of the family had. It was all the fault of that poor woman with mental health problems. She had found the confrontation with her upsetting.

*******

Towards the end of the train she found a loo with only three people waiting to use it.

Last in the queue was a young woman holding the hand of a little boy who, Debbie guessed to be about three. Next to them, was an occidental Buddhist monk; saffron robed and wearing flip-flops; his presence reminded her of the years she'd worked in the Far East. His shaved head reflected the cooling towers the train was passing.

Was he a convert from C of E? Catholicism? Converts were dangerous. She knew this from Geoffrey's enthusiasms over the years. Flora was in despair at the time Jock spent carving his totem pole and, as for Roger, and his mania for collecting the stickers wholesalers put on their hands of bananas, the least said, about that, the better.

At the front of the queue, was a middle-aged woman violating everyone's aural space by talking, very loud, without any inhibitions, into a mobile.

She was wearing a black trouser suit, a tight, bosom-enhancing, frilly white blouse and, sharkskin shoes with very high heels; so she could look tall men in the eye, Debbie thought, when she made them redundant; dark roots, like persistent weeds, showed through her dyed blonde hair: the total package? A JCB, designed to smash the 'glass ceiling' women of Debbie's generation never talked about... not even in the powder room.

'Yes ... yes ... how many times do I have to tell you ... Nigel, put that on hold ... we don't sell until I'm there ... this deal is my baby ... do you hear? Shit! I keep losing you ...' putting a finger in an ear, in attempt to enhance the signal and, when that didn't work, clamping the phone against her other ear. 'Nigel? I keep losing you ... Nigel?'

'S'cuse muh,' said a man with a paper cup of something hot in each hand and two bags of crisps in his mouth which was why he was mumbling.

Debbie moved aside. The woman with the little boy did the same.

'Bentley, move out of the way so the man can get through.'

'S'cuse muh.'

'I've told you before, Nigel you don't move without my say so. Nigel?'

'S'cuse muh.'

'What did you say?'

'S'cuse muh.'

'You're very faint.'

'Wee, wee,' said the little boy.

'I know, darling'.

'Wee, wee.'

'Bentley's just out of nappies,' the mother explained to Debbie. 'I'm trying to get him potty trained. This is a setback. If he pees himself he'll lose his confidence. He'll think it's his fault and it's not. It's not your fault, is it, Bentley?'

'Wee, wee.'

'S'cuse muh.'

'WHAT DO YOU WANT?' said the power dresser.

'S'cuse muh.'

'I know what you want, Nigel. I wasn't talking to you. I'm standing in a queue for the loo and some fucking idiot wants past ... as if I didn't have enough to do.'

The power dresser was blocking the aisle because she had taken up the rail equivalent of the airline 'brace' position; that is to, say, she was wedged at forty-five degrees across the aisle and bugger anyone trying to pass.

'Scuse muh.'

'Nigel ... can't hear you ...'

'Scuse muh.'

'Nigel ...' said the woman on the phone, looking straight at the man with the packet of crisps in his mouth and, moving a leg, not to let him pass but to try and hear better, 'Nigel, are you there?'

Carpe diem, the man squeezed by.

'Do you mind? What are you doing? Nigel, are you there? Nigel ... shit!'

'People shouldn't use words like that in front of children,' said Bentley's mother. 'We call it poo, don't we, Bentley?'

'Poo,' said Bentley.

'I gave him syrup of figs last night,' lifting Bentley up and smelling his bum.

'Nigel ... '

'Whoever is in there has been in there a long time,' said Bentley's mum.

'Constipation?' suggested Debbie.

'I've never been regular since I had Bentley.'

To calm himself the Buddhist monk began to chant.

'It takes all sorts, doesn't it?' Bentley's mum whispered to Debbie.

'If it takes his mind off his bladder ... I'm all for it.'

'If Bentley pees his pants he'll have to stay wet. He won't like that. Bentley doesn't like wet undies. Do you, Bentley?'

'Wee wee.'

*******

Debbie's position at the back of the queue gave her a bird's eye view of a young man's laptop. He was what she believed was called a 'Goth'. Of course, she knew about such people, it was just that she'd never spoken to one. There were lots of Tories in Jesmond but not many Goths. He'd a ring through his nose and a row of silver clips outlining the tip of one ear, made that pinna look like a horse shoe. In his other ear he had a collection of safety pins. Debbie kept her safety pins in her sewing basket. He was having IT trouble.

All her long life, Debbie had belonged to the pearls and twinset brigade. All her long, life she'd conformed. She knew the rules. You let men take the credit. She drank little, had never taken drugs. She found people with dragon tattoos on their forearms, as this young man had, difficult to understand … yet, she'd a weakness for eccentrics. After all, she'd married Geoffrey. Was she a coward for not having the courage to have 'fuck-u' tattooed on her forehead? On the other hand, long ago, when she was young, she had saved Geoffrey from being eaten by a crocodile in Australia with a Bowie knife.

Her favourite café in Newcastle (Gino's was in Jesmond) was 'Frenchies'. She liked it because it was different … such a mix of customers … students, lecturers, business suits and old people like herself, who'd time to spare.

She liked watching the young hold hands and fall in love over a latte.

She called it 'Frenchies' because its owner was French. He spoke French to his customers. If you ordered hot milk on the side with your Americano he wagged a finger … 'in Paree … never.' He spoke French, English and Geordie. He supported Newcastle United. She loved him; sadly, because of 'Brexit' he was packing up and leaving.

The Goth was pressing all the wrong keys. She didn't know why but she liked him.

'Press PXY and control,' she told him.

'Eh?'

What the Goth saw didn't grab him by the balls. She was old. When she went on holiday she probably packed a coffin, you know … just in case. She made his gran look like a teenager … but, and this was the funny thing, he liked her.

'Press PXY and control.'

'Eh?'

'PXY and control.'

'You sure?'

'Yes.'

'Now look what you've done.'

The laptop's screen had blanked.

'Ah! You have the upgraded version; may I?'

The fierceness of her attack on its keys made the Goth nervous. What if she broke it? He was still paying for it. Twenty pound a month for two years but … bloody hell, the old girl was a goer.

'There.'

'Wow! Wow! And, Wow! Again,' said the Goth.

His new screen saver showed ghosts playing hide and seek in a graveyard.

'How'd you do that?'

'I wrote the program.'

'But you're old and … you're a woman.'

'I have always been female but, never, always old.'

'I think you're wonderful.'

'That's what my husband says when I cut his toenails. Would you like me to show you how to open the graves? Press AZL and ALT.'

'It's no good queuing here,' said Gordon, squeezing past Debbie to get to the front of the queue, 'this facility is out of order.'

'What did you say?' said the power dresser, 'Nigel … Nigel … just a mo. What did you say?'

'The toilet is broken, madam … please use the facilities in the other carriages. There's no one inside waiting to come out. The door is locked because what's on its other side is not working.'

Molto prestissimo, the Buddhist monk, clearly in a state of panic, pushed past the power dresser to set off in search of a loo that worked.

'Do you mind?' said the power dresser, full of indignation. 'You might say, "Excuse me"; Oriental hooligan.'

'I think,' said Bentley's mum, 'his "need" must be very urgent if it's made him forget his manners.'

'Nigel ... are you there? I'll have to go. I know you heard the loo isn't working. I didn't mean "go on the loo" ... Nigel, I'm losing you. You might have put up a notice,' she told Gordon.

'That's what I'm about to do, madam, now, if you wouldn't mind?'

Passengers ... he was sick of them ... their moans and groans ... it wasn't his fault every toilet on the train was bust and smelly ... this was a bleeding train, not the Ritz ... and ... he thought he'd seen it all but he hadn't ... that bloke with the bow tie ... him, what kept chopping and changing between First and Second ... first time he'd had to deal with a 'chopper' and 'changer' ... bloody galley broken as well ... unless he could persuade Gloria ...she who pushed 'trolley service' up and down the train with her tits ... to give him some hot water from her thermos flasks he'd have no hot water for his pot noodles.

'Nigel, that's not funny. I know there are loos in the office.'

'Excuse me, madam,' said Gordon, 'you wouldn't by any chance happen to have some blu-tac on you ... would you?'

'Why should I? Nigel ... hang on a sec some fucking idiot thinks I'm W H Smiths.'

'Well,' said Gordon, 'you look like an office worker to me ... someone used to staplers and paper clips and ... blu-tac.'

'Are you mad? No ... not you, Nigel ... I am an executive ... a senior executive ... my staff, staple ... I do not ... nor am I W H Smith. I am a passenger ... a paying passenger ... not a provider of stationery.'

'In that case,' said Gordon, shrugging, 'I'm off back to my cubby-hole to see what I can find to stick up my notice. It's not my fault my boss doesn't give me anything sticky to stick up my notices. If anyone wants the toilet would you mind telling them it's out of order?'

'Tell them! No ... Nigel ... not "sell" ... I haven't changed my mind ... Nigel? Bloody signal.'

'I think that Buddhist's as desperate as Bentley,' said Bentley's mum. 'I wonder if it's the curry. Buddhists eat a lot of curry, don't they? I wonder if curry would help my constipation ... there's a thought ... come on, Bentley; if you feel it coming, cross your legs.'

'Good luck,' said Debbie.

'Can you make it so I can write names on gravestones?' said the Goth.

Helping the Goth made Debbie feel wanted, needed and useful. She wasn't an out of date coal fire, after all. Once again her fingers flew over the keyboard. Her total absorption in what she was doing, made her forget her aches and pains.

'Wow!' said the Goth, 'A-mazing! Your earrings, lady, studs or pierced?'

'Pierced.'

The Goth, nodding that, that suited him just fine, removed a safety pin from an ear.

'Here, lady ... wear it in your lug. Any Goth sees it will buy you a coffee.'

The Goth had kind eyes. He made her feel as young as seventy.

'Go on, put it in your lug.'

'Now?'

The Goth nodded.

What on earth did she think she was doing replacing a pearl earring with a safety pin?

'How's that?'

'Suits you … what about a castle with a dragon that breathes ghosts?'

Once again Debbie's fingers flew over the keyboard.

'Wow!'

*******

Back, sitting with Jock and Beryl, Jock said to Debbie, 'Am I seeing things or is that a safety pin I can see in your ear?'

'Do you like it?'

'It reminds me of nappies,' said Beryl. 'In the old days, before, Velcro, we used pins like that to pin the sides of nappies together.'

'I think I've scored,' said Debbie.

'What were you playing? Rugby, cricket or football?' said Jock. 'Ha! Ha!'

'I mean "scored" in the romantic sense; please, don't laugh. I have become the apple-in-the-eye of a man four times younger than myself. He's a Goth. He gave it to me for helping him with his computer. He told me, it's a Goth symbol; you know, like the Christian cross. Any Goth who sees it will buy me a cup of coffee. I don't know if he meant they'd literally buy me a cup of coffee or, whether he meant, they'd be kindly disposed towards me and, you know, give me a high-five.'

'I think,' said Jock, eyeing the homemade piece of jewellery in Debbie's ear, 'the safety pin is like that button … I think it was a button, Alan Breck gave David Balfour in "Kidnapped"; show it to a Jacobite and he'd give your horse hay; show that earring to a Goth and he'll let you share his coffin. Debbie, I know your hearing is better than mine, but, are you sure the Goth said, "Coffee"? He might have said "Coffin", you know; they sound the same.'

'He said, "Coffee". I know he did. And, I know something else, as well, it's stopped me wanting to go for a pee.'

'In that case, can I have one? And, get one for Geoffrey, as well.'

'I shouldn't tell you this but, to control his bladder, Geoffrey's been experimenting with alternative medicine. He has a friend who goes water divining with a hazel wand in the Atacama Desert. He advised him to put two horse chestnuts in his underpants.'

'Did it do the trick?'

'Not with boxer shorts, it didn't. They kept falling out.'

'Y-fronts?'

'They were better at keeping the chestnuts in but, Geoffrey doesn't like wearing y-fronts. He says he refuses to be an advert for the "Battle of the Bulge".'

'I've always found wearing a kilt makes me want to pee more. When it's windy in the glen; expect rain.'

'If Roger thinks you get a free coffee if you wear a safety pin earring, he'll want one,' said Beryl.

'He'd have to have his ears pierced,' said Debbie. 'Do you think it suits me? I wonder what Geoffrey will say.'

'I'd happily pierce Roger's ears. I believe you use a red-hot needle.'

\* \* \* \* \* \*

At Newark two women entered the carriage in which Debbie, Beryl and Jock were sitting. One of the women, asking if the seat next to Debbie was free and being told it was, sat herself down in it. The woman she was with, putting the same question to the passengers in the seats across the aisle and being told one was free, likewise made herself at home.

Jock warmed to the woman sitting next to Debbie. She was carrying a baby in a papoose. The 'papoose' reminded him of the Indians of North America, which in turn reminded him of his totem pole.

As the train pulled out of Newark, Beryl shouted, 'Look! A monk, a Buddhist monk, is chasing the train; Oh dear, he's lost one of his flip-flops.'

'A what?' said Jock. 'A monkey?'

'No,' said Debbie, 'a monk … as in, monastery.'

'It's not a monkey,' said Jock, looking out of the window to see for himself, 'it's a monk … a Buddhist monk.'

'That's what Beryl said,' said Debbie.

'I thought she said "Monkey".'

'I know you did.'

'Why's he running and waving? Is the Dalai Lama on our train? If he is I'll bet he's in First class.'

'I know him.'

'From when you worked in Java?'

'He was in the queue I was in waiting to use the loo.'

'The broken one?'

'You know what I'm thinking; I think he got off the train, not because it was his stop but to use the station's loo.'

'Are there no working toilets on the train?'

'If there are, I don't think the poor chap found one. He's not waving the Dalai Lama off, Jock; he's trying to stop the train.'

'When you were being awarded your "safety pin" for "services rendered",' said Beryl, 'monks kept passing us, didn't they, Jock? I thought there must be lots of them on the train. But, you think there was only one? And you think he got off because he needed to use the loo … because, none of the toilets on the train are working?'

Debbie nodded.

'That's sad.'

Jock said: 'When we have our debrief, I'll ask Roger if he thinks the monk will be entitled to a refund. Roger will know. If he doesn't, he'll find out, I mean, in case it happens to him. You know him and the law. If he can cite a precedent, he will.'

'If there had been lots of monks on the train,' said Beryl, pursing her lips in thought, 'what would we've called them? I mean, what is the collective noun for "monks".'

'A tonsure of monks,' suggested Jock.

'That fits Friar Tuck and his ilk but not Buddhist monks in saffron robes.'

'What about a … crocus of monks,' said Debbie, 'their robes are saffron and saffron comes from the crocus?'

'I like that,' said Jock.

'Or,' said Beryl, 'because they play finger cymbals … I think they do … what about a tintinnabulation of monks?'

'What was that, Beryl?' said Jock. 'A "tinnitus of monks"? I don't like the sound of that. Ha! Ha!'

'Tinnitus is terrible,' said Debbie.

'I like a "crocus of monks" best,' said Jock.

'What?'

'Would you mind keeping your voices down,' said the woman sitting next to Debbie, 'I'm trying to breastfeed. When you said "tintinnabulation" Norman lost the nipple.'

'I do apologise,' said Debbie. 'We have to raise our voices because Jock is deaf.'

'I'm hard of hearing,' said Jock.

'A boy?' said Debbie.

'Norman.'

'Boys take a lot of feeding.'

'Boys are very demanding,' said Beryl, 'even worse when they grow up. I should know, I married one.'

'That him?' nodding at Jock.

'No, he's in First class.'

'Typical that. I should be surprised but I'm not. The "little woman" in Second, while he who thinks he rules the roost enjoys the extra legroom in First.'

'I'm thinking,' said Jock, plucking up courage to speak up and remind everyone that he wasn't that hard of hearing, 'that breastfeeding is a bit like refuelling a jet fighter in mid-air.'

'I'm a pacifist, mister. I don't want Norman hearing any talk about fighter aeroplanes. And, what would you know about breastfeeding? You got tits? When Norman grows up he will know how to cook and iron.'

'Quite right too,' said Debbie.

'You can try,' said Beryl.

Jock closed his eyes. Why had he bothered? He didn't like it when people criticised his similes. And, what was the world coming to? Breastfeeding in public? Still ... live and let live ... if that's what she wanted to do, why shouldn't she? If she felt relaxed about it, what was the problem?

Flora would never have breastfed in public, nor would his daughter. But, they, like him, belonged to a generation noted for its reticence; things were done differently in the past ... not necessarily better, just different.

He knew a lot about the chemicals that combined to make breast milk. It was a miracle. A woman suckling a child was an angel. Wonderful creatures, women, but, all a bit of a mystery. He knew more about galaxies than he did about women.

'I'd never have done that,' said Debbie.

'Done what?'

'Breastfeed in public.'

'Does it bother you?'

'Not at all.'

'What about the old geezer with his eyes shut?'

'Jock is asleep.'

'No, he's not. He's just pretending.'

'How'd you know that?'

'Because I know men ... hoy! Wrinkles, open your peepers.'

Jock opened his eyes.

'Does it bother you, me breastfeeding Norman? Don't look so bloody surprised you've been earwigging everything we've been saying. I know you have. You're an aural pervert, you are.'

'Am I?' said Jock. 'I've never been called that before.'

'First time for everything. I'll bet you know a lot about steam engines.'

'As a matter of fact, I do. I was born in the age of steam. I used to collect engine numbers. "Namers" were my favourite. By the time I was ten I'd seen every streak named in my "Allan's" book of railway engines.'

'I knew it. I'm Ruby. This is my wife, Jean,' leaning across the aisle to pat Jean on the arm. 'We met at a steam engine rally.'

'Hi!' said Jean, looking up from taking a packet of disposable nappies out of a Moses basket.

Nappies? Incontinence pads for babies. It was alright for babies to wear them. The very old and the very young had so much in common. Both caused the fit and healthy problems. 'Sorry, can't make the party, I've no one to look after baby. 'I can't meet for coffee, I have to take Dad to outpatients.'

'Did you want to be an engine driver?' said Ruby.

'Yes,' said Jock, 'of course, every wee laddie of my generation dreamed of being an engine driver. I used to go round the house pretending to be a steam engine … Ch! Ch! Ch! Woo-a-who!'

Norman screamed.

'Sorry,' said Jock.

'It's not you,' said Ruby, 'he's lost the nipple. Were you an engine driver?'

'My eyes weren't far enough apart,' said Jock shaking his head and shrugging as if to say … it wasn't my fault but … there you go … that's life.

'It's a joke,' said Beryl, 'we've heard it before.'

'Last week,' said Debbie.

'And the week before,' said Beryl.

147

'You see,' said Jock, giving Beryl and Debbie the raised-eyebrow, 'in my day shunting engines had two porthole windows and when I was little my dad told me ... "to be an engine driver, son, you have to be able to look out of both at the same time ... the way you look through binoculars ...'

For the life of him Jock couldn't understand why Ruby and Jean weren't laughing? Norman was laughing; why couldn't they?

'Wind,' said Ruby, rubbing Norman's back, 'up it comes ... tissue, Jean.'

'Don't mind Jock,' said Beryl, 'it's not his fault his jokes aren't funny.'

If he told them his hobby was carving totem poles, that would make them sit up. Not many people carved totem poles. OK, he'd told the joke before but, it was still a good joke ... people liked to hear him telling jokes ... sod them all. He closed his eyes.

'You can't trust men,' said Jean.

'But,' said Debbie, 'where would we be without them?'

'Happy,' said Ruby, 'that's why I married Jean.'

'Norman's off the nipple, Rube.'

'Norman's IVF.'

'I was wondering,' said Debbie.

'Cut out the middleman. The sperm bank assured us his donor had a high IQ ... if he can't find the nipple ... I'm wondering.'

'You think you might have been miss-sold?' said Beryl.

'I once bought a tin of peaches,' said Debbie, 'guess what? When I opened it ... pears.'

'We don't eat food out of tins,' said Jean.

'He's had enough,' said Ruby, 'better start getting our things together. We're getting off at Peterborough. Tissue ... thanks. You're a messy bugger you are, Norman.'

'Like all men,' said Jock, opening his eyes.

'What's up with "Old Father Time" calling his own sex?'

'I'll have you know, young lady, I've been married for sixty years.'

'Poor woman,' said Ruby.

'We pity her,' said Jean.

'Jock,' said Debbie, 'where are you going?'

'I'm going to see Flora.'

'That's his wife,' said Beryl.

'Don't spoil her day,' said Ruby. 'I think Norman's done one.'

'You get a second sense for it, don't you?' said Beryl. 'I know I did when my children were in nappies.'

'I think you've upset Jock,' said Debbie.

'Old Father Time?' said Ruby.

'I'll bet he's upset lots of us women in his time,' said Jean.

'About time we women had our own back,' said Ruby.

'Just because he's old doesn't mean he isn't dangerous.'

'Old men are the worst.'

'They have experience, see.'

*******

Ravi was competitive. When the 'Ensemble' debriefed he wanted his contribution to be the best. With that aim in mind, like a journalist going in search of a story, he excused himself to Shirley by telling her he wished to stretch his legs.

In his youth he'd played chess for India. He'd been a prodigy. In chess clubs around the world, in post-match discussions, his name, if not frequently mentioned, was not completely forgotten.

Would the two men he'd spotted, playing chess on a miniature board mind if he gave them the benefit of his experience? How good were they? Did they know how to play? Were they Premier League? Or, like Sunderland, were they in a league no one had heard of?

Both men were middle-aged. One of them looked like Albert Einstein; the other, because he was wearing a beret, looked like a priest or a French onion man. A plastic bag at his feet said: Buckfast Abbey.

At first, the two men, out of politeness, tried not to show how much they resented Ravi's poking his nose into their game. They wanted to tell him to mind his own business, but didn't because ... well, he was old; silly old fool probably had dementia ... probably didn't even know he was on a train ... with a bit of luck his 'minder' would take him back to his seat.

'Check!' said 'Einstein'.

'Move your knight,' Ravi told the 'Beret'. 'May I?'

'Do you mind?'

'Sorry.'

'Chess, old man, is a young man's game,' said 'Einstein'. 'Now, if you don't mind, go back to your care home; off you go, toddle!'

'My friend dislikes old people,' said the 'Beret'.

'What has your friend's dislike of old people got to do with me?' said Ravi.

'It's obvious, isn't it?' said 'Einstein'.

'Not to me.'

'You're old, aren't you? Not your fault; it's all to do with the passage of time; look, to iron out your wrinkles may I suggest you board a spaceship and take a five year return trip to somewhere at the speed of light.'

'I find that insulting,' said Ravi. 'In the name of Vishnu I challenge you to a game of chess. With your friend's permission I will take over his game. If I win you will apologise; tell me I do not look as old as I am. If you win I will give you an English twenty pound note.'

'Don't be silly ... he's lost his queen and two pawns. I'd feel guilty. It would be like taking candy off a baby.'

'Forty pounds,' said Ravi, his ire roused; slapping down two twenty pound notes to show he meant business.

The two Englishmen were the 'Raj'. He, Ravi, was Gandhi.

'Sixty pounds. Both of you take me on. I take over from where the game is now ... down a queen and two pawns.'

*******

Ravi routed his opponents in less time than it would have taken his grandmother to make a batch of chapattis. On his way back to First class, he bumped into Jock.

'Why are we shaking hands?' said Ravi.

'Stress,' said Jock. 'I'm on the run from two feminist carnivores. I'm lucky to be in one piece. What about you?'

'I challenged two men to a game of chess.'

'And, of course, you won.'

'Of course. They told me chess was a young man's game. I proved them wrong. I made them admit they were wrong. I made them apologise. When I left them they were in shock. I cut them up the way Lord Louis Mountbatten cut up the country of my birth; I was … ruthless.'

'It will give us something to talk about at the debrief?' said Jock. 'I do hope Doughty Street sell scones.'

To stop themselves falling over when the train braked, the two men grabbed hold of each other.

'If I bang one of my varicose veins,' said Ravi, 'there'll be blood everywhere.'

'We've slowed down,' said Jock, stating the obvious, 'look … there's a sewage works … very important for getting rid of the … you-know-what … remember those poo tests we used to get?'

'For bowel cancer?'

'Damn difficult getting a sample.'

'I once used a whole toilet roll.'

'I caught mine in a mug. When Flora found out, she wasn't pleased. I'd used the mug she puts her false teeth in … talking of which … shall we join her?'

********

Jock and Ravi's progress back towards those members of the 'Ensemble' sitting in First class was halted by a hyperventilating man, wearing a white shirt, spattered with blood like a Jackson Pollock painting.

'Would you mind waiting?' he said. 'There's been an accident. I don't know how it happened.'

'Are you alright?' Ravi asked him.

'Not really.'

'Sit on the floor; put your head between your knees. If you faint you might hurt yourself.'

Ravi spoke with such authority that the young man did as he was told.

'Is there a doctor on the train?' someone shouted. 'Someone with medical knowledge. We need a doctor.'

'I'll get Flora,' said Jock. 'Excuse me! Excuse me! Let me through, please.'

At the sight of the casualty, a man with blood pumping out of a wrist wound, Ravi told Jock, 'I'll stay. You get Flora.'

Ravi took charge. To those standing around, gawping, he seemed to know what he was doing. He was big. He was calm.

'When the train braked,' explained a passenger, 'that bottle,' pointing to a broken bottle of whisky on the table, 'fell out of the man's holdall up there in the luggage rack; how it slashed his wrist, I don't know.'

'It's a gusher,' said another passenger, looking at the blood pumping out of the injured man's wrist.

Is he going to die?' said someone else.

'No.'

'Dear me! Dear me!' said the woman sitting opposite the casualty. 'He's ruined my "Homes and Gardens". My "Homes and Gardens" is covered in blood. Where are my tissues? I need tissues.'

'I'm going to make a tourniquet,' said Ravi, removing his trouser belt, 'that will stop the bleeding.'

'He's in trauma, isn't he?' said an onlooker. 'I watch "Casualty".'

'Here comes the ticket inspector,' someone shouted, 'he'll know what to do. He'll have been trained in first-aid. Out of the way, old man. Let someone in who knows what they are doing.'

'Out of my way ...let me through ... there's been an accident,' said Gordon. 'Let me through ... Oh, my gawd!'

'Catch him,' said a passenger.

'Put his head between his knees,' said Ravi.

'Can't ... his ticket machine's in the way.'

'I've hurt my shoulder,' said one of the men who'd cushioned Gordon's faint.

'Excuse me ... let me through,' said Flora. 'Excuse me ...'

'Let my wife through,' said Jock. 'Flora, I'm right behind you ... push through.'

'There's been an accident,' said a bystander, 'this is no place for useless old folk. It's not a peep-show, you know.'

'We are here to help.'

'But ... '

'But ... what? Is it because my wife and I look too old to be of use?'

'No ... yes ... but ...'

'My wife is a retired anaesthetist.'

'The bloke on the floor is out cold, mate; he wants bringing round, not knocking out ... anaesthetist ... talk about "coals to Newcastle".'

'Let the lady through,' said a big young man with a broken nose and cauliflower ears. The 'Rugby is not for softies' t-shirt, he was wearing, explained his thug-like appearance. 'Medics, are you? Allow me to be your siren and flashing blue light. Out of the way! Move! Medics!'

As Ravi said, many years later; it was like watching Moses part the Red Sea.

No one argued.

*******

At Peterborough, the chap with the severed artery and Gordon who'd a bump on his head the size of a walnut, were put in wheelchairs.

Flora explained to the paramedics, who'd been waiting for the casualties, that the man who'd severed an artery needed to be taken to hospital as quickly as possible.

'Gordon', she told them, 'the "Carriage Care Assistant" has a nasty bump on his head. He needs an X-ray. He says he's fine but, I'm not sure. He keeps mumbling that passengers hate him.'

'I thought I heard him say he "hates passengers",' said one of the paramedics.

'Yes,' said Flora, 'when I think about it, that's more likely; dear me, such a nice man, as well. He was ever so helpful when we got into a bit of a muddle with our tickets; weren't you, Gordon?' patting Gordon on the arm, to show him that she cared.

The pat made Gordon scream. It made him bury his head in the blanket in which he'd been wrapped. It made him howl and blubber like a spoilt child.

'Now, now, Gordon, no need for that, is there?' said one of the paramedics. 'The nice old lady is only trying to be kind. Any more of that and I'm thinking Gordon will need to be strapped into his wheelchair two notches tighter. We don't want you falling out, do we; what would A and E think if I wheeled you in there with two bumps on your head? When I've radioed in, that you have one. Bumps, they don't multiply like cells; at least, not without help, they don't.'

*******

As the train pulled out of Peterborough, Jock, giving his wife a kiss, told her she'd done a good job, that he was proud of her and that, if she didn't mind he was going back to sit with Beryl and Debbie. He needed to sit down, his back was aching.

He returned to his seat feeling rather pleased with himself. He, Ravi and Flora had done a good day's work. For old people they were pretty damn good; also, the breastfeeding harridan and her pal were off the train, and, no doubt by now, would be breastfeeding Norman while ogling steam engines.

*******

In First class Ravi and Flora told Geoffrey, Roger and Shirley all about the man with the severed artery and Gordon's bump. 'It was as big as a hen's egg,' said Ravi.

'Ravi, my darling,' said Shirley, 'you are my hero. I am so lucky to have married you.'

'That's what I say every time Beryl buys a new pair of shoes,' said Roger. 'You two didn't do any more than I'd have done.'

'Flora had the expertise,' said Ravi, 'she knew what to do.'

'Thank you, Ravi,' said Flora. 'If you'd not applied a tourniquet so quickly the man would have lost a lot more blood.'

'I think,' said Geoffrey, 'it would be best if we kept our stories for Doughty Street.'

'Geoffrey,' said Shirley, 'I do believe you are jealous. You don't like my darling Ravi and Flora taking centre stage, do you? Ravi, my darling, when we debrief at Doughty Street, do not forget to mention how you used your trouser belt as a tourniquet; such quick thinking. I hope your pants don't fall down. You are very backward in coming forward for a Brahmin.'

'Flora was the real hero,' said Ravi. 'She knew what to do. It was her expertise stopped the poor fellow bleeding to death.'

*******

In Second class Jock told Beryl and Debbie all about what he called the 'siren and flashing blue light' incident.

'Good job Flora knew what to do,' said Beryl. 'If I ever have a heart attack I hope she's there to take out my false teeth and put me in the recovery position. If Roger has a heart attack, I hope she's stuck in a loo.'

'I have a new name for Ravi,' said Jock, '... "Clematis". In my garden, behind my totem pole, I have a clematis. Last year it succumbed to ... wilt; clematis are prone to do that, you know. I thought it was dead. This year, I noticed ... just before we set out on our wee jaunt ... signs of green shoots. It wasn't dead after all. I've thought for a while that Ravi wasn't looking one hundred per cent.'

'Ravi's not dying, is he?' said Beryl. 'Poor Shirley.'

'No ... no ... all I'm saying is ... I thought he looked as if he was dying. I was wrong. The way he took charge of everything ... helping Flora ... showed me a glimpse of the Ravi I used to know ... just a glimpse ... a glimpse of a green shoot ... Ravi, the "clematis".'

'What was your clematis called?' said Debbie.

'"Resurrection".'

'This seat free?'

Jock nodded that it was.

The man asking was middle-aged and wearing an 'NAHT', t-shirt. Debbie and Beryl thought it needed ironing. His gingery-fair hair was thinning. His blue eyes were dull and lacked sparkle, like the sea on a dull day. In one hand he carried a small canvas hold-all of the sort given as a free gift by mail order firms when you spent twenty pounds or more. In his other hand, causing him much difficulty because of their length, he carried two six-foot poles strapped together with Velcro.

'Having trouble with your fishing rods?' said Jock, when the man, having failed to fit the two poles into the overhead luggage rack, sat down and settled for holding them by his side, upright, the way a beefeater holds his pike.

'When I fish the Tweed,' said Jock, 'I leave my rods with my gillie … saves a lot of bother. What you after? Sharks? Your rods look as if they're meant for big fish.'

Jock knew the poles weren't fishing rods. In the spirit of OPAC he was trying to get the man to talk. Debbie and Beryl weren't so sure. But, if Jock said they were fishing rods then, they must be. Everyone in the 'Ensemble' knew Jock to be a keen fisherman. Jock knew about things like that. They knew about breastfeeding and changing nappies. Jock knew about fishing.

'They are not fishing rods,' said the holder of the poles looking at Jock the way a cat looks at a tortoise.

'If they are not fishing rods,' said Jock, 'what are they? That is, if you don't mind my asking?'

'If you were a fisherman you'd know they weren't fishing rods.'

'Aye … aye,' said Jock, emphasising the tartan in his accent, 'I suppose I would … silly me.'

'It is my Association's banner. I am on a march.'

'I do admire activists,' said Debbie.

'I'd have loved to have been a suffragette,' said Beryl.

'What is your cause?' said Jock.

'The education of children,' pointing at his t-shirt, "National Association of Head Teachers". 'For my sins,' sniffing, 'I am a head teacher.'

'Can we see the banner?' said Jock.

'No.'

'Oh.'

'Is it sacred?' said Beryl. 'Like the Torah in a synagogue?'

'Unfurled,' miming inverted commas with his fingers, 'it is too big for a railway carriage. It is for the great outdoors.'

People who mimed inverted commas with their fingers irritated Jock.

'If I unfurl it,' said the man, sniffing loudly through his nose, 'I'd not get it tied up again ... not as neatly as I tied it up last night. To get it into that shape,' patting his bundle of poles, 'I was up till two am ... two am and two cans of non-alcoholic lager it took me to do that. If mother had been alive she'd have worried I was overdoing things. "Mr Hardy," she'd have said ... she always addressed me as if she was one of my staff or, sometimes, if she'd had a sherry, in a squeaky voice, as if she was one of my younger pupils ... I am head of a First school ... Mother was good at impersonations ... it was our little game together, "Mr Hardy ... you are doing too much. Education will be the death of you ... it really will ... and, if that happened where would I be?"'

'A banner carrier's work is never done,' said Beryl.

'Being a head teacher these days must be terribly onerous,' said Debbie, 'from what I've read in the newspapers. I can understand why your mum worried about you ... can't we, Beryl? I'm Debbie, by the way ... my friend, Beryl.'

'I'm Jock,' said Jock.

'I'm Mr Hardy.'

'Surely,' said Beryl, 'you have a first name. Of course, you do not have to tell us if you do not wish to.'

'Wouldn't it be funny,' said Jock, talking about Mr Hardy as if that man wasn't there, 'if Mr Hardy's first name was Laurel; parents pick the strangest names for their children.'

'Jock, shut up.'

'Sorry.'

'As it happens my first name is not Laurel', sniffing, 'I suppose, if it had been some people, myself excluded, of course, would have thought that amusing and made jokes about it.'

'You don't have to tell me your first name if you don't want to,' said Beryl. 'My friends and I are not the Spanish Inquisition. We are on a daytrip to London. We are on an OPAC excursion.'

'OPEC,' repeated Mr Hardy. 'Organisation of Petroleum Exporting Countries ... you are, perhaps, retired oil executives?'

'Not ... OPEC, Mr Hardy ... OPAC.'

'OPAC? OPAC? I have made a study of acronyms ... strange I don't know that one.'

'Organisation of Pensioners' Adventure Club,' explained Beryl. 'Debbie, Jock and I are all members. Other members of our club are in First class. We are all going to London to visit Charles Dickens' house in Doughty Street where we will have tea and cakes.'

'And scones,' said Jock, pronouncing that noun to rhyme with 'on'.

'Surely,' said Mr Hardy opening and closing his nostrils as if pumping up what he was about to say, 'the noun "scones", when pronounced correctly must rhyme with "stones", or "bones", or "loans"; I could go on. I have an extensive knowledge of English rhyming words. At university my contemporaries called me "Tennyson". I had quite a reputation; you see, in my younger days I wrote poetry, not, free verse, but proper poetry what rhymed.'

Beryl did not fancy herself a poetry expert but she did know, beyond any shadow of a doubt, that she was a 'black-belt' in massaging and puncturing male egos; after all, that's how she'd come to marry Roger. Her flattery had made Roger think she loved him. In turn, his ardour had made her think that she did.

In Mr Hardy, fate had sent her an excellent specimen upon whom to try out a few of her old wooing techniques; even if for no other reason than to see if they still worked; besides which, what better way was there to pass the time on a boring train journey, than, to, as it were, defrock a priest.

'Jock is forgetting he is south of the Watford gap,' said Beryl, 'I expect, you know a lot about pronunciation, Mr Hardy ... being a teacher you will have to,' patting the back of Mr Hardy's hand.

Mr Hardy didn't know why, but he liked Beryl. Old women made him feel safe. Old women understood him. They weren't flirts. What he'd overheard some of the young female members of his staff say, had … well … he'd never dared talk about what he'd heard with Mother.

'And,' said Beryl, placing her hand on top of Mr Hardy's and keeping it there, 'you have such a famous surname.'

'Do I?'

'In nautical circles, you do.'

'You know,' said Jock, '"Kiss me Hardy".'

To reassure Mr Hardy that Jock was not asking him for a kiss Beryl squeezed Mr Hardy's hand. His fingers were cold, like sausages taken out of a fridge.

'Jock is not asking you for a kiss, Mr Hardy,' said Beryl, 'he is quoting England's national hero, Lord Nelson. When Nelson was dying he asked his friend, Captain Hardy to kiss him.'

'Did he?'

'A platonic kiss, Mr Hardy,' said Beryl changing her grip on Mr Hardy's hand from a gin trap to a flutter of falling rain, before again, gripping it and smiling sweet nothings at him.

'Mother used to do that to my hand; what you're doing. You remind me of Mother. I have her photograph; perhaps you'd like to see it.'

From his 'free gift', holdall, Mr Hardy took out and handed to Beryl, a postcard sized picture frame decorated with sea shells.

The picture in the frame fascinated and horrified Beryl.

'My eyes are not as good as they used to be,' she said, to hide her shock. 'Yes, she looks very peaceful. What do you think, Debbie?'

Debbie reacted to the photograph by, involuntarily, pushing up her bottom denture.

'Yes, she looks at peace,' said Debbie.

'I made the frame,' said Mr Hardy, 'Mother stuck on the shells. We collected them together on the beach at Yarmouth.'

'May I see?' said Jock.

'Aye,' said Jock, 'the wee lassie looks peaceful … very peaceful.'

'The undertaker said it was alright for me to take the photo if that's what I wanted to do,' said Mr Hardy. 'She does look peaceful, doesn't she?'

'Of course she does,' said Beryl.

Mr Hardy didn't dress like a ghoul but, that's what he was … a ghoul.

'Mother must have been very proud of you becoming a head teacher,' said Beryl.

'Mother always wanted a girl,' said Mr Hardy, 'she never wanted a boy. I think that is why she called me "Evelyn". People who know me only by my name … Evelyn Hardy … are surprised I'm not a woman when they first meet me, that is. Yes, for my sins, my first name is "Evelyn".'

'But,' said Beryl, doing her best to make a silk purse out of a sow's ear, 'you have the same Christian name as the writer, Evelyn Waugh.'

'I have of course heard of him but I've not read any of his books. I have no time.'

'They are very funny.'

'Are they? Do you think they would make me laugh?'

'Of course they would,' lied Beryl.

Debbie, Beryl and Jock shuffled in their seats; all three were thinking the same thing. You do not photograph your mother, dead, in her coffin. It was un-British. Ravi may have watched his mother and father cremated on an open fire but that was in India. This was the UK.

In an attempt to legitimise Mr Hardy's photographing of his mother in that way, Beryl suddenly thought of the film, 'Doctor Zhivago', which she'd watched, a few weeks ago, at Newcastle's Tyneside Cinema.

'Your mother was Russian, wasn't she? Russian orthodox?'

As Mr Hardy clearly hadn't a clue about what she was on about, Beryl added, by way of explanation, 'You know, "Doctor

Zhivago" where they show Yuri's mother, dead, in an open coffin?'

'Doctor Zhivago,' said Mr Hardy, 'your GP?'

'Mr Hardy is not Russian,' said Jock, miming inverted commas – one of the things he found irritating about people like Mr Hardy who fluttered their fingers to mime inverted commas or speech marks or whatever you wanted to call them was that, for some reason, it made him want to do the same – 'he's not Russian because he's not "rushing" anywhere … he's sat, all comfy in his seat; Ha! Ha!'

Mr Hardy did not laugh. Old people were mad … mad! He wasn't in a railway carriage, he was in a lunatic asylum.

'I know what Beryl means,' said Jock, unaware that he was in a hole and should stop digging, 'the open coffin scene, right? We saw the film last week at a special Silver Screen showing at Newcastle's Tyneside Cinema … we're from Newcastle. All of the 'Ensemble', that's what we call our group of friends, like going to Silver Screen viewings … you get coffee and a biscuit. To get in of course you have to be over sixty. They always ask to see my birth certificate, just in case I'm a teeny-bobber trying to sneak in for the coffee and biscuit.'

'They do one for "Mothers and Toddlers",' said Debbie. 'To get in you have to be a breastfeeder.'

What were the old fools wittering on about. The day was turning out worse than he'd thought possible. Mother would not have approved of him marching into Trafalgar Square carrying a banner. Mother had been a true blue Conservative and, so was he. He wasn't a socialist or, a horrid, trade unionist. The NAHT was an 'association', not a 'union'; going on 'demos' as the younger head teachers called going on a protest march was not his cup of tea; also, he'd voted for 'Brexit' in the referendum, something he kept quiet about at association meetings. The younger head teachers were all for staying in the EU. You had to keep in with them because you never knew when you might need their support.

He'd used school glue to stick the shells onto the frame. That was naughty. He hoped he'd not be found out.

'You one of us?' said a young man carrying poles similar to Mr Hardy's.

The salutation made Mr Hardy pull the sort of face you pull when you are peeling onions and your eyes are starting to water.

The two young males he found himself eyeballing were from another planet.

One had what looked like an orange lettuce on top his head. Mr Hardy knew the name of the hairstyle; it was called a 'Mohican'. His school had banned them. The other had long, blonde hair, kept tidy by a red bandana headband which made him look like a Red Indian.

'Jamie's asking you, sir, if you are one of us?'

Mr Hardy sniffed. The one who'd called him, 'sir', the one who looked like a Red Indian, sounded American.

The seams of white flesh he could see through their slashed jeans were a fashion statement beyond his comprehension. One of his staff had once come to work in sandals. He'd had a quiet word with the young man who'd left after a term.

'What I mean is, me old cock,' said the one with the 'Mohican', 'you on the march?'

'The gentleman is "marching",' said Beryl, 'but, not, I think, on your "march". He is marching to save "education" from Tory cuts. You, by the logos on your t-shirts, are marching to highlight the need for "food banks" and those who deny climate change … am I correct?'

'On the ball, doll; give me a five.'

Beryl had grandchildren, they were always doing high-fives. She knew what to do.

'What about me?' said Jock.

'And me,' said Debbie.

'Love the earring, baby. You don't look like one of us but, you know what, I think you are. What about you, sir?' holding up a palm for Mr Hardy to smack.

'No thank you,' said Mr Hardy.

'Suit yourself, "Mr Collar-and-Tie"; no offence taken. I won't take out my Bowey knife and scalp you. You guys "deniers" or, "believers"?'

'Young man,' said Beryl, 'if you are asking if I and my friends, excluding Mr Hardy, whom I have just met, believe the Earth is warming up because of human activity, it may interest you to know that, in my younger days, I published papers in "Scientific American" on the subject.'

'Oh, yeah? I'm familiar with the literature. What's your name?'

She told him.

'You are she?'

'Yes.'

'I thought you were dead.'

'May I shake your hand?'

'What about a high-five?'

'That happened to me,' said Jock, 'coming down from Edinburgh. Do you think we have lived too long?'

'Certainly not,' said Beryl.

Subsequently Beryl was visited by at least twenty other marchers; all young; all wearing t-shirts stating that global warming was no longer a theory but a fact.

'Beryl,' said Jock, 'you have become a celebrity. If I was wearing a t-shirt would you sign it?'

'You have become the "Fatima of the East Coast Main Line"; a shrine,' said Debbie, 'wait till I tell Roger.'

'Of one thing I am certain,' said Beryl, 'if I have become a shrine, it will be a shrine at which Roger will never light a candle.'

'It's funny the people you end up marrying; isn't it? Why did you marry him ... Roger, I mean?'

'I don't know. I find that question as unanswerable as, "why are we here?".'

'On the train?' said Jock.

'You know what I mean.'

So much water had flowed under the Beryl and Roger bridge. If he popped his clogs would she miss arguing with him? Probably. He was like that filthy old cardigan she liked to wear when she weeded the garden. Over the years it had become part of her life, like her toenails which, these days, always seemed to need cutting. You never saw a chiropodist at a food bank.

Why had she married the tight fisted old bugger? She'd always liked a challenge. Is that why she'd married him? She thought she could change him. The power of 'love'.

When they'd first met at a university bash she'd offered him a tongue sandwich. Did anyone eat tongue sandwiches these days? She'd never heard anyone mention 'tongue' for years. There were fashions in food just as there were fashions in everything else – medicine, clothes and pets; in the fifties, who'd have thought of having a gecko as a pet?

The mini-skirt she'd been wearing when she'd proffered him the tongue sandwich had made his eyes pop; she remembered that.

'Don't you like tongue? Is it because it's from an animal's mouth?'

'Not a pleasant thought, is it?'

'What about a boiled egg?'

'That's more like it. I like egg and cress sandwiches.'

That's when she knew he had a problem. She liked a challenge. If she could give him a sense of humour, she'd make a man of him.

'I married Geoffrey,' said Debbie, 'because he's a thespian. I have a soft spot for thespians. I like a man who can put on a show; watching Geoffrey work a room is like watching that documentary about Picasso, the one where he's painting on glass and you are looking at him through the glass; those eyes! Never a brush stroke wasted. In his prime, that was how Geoffrey worked a room; never a handshake wasted. In a seminar he always tried to ask the first question. "Get in first", he always tells me, "before someone asks the question you are going to ask". Are you married, Mr Hardy?'

Mr Hardy intimated by a sniff that he was not.

'No, well, it's not for everybody.'

'Aye, that's true,' said Jock, 'it's a deep question you are asking, Debbie. I don't know why I married Flora.'

'Do you love her?'

'Aye, I do.'

'How much do you love her? If your house went on fire, would you save Flora or your totem pole?'

'I couldn'a carry my totem pole, it's too big; I happen it would be Flora I'd carry out the blaze.'

'I married Roger,' said Beryl, in a voice meant for Mr Hardy to hear, 'because he had a big penis.'

Mr Hardy twitched like a dead frog's leg touched by an electric spark. Why was the old crone ogling him? Surely she wasn't going to ask him if he had a ... she wouldn't dare.

'You mustn't mind Beryl,' said Jock, 'it's her sense of humour. She's an agent provocateur. Fight back, man. Put wind in your bagpipes; look her in the eye and say, "vagina".'

'See how men stick together,' said Beryl.

'Jock,' said Debbie, 'pray do not forget you are a member of the "Ensemble" and not Mr Hardy's defence attorney. A Second class carriage on the north-east coast line is not the place to answer such profound questions as why clever women marry stupid men.'

'Or,' said Jock, 'why clever men marry stupid women.'

*******

As soon as Debbie saw Geoffrey swaying his way towards her she knew what he wanted; the look of panic on his face told her everything she needed to know.

'Debbie, the bottle,' said, Geoffrey. 'All the toilets are locked and out of order. The bottle, Debbie. Plan B.'

'It's not far, to King's Cross.'

'Debbie … the bottle. I know the timetable. I also know my bladder.'

Like the good wife she was, without so much as raising an eyebrow, well used to her husband's little ways, Debbie took out from her bag an empty bottle of Highland Spring Water.

'Do you want the funnel?' she asked.

'What's that in your ear?'

'A safety pin. Do you want the funnel?'

'Where's your pearl? You have a pearl in one ear and a safety pin in the other … give me the funnel.'

'Don't snatch.'

'Debbie … I'm desperate.'

'Where are you going to do it … I mean, if all the toilets are locked?'

'I'll find somewhere … that safety pin in your ear … I'd better go. I'd better go.'

'Give him your safety pin earring,' said Jock, 'you said wearing it stopped you thinking about your need … you know, to go to the loo. Anyway, we'll soon be in King's Cross. Why can't he cross his legs … that's what I do?'

'Because, Jock, as you well know, Geoffrey has prostate problems. When he has to go … he has to go. He has no control. It's not his fault. I'm going to see if he needs help.'

'Is your husband not well?' said a woman in a seat across the aisle, wearing a 'FOOD FOR FOOD BANKS' t-shirt. She wasn't wearing a bra.

'He has prostate problems,' explained Debbie.

'My husband has urticaria.'

'Nettle rash.'

'Urticaria … the doctor said.'

'That must be most unpleasant.'

'It is … believe me. Unless you've had it you wouldn't believe how bad it is and … how do those science guys know about things like how far from us are things like stars? How'd they know how big the sun is? Fake news … that's what I think … fake news. They tell us anything. Now, urticaria … that's real, that is … you ask my hubby.'

'If you'll excuse me … I'm going to see if I can help my husband.'

Not to be denied someone with whom to share her thoughts, the woman, in between tucking into a jam sandwich, said to Mr Hardy, who, it was obvious, had no wish to talk, to anyone, 'I'd offer you half but I've not had any breakfast … well, a bar of chocolate. You on a 'march', like me? The train's full of "marchers". I'm marching for "Food Banks" … shouldn't need 'em … not these days. You know, I'm looking at you … know what I'm thinking? You'd suit a tattoo … a little bible on your neck, is what you need. OT and NT.'

*******

On his way back to his seat in First, Geoffrey pondered how he might pee into the bottle without been arrested for indecent exposure. It wasn't his fault that all the toilets on the train were bust; if caught, he'd plead mitigating circumstances. If people had sex in a Jumbo jet at thirty thousand feet surely it would be ok for him to pee in a bottle. Voiding one's bladder when one had to 'go' was a necessity; having sex at thirty thousand feet was an option. He was damned if he was going to walk round London smelling like the 'Phoney'.

*******

The female Geoffrey found sitting in his seat with a poodle on her lap, momentarily made him forget his need to pee. He might be old but he knew a 'stunner' when he saw one. She was absolutely gorgeous. If she'd been a hotel, she'd have been the Ritz. She had style. And, so had her poodle.

Like Geoffrey, it, that is, the poodle, was dressed to 'kill'. Geoffrey had a bow tie and a drizzling, breast-pocket handkerchief; the poodle had a red, white and blue French flag tied around its neck with a bow fastening.

'You can't sit there,' the man with the three legged bulldog was telling the young woman, 'there's an old man sitting there; speak of the devil, here comes "Mr Resurrection" himself. Tell her to move, mate; that's what I'd do. I know one thing … me, and my dog, aren't moving; are we, Brexit? And, another thing, young woman, tell your poodle to stop kissing my bulldog. She's sitting in your seat, mate; tell her to move.'

'I am seeing hair,' the 'stunner' told the man with the bulldog, 'because, you, monsieur, are seeting in my seat.'

'Bollocks!'

'I arv ze billet … see?' waving a ticket which, the bulldog thinking it was a biscuit, tried to bite.

'You are, French?' said Geoffrey.

'Mais, oui.'

'It's quite alright,' said Geoffrey, in French, 'I am more than happy to sit with my friends. I insist you have my seat. I take pleasure in letting you have it. I apologise for the boor with whom circumstances are forcing you to share a table. Vive la France!'

'Hoy! Stop your poodle doing you know what to my bulldog.'

'But, monsieur, they kiss … they are in love. The English are scared of love; are they not? Why do they use the "F" word to describe kisses and cuddles, why?'

Understanding the urgency of Geoffrey's need to 'go', Ravi and Shirley indicated to Geoffrey that he was to use a corner seat.

As soon as Ravi and Shirley were out of their seats, Geoffrey slid into their places. While Geoffrey did the necessary Ravi covered his friend by spreading himself like a goalkeeper.

On the other side of the table Flora, knowing what Geoffrey was doing, was sympathetic but wished her old friend could have just held on a bit longer; after all they were nearly at King's Cross. She was concerned that if a passenger reported him, that he might go to jail.

What Geoffrey was doing was beyond Roger.

'I keep control of my bladder the way I keep control of my money,' he said.

In situations such as this he disowned Geoffrey. If Geoffrey wasn't careful he'd be arrested for exposing himself ... caught in the act like a homosexual in a public toilet in the days before the law was changed.

'Oh, dear me,' said Flora.

As his bladder emptied, Geoffrey had a post coital look about him. His sense of relief made him indiscreet. With theatrical aplomb he brought the brimming bottle out from under the table, and said, 'That, could be IPA.'

'Debbie,' said Flora, 'thank goodness you are here.'

'Geoffrey needs looking after,' said Shirley.

'He'll get us all locked up,' said Roger.

'I'll take that,' said Debbie. 'Is the top screwed on?'

'Yes.'

'Tight?'

'Yes.'

'You sure ... your hands are not as strong as they used to be?'

'Of course I'm sure.'

'Give it here,' said Ravi. 'Geoffrey, it's like a hot water bottle ... you running a temperature?'

'Out of sight, out of mind,' said Debbie putting the bottle in her handbag.

'What will you do with it?' said Shirley who in the reshuffle had been left standing in the aisle.

'Shirley ... for goodness sake ... what do you think?'

'Hoy! "Resurrection",' said the man with the three-legged bulldog, 'if you want your seat back, mate you'll have to ask this piece of French pastry with a jam filling to move. And you,' meaning Brexit who was on the table, rolling on his back, three legs up in the air, while the poodle sniffed his private parts, 'remember who you are …stand up. Bloody dog would vote "Remain" if she had her way.'

'Your doggy is a tripod,' said the French woman. 'Asterix, my beloved, Asterix, he has the soft spot for the cripples.'

The ensuing conversation, in French, between Geoffrey and the 'stunner' annoyed the man with the three-legged bulldog. Why were they laughing? What were they saying? They were talking about him. He knew they were.

'Hoy! Speak English. Bloody foreigners. This is England. In England we speak English.'

'In Wales we speak English and Welsh,' said Shirley. 'Nadolig Llawen.'

'What's that mean?'

'Merry Christmas.'

'But it's not Christmas.'

'You're not as daft as you look, are you?'

'Watch it!'

The train began to slow.

'There's the Emirates Stadium,' said Roger, 'we're there.'

'Next stop … Doughty Street,' said Shirley.

'Tea and cake,' said Ravi. 'I have always liked English afternoon tea. In the days of the Raj my parents were not allowed tea and cake. Being allowed to take "tea and cake" makes me feel that I belong.'

'Ravi, darling, do stop moaning,' said Shirley. 'The English have treated the Welsh much worse than they treated your mother and father. If Jock could hear you, you'd set him off about Flodden and the Highland clearances.'

The train had stopped. Why?

In French, Geoffrey told the 'stunner' that he hoped his need to urinate had not embarrassed her; that his name was Geoffrey. And she was? Bridgette. A beautiful name. If she had children they would be good looking. Did she know why? Because they would look like their mother.

Debbie rolled her eyes. Her husband was such a flirt. If he said anything about her affair with the Goth, touching her safety pin earring, she'd remind him of Bridgette.

'Your attention please. The company running the east coast line, I've forgotten its name, we've had so many changes of ownership during the last few months, Ha! Ha! Wishes to apologise for the delay but ... I'm not making this up, there is an, elephant on the line.'

*******

In their different carriages the 'Ensemble' recorded the following responses from their fellow passengers.

'I knew I should have brought my shaving kit.'

'I'm a regular. I always pack a change of underwear.'

'Last year I finished "War and Peace" on a stoppage.'

'Wonder what it's like sleeping in a luggage rack?'

On a mobile: 'My apologies ... tell Gerald I may be late for our meeting. There's an elephant on the line ... pause ... no, I am not making it up ... pause ... no, I am not like the little boy who told his teacher the dog has eaten his homework.'

'No, it's not leaves on the line; it's an elephant.'

*******

'I am beginning to feel quite at home in England,' said Ravi, 'afternoon tea and now ... an elephant on the line. The last time an elephant stopped a train I was on was when Mumbai was still called Bombay.'

'If we are more than thirty minutes late,' said Roger, 'we'll get our money back.'

'The smell from the loos is getting worse,' said Flora.

'Flora, I wish you'd not mentioned loos,' said Debbie, fingering her safety pin earring, 'until you did I'd quite forgotten my need … you know.'

'I'll bet it's a circus elephant,' said the man with the three-legged bulldog to the 'stunner', 'done a runner. Good on it, that's what I say. What do you say, Brexit? Immigrants!'

On cue the bulldog whimpered.

'Your dog, monsieur … sounds like an, howl, 'ooting',' said the 'stunner'.

'I beg your pardon … that's his coyote howl, that is. Good dog. Good dog. Elephants shouldn't be on the Tottenham Court Road or wherever it's run away from … they should be in Africa.'

'Or, India. Ve do not know if ze elephant is from Africa or India.'

'You can tell by the size of their ears.'

'You are tres knowledgeable, monsieur.'

'Yeah … suppose, I am … pub quiz last week.'

'I like a man with a brain. Asterix, give the roast beef sitting in my seat a kiss.'

'Hoy! That's enough of that.'

'But, he likes you. You have a dog. You like dogs. You care about elephants. I too care about elephants and love dogs. Asterix is a dog …'

'I likes dogs better than I likes people.'

'Monsieur is a philosopher. Monsieur loves animals. Me too. Monsieur knows all about elephants.'

'Well … not everything but, some things.'

'Modest, as well. If not a kiss … a paw? Asterix … patte.'

'There,' he said, shaking the poodle's paw, 'happy now?'

'He is not 'appy, monsieur.'

'I've shaken his paw. What more does he want?'

'You must kiss his patte.'

'What?'

'Kiss his paw like a Frenchman kisses a lady's hand … see how he cries … poor, poor Asterix … will the naughty "roast beef" not kiss Asterix's paw?'

'I'll do it … but only 'cos I hates to hear a dog crying.'

'There … you have made Asterix an 'appy dog. Say "thank you", Asterix. Asterix … "merci".'

Asterix barked.

The train began to move.

'On behalf of whoever runs the east coast line; apologies for the delay. When you leave the train …'

\* \* \* \* \* \* \*

As the train pulled into King's Cross, Debbie re-joined Beryl and Jock in Second class.

'Where's Mr Hardy?' asked Debbie.

'Up and off,' said Jock.

'I don't think he liked us,' said Beryl. 'I can't think why.'

'Bit of a weirdo, that one, if you ask me,' said the woman whose husband had nettle rash. 'He kept sniffing; all the time. In the end he had me sniffing. Next time I sees me doctor, I'm going to ask him – he's a lovely man – I'm going to ask him if "sniffing" is infectious, you know, like what the measles is. He's going on a "march", isn't he? That's what I heard him telling you; not that I was earwigging. It's just as I happens to have very good hearing. I told him I was going on a "march" but I ain't. I'm off to see my boyfriend for a bit of how's your father. Don't look so surprised. I've had my beady little eyes on you three … you are "naughty", you are; you three is like cream cakes; especially you,' pointing at Beryl, 'you have a twinkle in your eye.'

'I may have a "twinkle" in my eye,' said Beryl, 'but, what I need is a "tinkle".'

'Don't let me stop you … Nice talking to you. By … ee.'

'What a nice woman,' said Jock, 'the salt pork of old England.'

'You've had a narrow escape, Jock,' said Beryl.

'Have I?'

'She was giving you "hungry looks".'

'Do you think so? I don't wish to sound big-headed, but I can understand that.'

'Jock … I was joking.'

'There's many a true word spoken in jest.'

'Debbie?'

'Yes, Beryl?'

'Did Geoffrey manage to do … you know what?'

'Yes … it's easy for men.'

'He didn't get arrested for indecent exposure?'

'He was discreet.'

'If he'd been arrested and taken to Bow Street magistrates' court it would have been like … something out of Pickwick; wouldn't it? I'd have liked that.'

'It's Geoffrey', said Debbie, checking a text on her mobile, 'bless his prostate. He wants to know where we are. Now he's emptied his bladder he's full of vim; some things never change. If Geoffrey had been arrested and taken to Bow Street I think he'd have enjoyed playing the part of Mr Pickwick; real life, imitating art; that worries me.'

# KING'S CROSS

Not for the first time the 'Ensemble's' choice of rendezvous caused mayhem. To the passengers trying to leave the station they were the platform equivalent of a fat-berg in a sewer.

'Where is everyone going?' said Flora. 'It's so busy. So many people. Jock, give me your hand.'

'I know where I'm going,' said Debbie, 'the loo. My safety pin is like ibuprofen; it's worn off.'

'Me too,' said Shirley. 'I'm like one of those dams you see on television with water trickling over its top just before it bursts.'

'Everyone follow me,' said Geoffrey, 'stick together. I know where to go … and watch out for pickpockets. Look, there's the "Artful Dodger". London! London! So full of life. "If you are tired of London, you are tired of life." Gangway please! Human organs for St Bartholomew's. Excuse me … thank you … do you mind?'

'Geoffrey's on a roll,' said Debbie, 'it's so nice to see him enjoying himself.'

'What's he like?' said Flora.

'If Geoffrey's on a "roll",' said Beryl, 'Roger's on his knees. He's spotted a twenty pence someone has dropped. He'll do anything for money. Bending down causes him a lot of pain.'

'Finders, keepers,' said Roger.

'Onward!' cried Geoffrey, 'stick together. This way to the loos.'

Ahead of the 'Ensemble', appearing and disappearing in the crowd, were Bridgette and Asterix and the chauvinist with the three-legged bulldog.

Asterix, full of doggy beans, was lolloping along as if each of his four legs was a pogo stick. Brexit's three legs were pogo sticks with busted springs. He was doing his best to keep up but, when you are a bulldog with only three legs you can't be a greyhound.

At a bottle-neck caused by a confluence of passengers, Brexit, needing a rest, stuck her backside up in the air and, breathing heavily, rested her slavering jowls on her single front leg.

Asterix, not being the sort of dog to look a gift horse in the mouth, without a, 'vous permettez?' mounted Brexit and began, with vigour, to inseminate England's national symbol.

'Hoy!' exclaimed the chauvinist. 'Look what your poodle's doing to my bulldog.'

'It is "amore", monsieur. It is "love". Asterix is in love with Brexit. Do not worry, I will not charge you. When Asterix goes … how do you say? To stud, his 'perm costs one thousand Euros.'

To the 'Ensemble' the rape of Brexit by Asterix was of secondary importance to their need to find a loo. They urgently needed to empty their bladders … that's all they wanted to do … empty their bladders.

*******

Flora thought leaving the station, the nautical equivalent of crossing the bar. It had been busy inside the station but its concourse was – white water; suddenly she was in a cataract of people and struggling to keep calm. Where was everyone going? She knew there were too many people in the world but why had they all come to London? And why did everyone seem to be going on a protest march? To make her feel safe she held Jock's hand.

A man and a woman; the woman dressed as a ladybird, the man dressed as a beetle, were holding a banner which said: SAVE THE PLANET SAVE ITS BUGS.

Beside them, a man with dyed blonde hair, dressed as a caterpillar, was giving would-be supporters of this cause directional advice, through a megaphone.

'If you are marching from Trafalgar Square follow the ladybird markers. Every one-hundred yards you will see a ladybird. If you are marching from the Natural History Museum, follow the beetles. Every one-hundred yards you will see a beetle. Trafalgar Square! Ladybirds! Natural History Museum! Beetles! Save the planet! Walk! Leave the car in the garage. If you are …'

'There's that awful man with the three-legged bulldog,' said Debbie, 'look who he's talking to.'

'An organiser for the National Front,' said Geoffrey. 'I am not surprised.'

177

'It's a flower bed of protest,' said Beryl, 'just look at all the "March Marshals", and all the banners. It is positively, mediaeval.'

'The bunting of protest,' said Ravi. 'It is very Indian.'

'Everyone except us seems to be going on a march,' said Shirley. 'What I want to know is, where are the Welsh nationalists?'

'It's like "Fresher's week",' said Jock, 'you know … established students, out and about to help the new boys and girls.'

'Oh, dear me,' said Flora, 'look at those policemen … they have guns. I suppose that should make me feel safe, but it doesn't.'

*******

'The loo is twenty pence,' said Geoffrey. 'Do we all have change?'

'I'm not paying that,' said Roger. 'Beryl … you got twenty pence I can have?'

'No.'

'Let me squeeze in with you.'

'Roger …'

'Two for the price of one … go on … keep moving.'

*******

Outside the loo, Geoffrey, very much in charge, said: 'Is everyone here?' No one left in the loo, is there?'

'Have you men zipped up?' said Debbie.

The men checked their flies.

'Would it help if we held hands and lined up in two's like we did at school?' said Jock.

'Geoffrey,' said Debbie, 'do you know which way to go?'

'What if we get separated?' said Flora. 'There are so many people. It's so busy and the policemen have guns.'

'The bother I had getting rid of Geoffrey's bottle. When I think about it … it was your pee, Geoffrey, you should have got rid of it.'

'You spoil Geoffrey,' said Shirley.

'You won't believe this, Shirley, but last year he ironed a shirt.'

'Roger,' said Geoffrey, 'hold up your stick; everyone, follow the stick.'

'Excuse me,' said someone wearing a Donald Trump mask, 'you marching? I'm "marching" for the planet ... climate change. What's your whizz?'

'We are ... OPAC,' said Geoffrey.

'Wasting my time then ... aren't I. Oil men, are you? You should be castrated.'

'I said, "OPAC" ... not, "OPEC",' said Geoffrey.

'Fancy threatening Geoffrey with "castration",' said Debbie. 'If that is not closing the stable door after the horse has already bolted, I don't know what is.'

'Do you mind?' said Geoffrey. 'That info is confidential. Roger, up with your stick; everyone follow the stick. Last one to Doughty Street's a cissy.'

*******

It was a hot summer's day, the air hazy with diesel.

'Put a dollop of lard on the pavement,' said Jock, 'and I'll bet you could fry an egg.'

'If the black smoke pumping out of that white van's exhaust pipe was pollen,' said Flora, 'London's bees would make wonderful honey.'

'In Wales,' said Shirley, 'that van would have failed its MOT.'

'Perhaps,' said Ravi, looking thoughtful, 'it is sending smoke signals to other white vans.'

'What makes you think that, Ravi, my darling?' said Shirley.

'It's obvious, isn't it?' said Roger, butting in, 'it is to me at least but then, I went to a grammar school. By the way, it was fifty pence I found. It wasn't twenty pence like you said, Beryl. I wouldn't have bothered picking up a twenty pence piece. Ravi's

Indian, isn't he? Indians communicate through smoke signals; everyone knows that. End off.'

'Roger,' said Ravi, 'I am a Hindu, not an Apache. I do not do war-whoops; the occasional "Hare Krishna" chant, maybe, but that is all.'

'Motor cars are no respecters of ethnicity,' said Geoffrey. 'Please, everyone, concentrate on looking where they are going.'

'It's so busy,' said Flora, 'it makes Newcastle seem like a village.'

'Flora,' said Beryl, 'do stop repeating that London is busy. I can see; we can all see that London is "busy".'

'Ha! Ha!' said Roger. 'At least when she's lashing out at you, Flora, she's not getting at me … makes a change.'

'Flora, I am not getting at you. Roger, shut up! Crossing these roads is like playing "Russian Roulette".'

'Follow me,' said Geoffrey. 'Roger, stick up, hoist the top sails; give us a marker to follow.'

*******

Both physically and mentally, the 'Ensemble' was going downhill, fast. They were weight lifters who, having done the 'lift', can't manage the 'press-up'.

'I think I've joined the Foreign Legion,' said Jock. 'Look, there's a camel.'

'It's painted on the side of a van,' said Flora.

'At least I'm not seeing things … you know … lakes of shimmering water in the desert … that sort of thing.'

'It's a "scorcher",' said Shirley.

'Aye,' said Jock, 'it's a wee bit warmer than that hot day in Glencoe in sixty-three.'

'No sea breezes here,' said Ravi.

'Come back the north east wind,' said Debbie, 'all is forgiven.'

'I'll have to stop,' said Flora. 'How much further?'

'Jock, your wife needs you,' said Geoffrey. 'You take that arm, I'll take the other. One for all and all for one. Onward ...'

'Geoffrey,' said Debbie, 'cut out the theatricals ... this is real life. Flora is exhausted and so am I.'

'Halt!' said Geoffrey, happy to take the hint because he too was exhausted. 'I spy an oasis.'

What Geoffrey called an 'oasis' was a small café cum general dealers. Its forecourt was full of boxes of crisps and bottles of water. Under its awning were three, orange coloured, metal tables with matching, seats.

Sitting beside them, on a wooden chair with a leather covered seat, from which feathers of horse hair were waiting to be blown away as soon as a wind got up, sat an Asian gentleman, dressed as an Indian rajah. He'd his head in his hands as if resting. In fact he was viewing the approaching 'Ensemble' through his spread fingers the way nosey folk peek at their neighbours through twitched back net curtains.

Customers? Tourists? They looked all-in; should they not be at home being looked after by their relatives? The English did not look after their old people.

'"Sammy Sikhs",' said Shirley, reading the shop's name.

'That is me,' said Sammy, standing and bowing. 'You wish for refreshments? Tea? Coffee? I know, Sammy can read minds, he is from the mystic east; you "guys" want a cold drink, yes? Feast your eyes on Sammy's chiller cabinet,' gesturing to the chiller cabinet on the pavement, under the awning. 'All one price. All, very icy, cold. Three Great British pounds a tin ... very good value. The hot weather puts up the price. Fair do's .... Up the "Blues and Royals".'

'We are ... OPAC,' said Roger, 'what about a discount?'

'OPAC? Ah ... QPR ... you are football fans.'

'Old Persons' Adventure Club,' said Geoffrey. 'I ask you, do I look like a QPR supporter? We are from Newcastle upon Tyne.

That's way up North. We are Newcastle supporters. We all have season tickets. Never miss a game.'

'There are eight of us,' said Roger. 'What about if we buy seven tins and get one free?'

'Like in the bookshop … three for the price of two,' said Shirley.

Sammy shook his head. 'I am not a bookshop. I am, Sammy Singh … entrepreneur. I run the first auto-rickshaw taxi in London. It is all electric. It makes no bad smells like my granddad when he eats too many poppadums. Please to look and admire my auto-rickshaw?' drawing the 'Ensemble's' attention to a customised three-wheeled vehicle parked on the road outside his shop. 'Is she not beautiful? Is she not brighter than a thousand suns? I quote from the "Bhagavad Gita".'

'The colours of the land of my birth,' said Ravi, commenting on its orange, white and green, canvas roof.

'It's very colourful,' said Shirley.

'Very "Bollywood",' said Beryl.

'I'm going to sit down,' said Flora.

'Me too,' said Debbie. 'Geoffrey … eight tins of chilled coke … pay out of the kitty.'

'Eight tins of coke, Sammy, please,' said Geoffrey.

'You will pay in "readies"?'

'He wants us to pay in rupees?' said Jock. 'We can't do that.'

'He said "readies", Jock,' Flora told her husband, 'he wants cash.'

'Do not fear, Sammy,' said Geoffrey, 'in its wallets and purses the 'Ensemble' has enough "readies".'

'He didn't say "Rennies", did he?' said Jock. 'I can pay in Rennies.'

To get their order Sammy walked backwards away from the 'Ensemble' as his ancestors might have done in the days of the Raj.

'The cash we hand over won't see the tax man,' said Roger. 'I wonder if he sells bananas; sort of shop like this, on the fiddle, a bit dodgy, might get its bananas from, goodness knows where.'

'I like him,' said Geoffrey. 'He has style.'

'Jock,' said Flora, 'you haven't shaved properly. You have fluffy bits under your chin. They make you look like an old man.'

'That's because he is old,' said Roger, 'we all are. Ravi, what about you chatting up the Rajah in Hindi ... if you and him speak the same language you might be able to cut a deal ... you know ... knock a few pence off the price of a can; never mind, buy eight, get one free; what about, two for the price of one?'

Sammy, whistling 'Cockles and Mussels' and singing, 'Alive, Alive, O,' delivered the 'Ensemble's' order by an indirect route, like someone living in London travelling to Newcastle, via Cardiff.

To serve them he walked twice round a rail of saris; all the time whistling 'Cockles and Mussels'.

'My establishment is so very big', he said, at last reaching the 'Ensemble'. 'I apologise for the delay. Up the Blues and Royals.'

'My good man,' said Ravi in Hindi, 'what are you doing selling overpriced tins of coke to tourists dressed as a rajah?'

'Me old cock sparrow ... I've not a "morning dew" what you're on about.'

'"Morning dew"?'

'"Clue",' said Beryl. 'Cockney rhyming slang ... this is wonderful.'

'You do not speak Hindi?' said Ravi.

'I speak English; everyone speaks English. If everyone speaks English, why should I speak Hindi?'

Saying which and shaking his head as to why he should be expected to speak Hindi, Sammy went back into his shop humming, 'God save the Queen'.

'Not to be able to speak the language of your ancestors,' said Ravi, 'is that right?'

'He has forgotten the village of his birth,' said Jock. 'I'll never forget Edinburgh.'

'I speak Welsh,' said Shirley, 'and I've lived in England longer than I ever lived in Wales.'

'She was on the phone to her brother in Crymch for an hour last week,' said Ravi, 'speaking Welsh ...'

'"Up the Blues and Royals",' said Geoffrey. 'I am much taken with Sammy. I wish he'd brought glasses with the tins ... I don't like drinking out of a tin.'

'I'd drink out of a dirty chamber pot,' said Jock, 'I'm so thirsty.'

'That's a sign of diabetes,' said Flora.

'Flora, you know I don't have diabetes ... I've had the test. It's London ... it is so hot.'

'Geoffrey, what will we see when we get to Doughty Street?' said Beryl.

Geoffrey, never one to hold back, at once began an impromptu lecture.

'Sink the "Bismark",' muttered Roger. 'It's all go.'

*******

Sammy eyed the 'Ensemble' from behind a rack of 'fifty per cent off ticket price' saris. Could he sell a sari to one of the women? It was six months since he'd sold one. An uncle who ran an emporium in Bradford had told him, 'Sammy, there is money to be made up North'. These people were from the North of North. Did that mean the further North you went, there were ever more opportunities to make money?

The problem he'd to solve was how to make them put their hands in their pockets and take out their wallets. They were old but they had all the buttons on. The way they were dressed told him they were 'posh' English. He prided himself on his ability to 'read' his customers.

The woman with a safety pin earring, puzzled him. The safety pin just didn't 'go'. It looked wrong. The anomaly made him feel the way he thought he would feel if he stopped wearing his turban.

These old people were very tired. It was a hot day. From his eavesdropping he knew where they were going; then, it came to him; they didn't need saris, what they needed was transport.

'Geoffrey!' said Mr Singh, clasping his hands and bowing.

'How'd you know my name?'

'Ravi calls you Geoffrey. I know all your names. It is good for business, to know a customer's name.'

'A man after my own heart,' said Roger.

'I heard you "rabbit and pork",' said Mr Singh. 'You are going down the "frog and toad" to Mr Dickens' house … four "pots and pans" out on a jaunt with their "troubles and strives" … up the "Blues and Royals" … long live the Queen … we cut a deal? Eight cokes chilled, free use of my family loo … I heard your "rabbit and pork" about "incontinence". That is a long word … many letters. I admit my great ignorance. I "googled" it. I now know of your needs to use the little boy's room … no extra if you do a "Richard the Third" … Ha! Ha! And I drive you there in my electric auto-rickshaw … no pollution. You arrive in style … cool as the cucumber. You have money … I know. You are posh English.'

'I wish I had,' said Roger. 'Anyway, Sammy, what's all this going to cost?'

'Let me do some "mouth of the Humber" … eight cokes … chilled, use of private facilities, electric rickshaw hire … is … twenty … no, that is too much … fifteen Great British English pounds … cash … no lumps of lard.'

'I take it "lumps of lard" means my "credit card" … you want cash … in that case … ten,' said Roger.

'Thirteen,' said Sammy.

'Twelve-fifty if you sell bananas and I can inspect your bananas without being expected to buy any.'

'How's that! You have me stumped, Mr Roger.'

'My husband collects banana stickers,' explained Beryl.

'OMG,' said Mr Singh, 'you are one of those.'

'I have more than five hundred at home,' said Roger.

'You have the collecting bug,' said Sammy, shaking his head. 'My wife she has so many saris you wouldn't "Adam and Eve it" … for thirteen Great British Pounds I take you to see Mr Patel …. Mr Patel is your man. Fruit and veg. … round the "Jack Horner" from Doughty Street. I take you there … no extra charge. Up the Blues and Royals. I am not Oliver Twist … I do not ask for more.'

*******

The electric rickshaw had seats for eight, including the driver.

'I volunteer to walk,' said Geoffrey, 'I know where to go. It isn't far.'

'I squeeze you in, Mr Geoffrey,' said Sammy, 'beside your wife … you make babies … no seat belts … up the Blues and Royals … Ha! Ha!'

'This is so like Mumbai,' said Ravi. 'The heat and the crowding together. The lack of social space. The intimacy.'

'Get your leg in, Geoffrey,' said Debbie.

'There's no room. I can't.'

'Ah!' said Sammy. 'Mr Geoffrey, thank you so very much, you will be my foot brake.'

'I'm alright,' said Roger.

'I'm not,' said Beryl. 'Roger, I've not been this close to you since that New Year's Eve party, thirty years ago, when I drank too much champagne and forgot myself.'

'Foot off the ground, please, Mr Geoffrey. We cannot go down the "frog and toad" with the foot brake on. Ha! Ha!'

The trip to Doughty Street took less than a minute. Even in that short time, Geoffrey's brogue, the one sticking out of the rickshaw, through intermittent contact with the road, had a centimetre shaved off its heel.

'I pick you up ... yes?' said Sammy. 'To save your "plates of meat" ... up the Blues and Royals ... twenty Great British English Pounds in advance ... if you please ... thank you very much.'

'Ten Great British English Pounds, cash in your hand, when, in two hours' time, you come back to take us to King's Cross ... take it or leave it,' said Roger. 'Where's this fruit and veg shop?'

'Do not fear, Mr Roger, I will take you there. You do not want Mr Dickens?'

'My hunt for banana stickers far exceeds my curiosity to see where Mr Dickens combed his hair and brushed his teeth ... five more stickers and I'll be in the Guinness Book of Records.'

*******

'When I married Roger,' said Beryl, watching the rickshaw turn a corner on two wheels, 'it was triangular shaped stamps ... in his middle years ... match box labels ... now it's banana stickers ... so what? Quite honestly, I'm glad to see the back of him. I told him, "Break a leg".'

'But, Beryl,' said Flora, 'that's what you say to wish an actor good luck ... Roger is not into amateur theatricals ... Geoffrey is, or used to be ... but, not Roger.'

'I know that ... when I told him, "Break a leg", I meant it.'

'Beryl, that's an awful thing to say ... I'm sure you don't mean it.'

'Before we enter this hallowed edifice,' said Geoffrey, 'I think we need to focus our minds.'

'I do that when I play golf,' said Jock.

'I think Geoffrey means, showing respect, like a man taking off his cap before going into a church,' said Flora.

'Or, a Moslem taking off his shoes before going into a mosque,' said Ravi.

'Or, in the old days, in the village of my birth in Wales, not buying a Sunday newspaper,' said Shirley.

'This is where the "Inimitable" finished "Pickwick" and wrote "Oliver Twist",' said Geoffrey.

'The last time I remember feeling this emotional,' said Beryl, 'was before I went into Notre-Dame ... and I'm not a Catholic.'

'You really are into Dickens, aren't you, Beryl?' said Flora.

'Emotion is making me go all shivery. I wouldn't be surprised if I saw Mr Dickens' ghost. I hope I do.'

'I need the loo,' said Jock.

'The museum will have facilities,' said Geoffrey.

*******

'Excuse me,' Geoffrey asked a large black woman sitting behind a desk, 'where are the toilets?'

She had bell cheeks, this black woman ... cheeks as large as Louis Armstrong's when he was blowing his 'horn'. The whites of her eyes were ... fresh as fallen snow ... not a red vein in sight; her Afro ... a piece of topiary. The gold chain around her neck ... big and heavy like a Lord Mayor's chain ... not a trinket from a 'Pound Shop'. Her name pin said: 'Gloria'.

'The "facilities", sir, are for visitors who have paid. The home of the great writer Mr Dickens is not a public facility ... you ... American?'

'Certainly not,' said Geoffrey, 'whatever made you think that?'

'The bow tie ... been doing this job for ten years ... you the first Brit I've had in wearing one ... you are a Brit?'

'Of course I'm British. My friends and I are Novocastrians.'

'That a religion? Once had an affair with a Rastifarian; didn't work out.'

'My friends and I hail from Newcastle.'

'Now, where would that be … Scotland?'

'Try again.'

'But I knows you have a football team.'

'You can say that again.'

'But I knows you have a football team.'

Geoffrey looked at the woman and smiled. She smiled back.

'You have a sense of humour.'

'You can say that again.'

'You have a sense of humour.'

'Young man …'

'You mean me?' said Geoffrey. 'Let me assure you, young lady, I am immune to flattery.'

'Flattery, huh! Don't you go getting a head shine at the barbers to impress me with your … word fun. If you and your friends don't buy tickets pretty soon whoever is needing to use the "facilities" won't be needing them … they'll be with the angels; excuse me for being so blunt but none of you guys and dolls are twenty one … are you?'

'Gloria …' said Geoffrey.

'And don't you go thinking because you can read and knows my name that I'm going to let you use the "facilities" without paying … Mr Dickens wouldn't like that. Mr Dickens was "sharp" that's what I've heard the professors say when they gives their talks and I earwigs.'

'I have a pre-paid ticket to admit eight people,' said Geoffrey.

'You are one short.'

'That is correct. We do not wish for a refund. I and my friends wish, merely to be, admitted.'

'To an old folks' home or a lunatic asylum?'

'And,' said Jock, 'to use the "facilities"; dinna forget the facilities.'

'If the eighth member of our group arrives later on,' said Geoffrey, 'I'm sure you'll let him in. He will tell you he is from

OPAC … Old Persons' Adventure Club. We, you see,' pointing at the group, 'are OPAC.'

'Like the "Pickwick Club",' said Beryl.

'Halleluiah! Excrement and poo,' said Gloria, 'the computer's gone down … it's always happening. I will have to trust you that you've pre-paid … huh! What's your name?' picking up paper and a pencil. 'When "Clark Gable" comes back on, I'll check your bona-fides. "Clark Gable" is what I calls my computer … everything should have a name … what's yours?'

'William Shakespeare,' said Geoffrey.

'And I'm Scarlett O'Hara.'

'I like you, Gloria. You are quick witted and have a sense of humour. You are sugar and honey. I'll bet you cook as well.'

'Sure, I can cook; you stop flattering me, sir. I'm weakening. You're a real ladies' man, you are.'

'Have I scored?'

'Old man, you've hit the Bull's Eye; happy? Now, what's your name; your real name?'

'Geoffrey, do stop flirting, Jock is bursting to "go".'

'So, you are called Geoffrey,' said Gloria.

'Geoffrey, with a "G". I am not a "Jeffery" with a "J". When "Clark Gable" decides to roll up his sleeves and do some work, look me up under OPAC … a block booking.'

'Geoffrey … that's a nice name … once had a boyfriend called "Geoffrey". We didn't get on … know what I'm saying? In you go … facilities that way … no photography.'

*******

In the 'Ladies' Beryl wondered why the woman selling tickets hadn't called her computer after a Dickens character. 'Mr Bumble' she thought, would have been apt.

In the Gents, Jock said he hoped the café sold cheese scones.

'We take our victuals after we've looked around,' said Geoffrey. 'If we sit down in the café first we may not have the willpower to get up off our bums and see what we have come all this way to see.'

'I think I'm getting a spot on my nose,' said Ravi.

'Let me see,' said Jock, taking out the magnifying glass he used to read small print. 'It doesna look cancerous.'

\*\*\*\*\*\*\*\*

There is a law which says nothing can travel faster than the speed of light; there is a law which says a gentleman in the Savoy must not lick gravy off his knife. A lesser known law says that when people, both young and old, visit a museum or art gallery the museum or art gallery's coffee and gift shop will always have more pulling power than what is being exhibited. No Van Gogh, Egyptian mummy or the bottle in which the murderer, Crippen, kept his poison, can compete with buying a bookmark or, in the case of the 'Ensemble' sitting down to enjoy tea and cakes and, hopefully for Jock, a cheese scone.

Thus it should not come as a surprise to learn that, while the 'Ensemble' found what was on show in Doughty Street 'interesting' they did not find it as compulsive as their need to sit down and drink tea.

They were tired. They were hot. Their bodies were telling them, indeed, were yelling at them: Stop! You need to rest.

'I fear Dickens would not like us nosing around his personal things,' Geoffrey told the 'Ensemble'. 'He wanted to be remembered for the books he'd written not for combing his hair at the dinner table or for doing awful things to his wife.'

'Did he write with a quill pen?' asked Flora.

'I think so.'

'When did steel nibs come in?' said Ravi.

'That is something we can look up on the internet. I'm sure I read somewhere that when steel nibs began to be used, he couldn't adapt to them.'

'They used goose feathers, didn't they?' said Debbie.

'When they stopped using them the … you know,' said Flora, 'I was going to say, "gooses" instead of "geese". I do worry about such … tendencies.'

'It is because you are tired,' said Debbie, 'Geoffrey …'

'I know, dear, we are all tired. It is not a large house … even with the museum annexe. I want to see where he wrote "Oliver Twist".'

'And the room where his sister-in-law passed away,' said Beryl.

'Don't talk about "passing away",' said Shirley. 'I do wish that chair did not say: DO NOT SIT ON ME.'

'Stiffen the sinews,' said Geoffrey, 'once more, members of OPAC, into the breach … up the stairs.'

'Geoffrey,' said Debbie, 'do stop quoting Shakespeare. We are in Doughty Street, not Stratford upon Avon.'

'If Roger was here,' said Beryl, 'he'd do the whole house, even if it killed him … to get his money's worth.'

'Motivation,' said Geoffrey, 'motivation … ignore the pain … life is a marathon, not a sprint. Last one to the top of the stairs is a sissy … it won't be me.'

'The others aren't coming,' Beryl told Geoffrey, when they met at the top of the stairs, 'they are going to the café. They want a sit down.'

'I sometimes wonder why I bother,' said Geoffrey. 'I sometimes think people take my organisational skills for granted.'

'I want to see everything,' said Beryl. 'It says here that this is the room in which his sister-in-law died. Poor, Mr Dickens. A sad room. I feel its sadness.'

On seeing the desk at which Dickens had written many of his greatest works, Geoffrey said: 'It reminds me of a stuffed tiger. I know that it once roared and had sharp claws but, what is it now?

It is a piece of wood. If only it could talk … if only it could talk … let's join the others.'

*******

'Who picked this table?' said Geoffrey, in the al fresco seating in Doughty Street's back yard. 'It's in the sun. On a day like today one needs shade. We'll fry if we sit here. There are seven of us … we'll need another table. I'm right, aren't I?' Looking round. 'Ravi, help me … come on, don't just sit there.'

Together they dragged two tables into the shade.

'There, that's better. Have you ordered?'

'We were waiting for you and Beryl,' said Shirley. 'You have the kitty; all I wanted to do was sit down.'

'There's no cheese scones,' said Jock. 'I've looked.'

'But, have you asked?' said Geoffrey. 'They may have some under the counter … always ask.'

'I asked,' said Flora, 'they do not sell cheese scones. It reminds me of that time in Edinburgh, Jock, when the one o'clock gun didn't go off on time. You were disappointed … but you got over it.'

'I hope Roger gets his banana stickers,' said Beryl. 'He's determined to get into the Guinness Book of Records … not that I care either way … except … I don't want him sulking all the back to Newcastle.'

'On the way back,' said Ravi, 'are we all sitting together?'

'Yes,' said Geoffrey, 'two tables of four … better for the debrief. I know I've kept saying we'd debrief here but, quite frankly, I'm knackered.'

'If you were a horse,' said Shirley, 'they'd shoot you.'

'I wish someone would shoot Roger,' said Beryl.

'Let's order,' said Geoffrey, 'seven fruit scones with cream and strawberry jam and tea.'

'Is that a suggestion or an order?' said Jock. 'As far as I'm concerned a fruit scone is not a substitute for a cheese scone. I'm not sulking … just saying.'

'Geoffrey,' said Debbie, 'I know you mean well but, I think we are all old enough to choose our own menu. May I suggest we all go into the café and order, individually; Geoffrey, you will be last because you have the kitty.'

'Yes, Geoffrey,' said Shirley, 'you are in charge of the kitty but you are not in charge of our taste buds. I'm having a cold drink and a chocolate éclair. They have a chilled cabinet full of creamy goodies. And I'm sitting in the sun …put that in your hookah and smoke it.'

'It's the heat,' said Ravi.

'Ravi, darling, stop apologising for me; we all know Geoffrey's a control freak.'

'But we all love you to bits,' said Flora, 'because if we didn't have you to organise us we wouldn't be out, in London, on this very agreeable jaunt.'

'Here! Here!' said Beryl. 'Geoffrey, help me up, my leg's gone all stiff.'

'Keep your hands off my husband, Beryl,' said Debbie.

*******

As they sipped their drinks and bit into the various cakes and pastries they'd chosen, the topic uppermost in their minds was their various aches and pains.

'My ankles are swollen,' said Shirley, 'look …'

'I'm running out of deodorant,' said Beryl, smelling an armpit.

'Where's my sunglasses?' said Debbie. 'I must have them.'

'Something stuck under my palette,' said Jock, taking out his bottom denture. 'It's a currant … if I'd had a cheese scone instead of a fruit scone that wouldn't have happened … cheese scones are kinder to dentures than fruit scones.'

'Jock,' said Flora, embarrassed, 'you shouldn't do that.'

'What?'

'Take out your denture … not in public. People are watching … what must they think?'

'I'm sure there's something wrong with my back,' said Geoffrey.

'Roger is always complaining about his back,' said Beryl. 'I take it with a pinch of salt. I mean, he bent all the way down to pick up that fifty pence; let's get real. If he can do that there's nothing much wrong with his back. I can't bend down like that … I wonder if he's got his banana stickers …'

'Ah!' screamed Ravi, grabbing the shoulder of the young man sitting at the next table. 'Ah! Ah! Cramp,' stretching out his leg. 'Ah! Damn!'

'Terrorist!' shouted the young man in German.

'For goodness sake,' said Shirley, seeing that the young man was threatening her husband with a pastry fork, 'don't stab him, he's my husband not a slice of Victoria sponge cake.'

The German's white shirt dripped tea.

'I will, of course, pay for your shirt to be replaced,' said Ravi, 'cramp, sorry.'

'I do not want the money,' said the German. 'It was an accident.'

'We are worried about you,' said the German's friend, 'we have read how the English do not look after their old people.'

'Where are your minders?' said the German with the stained shirt.

'Och!' said Jock, 'we've given them the slip; they'll be here soon … they always find us … you know … to take us back to the …home. We escaped this morning out of a bedroom window.'

'Do they not lock the bedroom window?'

'It has bars but I unscrewed them,' said Jock.

'Should the bars that were screwed not have had screws that cannot be unscrewed?'

Speaking German, Geoffrey asked the two young men from which part of Germany they came. He told them he'd voted 'Remain'. Would they let him buy them another pot of tea? No thank you. They had a tight schedule ... the British Museum and now ... M and S to buy a shirt.

'Auf Wiedersehen,' said Geoffrey.

He liked saying 'Auf Wiedersehen'.

'Good bye', said the two, young Germans.

'They were from Dresden,' Geoffrey explained to the 'Ensemble' when the two young men had gone, 'they made a point of telling me that. I know they did ... letting me know they knew what we, the British, did to one of their most ancient and beautiful cities in the Second World War. No wonder they didn't want you to pay for a new white shirt, Ravi ... putting a stain on a white shirt is a mere nothing to wiping out a city.'

'They did nasty things to us,' said Beryl, 'they killed my uncle Rowley.'

'And now we are all driving Volkswagens and Mercedes,' said Jock, 'it's a funny old world.'

'Don't forget the Prussians saved us at Waterloo,' said Debbie.

'A pity they bothered. If Napoleon had won we might now be a republic and Scotland ... an independent country.'

'Jock,' said Flora, 'you love the Queen. You've been to one of her garden parties. You had four cucumber sandwiches. If Napoleon had won you wouldn't have had cucumber sandwiches.'

'People are looking at us,' said Debbie.

'Nothing wrong with that,' said Geoffrey. 'If they wish to look at athletes ... let them.'

'Better than being ignored, bored and lonely because you are old,' said Shirley.

'Geoffrey,' said Debbie, 'you have cream on the end of your nose.'

'Have I?'

'Yes ... I've just said so, haven't I?'

'I've a knot in my leg the size of the Bounder Stone,' said Ravi.

'Don't exaggerate, darling,' said Shirley.

A few seconds later, a man, carrying a copy of Proust's 'À la recherche du temps perdu' in an ostentatious kind of way, and bristling with indignation and not mincing his words, told the 'Ensemble': 'Old folk like you should be locked up. You are worse than cyclists ... the ones who ride on the pavement.'

'If you think I'm going to put that in my pipe and smoke it,' said Geoffrey, doing his best to jump up, which old age made difficult, 'you, can think again.'

'"Nelson",' said Debbie, 'do your "Nelson".'

'Thank you, Debbie. I think I will,' whereupon, closing an eye and putting a hand inside his jacket, Geoffrey said, 'Sir, I am Horatio Nelson. I see you speak French.'

'Eh?' said the malcontent.

'You have a copy of "À la recherche du temps perdu" in your hand... you speak French?'

'Fluent as a barmaid at the, what's it, Follies,' said the man, full of bravado and bluster. 'What's it to you, mate?' bringing his face close to Geoffrey's.

In French, Geoffrey told the obnoxious fellow that Ravi had had cramp; that anyone, young or old, could have an attack of cramp.

'If you had an attack of cramp, young man,' said Geoffrey, 'you'd have reacted in the same way as Ravi.'

'Eh? What you on about?'

'You don't speak French?'

'Never said I did.'

'Yes, you did.'

'You did,' said Shirley.

In French, Geoffrey called the man an ignoramus, a disgrace to French culture, a poseur ... the sort of fellow who would guillotine old people. One day he too would be old … heaven help him.

'You, sir,' said, Geoffrey, letting rip in French, 'are 'Fagin' and the 'Artful Dodger' all rolled into one.'

'Fuck you!'

As the man left, a man and a woman at another table in the yard, stood up and bowed.

'I am Japanese,' said the man. 'In Japan we look after our old people; that man should not have said what he said.'

'When I return to Japan,' said the man's wife, bowing, 'I will light a lantern for you at a Shinto shrine.'

'That's most kind,' said Geoffrey. 'Did you hear that, Debbie? I am to be venerated. I don't know about you, but I think that's wonderful.'

'What an obnoxious fellow,' said Flora; 'there'd be no heather in Glencoe if he had has way, I'll be bound.'

'Why did he pick on us?' said Ravi. 'I know we are old but we are not dinosaurs. By the way, if anyone is interested my leg is very sore.'

'Of course we are interested, darling,' said Shirley, 'just don't keep going on about it.'

'You are like the "gays",' said Jock, 'I'm weary of folk coming out. What do they want me to do about it? Last week … when was it, Flora? The plumber we had to fix a dripping tap.'

'Two weeks ago. It was the day we'd to put out the wheelie bin for garden waste.'

'Two weeks ago my …'

'Our …'

'Our kitchen tap was dripping. I …'

'I rang for a plumber.'

'Of course you did, dear … as I was saying Flora rang for a plumber. Next day … in he comes … parks his van so my neighbour can't get out of his drive … no thought for anyone but themselves … some people … anyway, in he comes. What does he say? "Where's your leaking tap?" No! He says, "I'm gay". I told him, "I'm heterosexual and this morning my stools were loose … what's any of that got to do with plumbing? Can you fix my … our, dripping tap?" I couldn't believe it when he said he wasn't sure.'

'Jock,' said Flora, 'the wee man was trying to be honest.'

'When he asked me where my stopcock was, I raised my eyebrows.'

'Jock, we are in Doughty Street not the D H Lawrence museum in Nottingham. As far as I'm aware Mr Dickens never used sexual innuendo … and do keep your voice down.'

'Am I loud?'

'Yes.'

'I didn't think I was.'

'That's because you are deaf.'

'I am not deaf. I am hard of hearing.'

'I still want to know why that horrible man picked on us,' said Ravi. 'Anyone want to feel the knot in my leg?'

'It was because he dislikes old people the same way as some people don't like prunes,' said Shirley. 'Ravi, I can see your varicose veins … please don't'.

'There was more to it than that,' said Geoffrey. 'I think he picked on us because when Ravi's cramp made him bump into the young German, he scuppered the man's plan to steal the German's wallet. Did you not see it sticking out of the German's back pocket? Proust's novel was his camouflage. It was to make him look literary; to make him look like the sort of person who'd visit Doughty Street. I think he was a pickpocket.'

'I suppose,' said Flora, 'if he'd been carrying a copy of "Oliver Twist" it would have been obvious that he was a pickpocket.'

'We have scuppered a crime' said Jock. 'All this way to stop a German losing his wallet. The Lord works in mysterious ways as my old father used to say when he tried not to let my mother see him smoking on the Sabbath.'

Beryl's phone played: 'Money! Money! Money!'

'Is it Roger?' said Debbie.

Beryl nodded that it was indeed her dearly beloved.

'So,' said Beryl, talking to Roger on her mobile, 'you are a happy bunny ... I don't hate you ... I AM happy for you .... What are you doing in St Pancras? I see ... don't forget our train back to Newcastle goes from King's Cross, not St Pancras ... I know you are not stupid ... bye.'

'What's Roger doing in St Pancras?' said Shirley.

'Busking ... there's a piano in the station. He's trying to get back the money he's spent on banana stickers. Mr Patel drove a hard bargain; to get the stickers he's had to buy the bananas. He has two carrier bags of bananas ... and, he had to pay for the bags. He's furious about having to buy the bags.'

'Ah! The collecting mania,' said Ravi, 'it does strange things to the brain. My grandfather had a "thing" about collecting elephant dung ... couldn't get enough of the stuff. It was for what you English would call his allotment. To collect elephant dung he would stay out all night.'

'To see his tart,' said Shirley.

'How did you know that?'

'Because, my darling, you tell that story every month.'

'It's a funny old world,' said Jock, 'but, in London you have to pay if you want a wee or a poo but you can play on a piano for free ... what would Pickwick have thought of that, I wonder.'

'I do hope the toilets on the train taking us back home are working, said Debbie.

'Which reminds me,' said Geoffrey, 'I must buy a bottle of "Highland Spring Water".'

'Geoffrey, I'm not being personal,' said Jock, 'but ... does it have to be "Highland Spring Water"?'

'It is my experience that "Highland Spring Water" bottles, fit my prepuce ... shall I ring Sammy and order his electric rickshaw to take us back to King's Cross? I don't care how much he charges. I'm not walking back in this heat.'

*******

While Geoffrey made the call the 'Ensemble' chatted.

'Do you think visiting Doughty Street has brought us closer to Dickens?' said Debbie.

'It would have been better if the café had sold cheese scones,' said Jock. 'A fruit scone is no substitute for a cheese one.'

'When Jock and I visited the "Victory" in Portsmouth,' said Flora, 'a placard told me that the piece of cloth I was looking at came from one of the ship's sails; looking at it didn't make me go all shivery like I do when I hear Andrew Lloyd Webber's, "Midnight". If I'm honest I thought it looked like something the moths had eaten and that the holes made by the cannon balls must have been very big moths.'

'I disagree,' said Beryl, 'sitting here … I can feel the spirit of Charles Dickens. I do believe Roger was scared to come. He'd die if Marley's ghost tapped him on the shoulder and turned him into a spendthrift.'

'That phial of Christ's blood we didn't buy in Bethlehem, did nothing for me,' said Ravi.

'That, my darling, is because you are a Hindu,' said Shirley, 'Geoffrey … do we have a problem?'

'I'm not sure,' said Geoffrey.

'Sammy is coming for us?'

'Someone is coming for us but, I'm not sure if it's Sammy. The man to whom I've been talking said he was, Sammy but … this is the funny thing … he didn't sound like Sammy. When I said, "Up the Blues and Royals" … trying to be friendly, he asked me if I knew what I was saying? Wanted to know my name … where I was calling from and, for how long had I known Sammy. When I reminded him he was Sammy and should know that, he told me to stay where I was and not to move … that he'd taken over Sammy's rickshaw taxi business and would be along to pick us up. I don't know why I should think this but I think the man who has taken over Sammy's business is a policeman.'

'I do hope we are not going to be arrested,' said Flora. 'I mean because of Ravi's attack on the nice German.'

*******

Within seconds they heard sirens.

'Police or an accident, I wonder,' said Ravi. 'By the way, I've an erection,' pausing to look at the 'Ensemble', 'on my calf … if anyone is interested; bloody cramp!'

'I've one on my foot,' said Shirley, 'it's called a bunion. Ravi, darling, do stop blowing innuendos and feeling sorry for yourself. Cramp is not cancer. You know I don't like men who feel sorry for themselves … if you'd been born a woman you'd have something to moan about.'

'I hope no one's hurt,' said Flora, 'I mean, if that siren we can hear means there's been an accident.'

*******

The 'Bow Street Bashers' as the 'raiders' liked to call themselves when team building over pints of, 'London Pride' in the 'Elephant and Castle', made a lot of noise, on purpose, when they barged into Dickens' house in Doughty Street.

In fact, they made so much noise that even Jock heard them and knew something was up.

They charged into the eating area, all six or eight of them – there seemed to be more than there were – banging truncheons on riot shields the way Zulus had banged knobkerries on antelope shields at Rorke's Drift.

'Police! Hands on heads!'

Beryl thought: It's years since anyone has told me to do that. In primary school a Mr Hall was always telling us: 'Hands on heads'; that's what we called him, 'Hands on Heads.' Look out, we'd say, here comes, 'Hands on Heads'.

'Oh, dear me,' said Flora, 'I'm dribbling.'

'Flora,' said Jock, 'put your hands on your head. If you don't they might shoot you.'

'I can't ... my arthritis.'

'Try ...'

'Which one of you is Geoffrey?' asked a very tall man wearing a Savile Row suit and a tie, which Geoffrey recognised.

'I am,' said Geoffrey, beginning to stand, as manners demanded.

'Sit down!' said a 'Bow Street Basher' pointing a gun at Geoffrey, 'and, stop shaking. I'm not going to shoot you ... silly old fool.'

'Fairbairn,' said the 'Savile Row' suit, 'watch it. I don't object to you pointing your gun at ... the elderly gentleman but, calling him a "silly old fool" is age discrimination ... that could land us all in a lot of trouble.'

'Sorry, sir ... it's stress ... raiding is stressful. I'd have felt better if I'd had to break the door down.'

Jock's fingers, sweat-glued to his scalp, knew all about the, Fairbairns. They were Scots, like himself. They were mad, bad and dangerous. He recalled stories his grandmother had told him, huddled round a peat fire. The Fairbairns didn't send their dogs into a fox's den, they went in themselves, on their bellies; a dirk clamped between their teeth. When they were hungry they ate other people's babies.

'Fairbairn ...' said the 'Savile Row' suit.

'Sir?'

'Put down your weapon ... '"before the dew doth rust it"; there's a good ... Othello.'

'Eh? You sure, sir?'

'Positive ... Nightingale' – this to a tiny woman whose body armour made her look like a table-tennis ball – 'take "Jean" back to the dog van; her teeth will not be needed.'

At the mention of her name, "Jean", an Alsatian with canines like inverted ice-cream cones, snarled.

'She's disappointed, sir,' said Nightingale, 'she was hoping to taste blood.'

'Give her a cheese and onion crisp. It is important that on very raid she gets a treat; tell everyone to stand down.'

'You sure, sir? These people look so old they could be wearing prosthetic masks ... I mean, sir, no one looking as old as they look should still be breathing.'

'Are you saying, "I am not what I am"?' said Geoffrey.

'Touché,' said the man in the Savile Row suit.

'Eh,' said Fairbairn, 'what's going on?'

'Sir Geoffrey is quoting Shakespeare, Fairbairn.'

'Is he?'

'Yes, he is. We are fencing, Fairbairn ... with words.'

'Eh?'

'You know I have a title?' said Geoffrey. 'Have you been investigating me?'

'Not at all. I've just recognise you. I was at your daughter's wedding ... Magdalene College. She married a rowing "blue". You made a very good speech.'

'May I take my hands off my head?'

'Oops, sorry ... of course. Nightingale, Fairbairn ... don't stand gawping ... off you go ... toddle.'

'What's this all about?' said Geoffrey.

'"Up the Blues and Royals", that's what it's all about, Sir Geoffrey. How do you know Sammy?'

Geoffrey explained. The man in the Savile Row suit nodded.

'Is Sammy not coming to pick us up?' said Shirley.

'Sammy ... by the way, let me introduce myself ... when dealing with desperate situations it is too easy to throw the good manners Nanny taught one out of the nursery window. Lawrence Kindley, MI5. I'm afraid Sammy is an illegal immigrant. He may also be a terrorist.'

'Might, he have murdered us?' said Flora. 'Oh, dear me. I thought him such a nice man, as well.'

'His affability was his cover,' said Mr Kindly.

'You're like a secret agent, aren't you?' said Debbie, clearly in awe. 'I think I remember you … just; at our daughter's wedding, I mean.'

'I don't suppose I'm the first to tell you this,' said Beryl, 'but you look a lot like Clint Eastwood.'

'Beryl, stop flirting,' said Jock. 'It's because her husband's not here.'

'Roger, that's my husband, collects banana stickers,' said Beryl. 'Sorry, I'm finding all of this very stressful.'

'Mr Kindly,' said Shirley, 'we're not going to be arrested, are we?'

'Don't be silly … of course not. The "Establishment" does not arrest other members of the "Establishment". Sir Geoffrey is one of us.'

'Me?' said Shirley. 'A member of the "Establishment"? But, I'm Welsh.'

'We are, madam, a … UNITED Kingdom,' said Mr Kindly, taking a Glock 9 automatic out of a shoulder holster. 'Just checking I have the safety on, don't want to blow a hole in my armpit'.

'What about me?' said Ravi. 'Am I part of the "Establishment"?'

'The "Commonwealth" is important, sir.'

'I have no doubt my brown skin made you think I was "Commonwealth" but I'm not. I am a citizen of the United Kingdom of Great Britain and Northern Ireland.'

'I understand your grievance, Ravi, I really do,' said Geoffrey, 'but, I wish to ask Mr Kindly a favour: Lawrence, dear thing; my friends and I have a train to catch. Your "raid" has put us behind schedule. Furthermore, your efficiency at catching "illegals" and "terrorists" has deprived us of Sammy's electric rickshaw taxi service.'

'You want a lift to King's Cross?'

'Would that be possible?'

'How many are you?'

'Seven.'

'Would one of you be prepared to go in the dog van?'

'I will,' said Geoffrey.

'Good man … don't worry, you won't be in the back with, "Jean"; she has her own cage. You'll be in the front seat with Nightingale. What time's your train?'

Geoffrey told him.

'In that case, there's no time to lose, is there? If the traffic's bad I'll put the siren on.'

# KING'S CROSS

The journey from Doughty Street to King's Cross took less than a few minutes and passed without incident. No sirens were needed and 'Jean' did not bite Geoffrey; even when he poked his finger into her cage.

At the station, they had no bother parking because they parked on double yellow lines; after all, they were the police.

Before going their separate ways, the retired and the active shook hands. Only Fairbairn declined to dance to the tune of civilised behaviour. He was checking his weapon. He was an armed patrol officer not a fucking taxi.

As they drove off Nightingale blew them kisses and Mr Kindly winked at Geoffrey while fingering the Windsor knot in his Guard's tie; as if sending Geoffrey a message.

'What nice people,' said Flora, as she watched the Range Rover and the police dog van with 'Jean' – standing in her cage, looking miffed that she'd not been allowed to bite anyone – merge and then disappear into the traffic.

Tired and more than a little bit shocked after what had happened to them in Doughty Street, the 'Ensemble', for a while, just stood and looked at each other; it was as if they couldn't be bothered to move.

Breaking the silence, Geoffrey said: 'Standing here, I feel as if the police have left us marooned on a desert island. I feel a little bit helpless.'

'Come on, Geoffrey,' said Ravi, 'show some leadership. The 'Ensemble' needs you.'

'Let's find Roger,' said Jock.

'Do we have to?' said Beryl.

'There he is, over there,' said Shirley. 'Coo-ee! Roger!'

*******

'What's happened?' said Roger. 'I can tell by your faces, something has happened.'

Geoffrey, his powers of leadership rejuvenated by Roger's question, gave Roger a précis of the police raid on Doughty Street and, sadly, that 'Sammy Singh' was not what he appeared to be and that he might have a finger in many naughty pies.

'Wow! So I didn't miss anything,' said Roger, ever the curmudgeon. 'It's all go.'

'It's not like you to be ironic, Roger,' said Debbie; 'are you alright?'

'If I know Roger,' said Beryl, 'and I do … he's on a high … probably because of something to do with his fetish for collecting banana stickers. Where are all the bananas you said you had to buy? I do hope you haven't eaten them. I hope you are not going to be sick, on the train.'

'You'd like that, wouldn't you, Beryl, me puking up … well, I'm not going to be sick … wouldn't give you that satisfaction. I

bartered them for two cups of coffee and a Danish. A nice guy …
Polish, took them off me. He runs a coffee shop but has ambitions
to own a fruit and veg stall; wants practice selling fruit.'

*******

Inside King's Cross, Geoffrey bought a small bottle of 'Highland
Spring Water'.

'What you looking for?' said Debbie.

'A drain down which to pour this water. If I drink it I'll need
the bottle before I get on the train.'

Flora bought 'sucky sweets'.

'As we're all sitting together, we can share them.'

*******

The 'Ensemble' found the station too busy; as, indeed they'd found
all of London, ever since they'd stepped off the train. For old folk,
a bit unsteady on their feet, the station, seething with passengers,
seemed a dangerous place to be; at least, that's how it felt.

'It's like standing in the middle of a motorway,' said Geoffrey.

'I feel like a hamster in a cage with a hungry python,' said
Ravi.

'Where is everyone going?' said Debbie.

'The people pulling suitcases on wheels are the worst,' said
Shirley.

'Look! There's Judi Dench,' said Jock.

'Where?' said Flora, who was a big fan.

'Made you look! Made you look!'

'What's he like?'

*******

When they'd 'made it' to a place on the station's forecourt where they could see the 'Arrivals' and 'Departures' screens, the 'Ensemble' formed a square as if they were redcoats and the King's Cross station concourse a field at Waterloo.

'Where's our train?' said Flora.

'It's not on the screen, yet,' said Jock.

'Can you read that? I can't.'

Every time the 'Departure' screen showed a new train 'boarding', a swath of passengers grabbed their luggage and took off, en masse, like a flock of starlings.

When this happened, for a short while at least, large areas under the screens would empty before, in no time at all, filling up again.

'It's like filling a bath and emptying it,' said Geoffrey, 'filling and emptying; filling and emptying; non-stop, all day long. King's Cross makes Newcastle Central look like a one-train-a-day station.'

'There's an empty seat,' said Roger, 'I'm going to sit down. I want to look at my banana stickers. It will take my mind off waiting. I hate waiting. It's all go.'

'Debbie,' said Geoffrey, linking arms with his wife to forewarn her that what he was about to say, was of a somewhat delicate nature, 'as we will soon be on the train and going home, do you not think it might be a good idea if you took that safety pin out of your ear … you know, just in case we meet someone on the train we know. I mean, I know Jesmond is Bohemian but we are, I put it to you gently, past the age of "Flower power" and all that.'

'It makes me feel empowered.'

'Debbie, it doesn't suit you; you are not a Goth; you are a pearls and twinset lady; furthermore, you are my wife.'

'It makes me feel liberated.'

'You said "Empowered" before.'

'It has "Empowered" me to feel "Liberated". For the first time in my life I feel I've done something daring.'

'I just hope we don't meet anyone on the train that we know, that's all.'

'Don't sound sulky. It doesn't suit you. It's not like you. You have the "Ensemble" to lead. We look up to you.'

'Do you really?'

'Of course we do; because of you we've all had a wonderful day out. Look at Roger, absorbed with his banana stickers. To see Roger looking happy, surely that's worth a safety pin earring. You never know, I might start a fashion. I think you are getting uptight, perfectly understandable, in case the toilets on the train aren't working. You have your bottle of Highland Spring Water?'

'It's full. I can't find a drain.'

'As soon as you get on the train, empty it down a loo. You'll feel ever so much happier knowing you have somewhere to go, you know, in a worst-case scenario; excuse me, but why are you looking at me?'

*******

Debbie's question was addressed not to her husband, but to, two steampunks; a woman and a man. The woman was dressed all in black; black leather bomber jacket, short black skirt, black tights (laddered) and, knee length, black leather boots with sledge hammer heels.

The white powder on her face made her look like a corpse; her black hair, lacquered into two peaks gave her a horned-look. The overall impression was that of looking at a bug through a microscope.

Her male companion was wearing a blue velvet frock coat and a black top hat; the hat been a display cabinet for a red rose, a chain from an old fashioned toilet (complete with wooden handle) and a pair of goggles of the sort worn by racing drivers in the nineteen thirties.

'Greetings, sister,' said the steampunk woman to Debbie, 'I'm Arlene. This is my mate, Bert. Bert's deaf so, just smile at him and give him the thumbs up; me and you is kin, sister; that's what I'm thinking; don't you be frightened to come out. I started with a safety pin in my ear, just like you; spotted it straight away; now, look at me. You're trying to say something, aren't you? Bert started with a top hat he found in his granddad's wardrobe; didn't you, Bert?' using sign language to include Bert in the conversation. 'May the force be with you.'

'And with you.'

'You marching? We're with Greenpeace; steampunk's got to do its bit to save the planet; see you in a cemetery, sometime, eh? Come on, Bert,' this in sign language, 'let's stroll.'

And off they went, arm in arm, bowing and waving like royalty at their many admirers.

'Geoffrey, what a lovely couple,' said Debbie. 'My safety pin earring is opening doors into cultures I know nothing about.'

'I'll bet you won't wear it at the Bridge Club.'

'You are probably right,' sighing, 'at my age I'm too old to ditch the pearls and twinsets look. I wonder if I should have a Goth funeral; that would set the tongues wagging, wouldn't it? I can hear them now, when I'm looking down at them from the clouds, "Well, well, well, who'd ever have thought, Debbie was a Goth. Poor Geoffrey. He keeps telling everyone it was in Debbie's will; her choice, nothing to do with me".'

'Would you do that?' said Shirley, who'd come to join in the conversation. 'I think I might organise myself a druid send off. I'd like to think that when I was dead I could shock the living.'

'I think we should be boarding soon,' said Geoffrey. 'Where's Roger?'

'I'm right behind you,' said Roger. 'I've been forced to leave my seat by an out of control child who wanted my banana stickers; took a real fancy to them, he did. His mother couldn't understand why I wouldn't let him have them; a woman, I fear, without, imagination.'

'May I see them?' said Jock. 'If I can see them I might be able to understand why you find them so fascinating.'

'No … exposure to sunlight will cause them to fade.'

'I wouldn't worry about that; they will outlast you.'

'I bought a plastic wallet from W H Smith to put them in. Do you know how much I paid for it? Three pounds … daylight robbery.'

'They must have seen you coming.'

'Roger doesn't care what he spends,' said Beryl. 'Ha! Ha!'

'This morning,' said Flora, 'when I was making Jock his early morning cuppa, before we left Edinburgh … to think, this morning we were in Edinburgh … a tea bag split open … tea leaves, everywhere … that's bad luck, isn't it?'

'This "morning" seems a long time ago,' said Debbie. 'The older I get the quicker time seems to fly. A day is not as long as it used to be.'

'We're boarding,' said Geoffrey, 'we're on the screen, look, "boarding". Debrief on the train over wine and sandwiches … maybe, even a cheese scone, Jock.'

'That I should be so lucky,' said Jock. 'I've been thinking, my craving for cheese scones … I wonder if I'm pregnant.'

'I wish men could have babies,' said Beryl, 'then they'd know what life was about.'

'No need to rush,' said Geoffrey, 'our seats are booked; all of us together in First class.'

'Lots of people going north,' observed Ravi.

'North is a lot more popular than those living in the South would care to admit,' said Roger. 'For a start it's cheaper up north … one's money goes a lot further.'

*******

The 'Ensemble' passed through the open gate and onto the platform more or less together.

'No need to show tickets,' said Geoffrey. 'First class is up front. Onward Christian soldiers. No need to rush. The train won't go without us.'

At first, Geoffrey led the way, then, out of consideration for Debbie, who was flagging, stopped to let her catch him up; letting Flora and Jock take the lead.

Hard on the heels of Flora and Jock were Roger and Beryl, who for once in their lives were walking side by side, as if they belonged to each other.

Ravi and Shirley were last because Ravi kept stopping his wife to ask her if she was serious about having a druid funeral.

# Epilogue

Of all the group only Ravi and Shirley remembered what happened next; only they were far enough away from the explosion to know it for what it was … a terrorist bomb. They remembered seeing a carriage somewhere at the front of the train disintegrate – its sides and windows blown out; turned into confetti by the powerful explosion.

They remembered smoke belching out of canisters thrown at them by men dressed in black … men with beards.

Beryl had vague memories of Roger, shouting, 'you bastards aren't getting my stickers'. She remembered one of the terrorists grabbing the end of his walking stick and Roger releasing its wooden sheath, to reveal a two foot long blade. She remembered how he'd stumbled forward to pick up the plastic folder containing his banana stickers, which in the mayhem, he'd dropped and, by default, stabbing his attacker in the heart.

Beryl fled, hysterical. If Roger had done the same he might have survived but he didn't. A banana sticker had fallen out of the plastic bag onto the platform; stooping to pick it up a terrorist decapitated him.

The rest of the 'ensemble' had no recollection of how they came to wake up in a hospital bed.

In the explosion, shrapnel had taken off Geoffrey's right arm; another piece had removed Debbie's left eye.

*******

A year later, at the inquest into the attack, Geoffrey and Debbie told serious looking legal men and women, that they remembered walking down the platform but, that was all.

Jock recalled Flora passing away in his arms. Her last words to him: I love you. He recounted to a silent courtroom how he remembered someone kicking him, hard; how the face he saw looking down at him should have scared the hell out of him but, he supposed, because he was in shock, didn't. Flora was dead, he kept repeating in the witness box. Flora was dead.

He narrated how the man kicking him had a beard and white teeth and a knife of the sort he, Jock, had used, many years ago, when the children were young, to carve the family Sunday roast. But this knife had a knuckle duster handle ... why? He didn't understand. Jock had aged.

*******

Afterwards in a wood panelled room, in a government building close to the Old Bailey, where refreshments had been laid on for those giving evidence, Jock thanked the policeman who'd shot the terrorist with the beard, the white teeth and the carving knife.

'He was going to slit my throat, wasn't he?' said Jock.

'That was my impression, sir.'

'What was he shouting at me? I know you told the inquest but I'd like you to tell me again ... in a strange sort of way it makes me feel close to Flora ... you know, my wife ... the terrorists blew her up, you know.'

'I know, sir.'

'What was he shouting?'

215

'He kept telling you ... "Allah is great".'

'In English ... not Arabic?'

'In English ... yes.'

'He wanted me to know why I was going.'

'Possibly, sir.'

'And ... I couldn't hear him.'

'So ... he failed.'

'Do you know why I couldn't hear him?'

'You were in shock, sir.'

'Yes, there was that ... also, I'm hard of hearing, not deaf, you understand .... Just a little hard of hearing ... but, I know this will sound strange, perhaps even unbelievable, but ... I was thinking about cheese scones.'

'Of course you were, sir.'

'I'm not going gaga, you know.'

'Of course you're not, sir. If you'll excuse me one of my colleagues wants a word with me.'

*******

Jock knew why the man who'd saved his life had given him the shove. His 'saviour' did not want to talk to an old fool. Jock knew what the man was thinking. He was thinking: All my marksmanship's gone and done is save the life of a 'wrinkly' registering nine on the doo-lally Richter scale.

*******

Jock had found his grief for Flora to be like England's weather; unpredictable. One minute of sunshine followed by rain. Sometimes, like now, he wanted to be by himself but he knew that was not the way forward. Where were Geoffrey and Debbie?

Looking round he spotted them through an open door, in a brightly lit room, been interviewed by someone he recognised as a BBC news presenter. Beryl was with them.

He'd declined to be interviewed. He was old fashioned Edinburgh. He'd no wish to share his loss of Flora with a gawping public.

Geoffrey was loving it; talk about giving a cat a saucer of milk. And, Beryl had a story to tell.

The attack had left so many people with terrible injuries. He counted the wheelchairs in the room ... gave up after reaching ten.

On the train coming down for the inquest, Geoffrey had made a stab at a wee joke ... the first, so far as Jock was aware, that Geoffrey had made since he'd come out of hospital.

Geoffrey had said – they were leaving Peterborough at the time – 'If I'd lost an eye as well as an arm, my impersonations of Lord Nelson would require no prosthetics. Every stage manager in the country would have wanted me. I'd be cheap.'

*******

Drifting towards the open door of the brightly lit room – full of lights on tripods – Jock heard Beryl telling the BBC presenter how her husband had saved her life.

'Your husband must be a huge miss,' said the presenter. 'How have you coped?'

'Roger was the love of my life,' said Beryl, shedding a tear. 'We were a close couple. I will never get over his loss.'

'Jock!' said Ravi.

'Jock!' said Shirley.

'Jock, there's a bar next door and ... it's free.'

'If only Roger was here. He'd borrow Geoffrey's bottle of Highland Spring Water and fill it with whisky.'

'We must be mad to have lived for so long,' said Jock, 'mad!'

'And,' said Ravi, 'if you don't think you are mad then you must be mad.'

'It's Catch-22,' said Shirley. 'Ravi, my darling ... next year ...'

'If we are all still here,' said Jock.

'Don't be such a pessimist, Jock,' said Shirley, 'next year, let's persuade Geoffrey to organise a trip to Stonehenge ... for the summer solstice. As we are none of us getting any younger I think our jaunts should be more spiritual than literary. We'll take our own cheese scones ... Jock?'

Ravi and Shirley watched their old friend fall, as if they'd been expecting it; they watched him slide onto the floor and into oblivion, the way you watch a house tumble over a cliff edge ... with a feeling of helplessness; you know there is nothing you can do. They did not scream or make a fuss. They knew he was dead; looking down at him, they pondered the change in his face; were in awe at how quickly, after he'd drawn his last breath, warm life had been replaced by cold death.

'He's at peace now,' said Ravi.

'He is with Flora,' said Shirley.